DAWN SKIES

Suzanne Cass

S C

STORM CLOUD
PRESS

Dawn Skies

Storm Cloud Press, Perth Australia

Copyright © 2022 by Suzanne Cass

Edits by Tanya Saari

Cover by Vikncharlie

All rights reserved.

To Kyle and Arran, my stars and my moon.

CHAPTER ONE

Warwick Nobles turned the air conditioning up another notch and squinted through the windshield, letting his gaze drift out over the scrubby plains. Glare from the fierce sunlight reflected off the dry earth, almost blinding him, even through his sunglasses. The temperature gauge on the dash said it was already thirty-four degrees, and it was only nine am. The sandy ground ahead shimmered with heat, concocting mirages that turned the earth into water and the outback bushland into sky.

The dirt track was faint, winding around and between stands of acacia and saltbush, but he was almost there. A two-hour drive, and another two hours back to the lodge. That was four hours out of his busy day he couldn't afford. But there was no one else to check on the water trough, so he had to suck it up. Wazza's boss, Steve, had noticed the camera wasn't working at trough number nineteen yesterday morning when he did his routine check, but the bore runner normally employed to check that all the bores were in top-notch working order was all the way out on the other side of the cattle station. Tad had called in this morning to say a broken bore pump had held him up, and he couldn't make it to number nineteen, so Wazza had drawn the short straw. The water troughs scattered around the large, outback station were vital for the cattle's survival during the extended heat of the dry season. It wasn't a job that could be left until another day.

Normally, he would've made sure he had some tunes to keep him occupied on the long drive. But he'd left in such a hurry, he'd forgotten to download a playlist onto his phone. And there was no radio reception this far out. So Wazza was left with nothing but his own thoughts.

As usual, his mind wandered to contemplation of Karri and what might have been. What would he be doing now if Karri were still alive? Would they be playing happy family's somewhere, together? Perhaps he'd have continued to work at Stormcloud, supporting Karri and the baby. She might've wanted to be a stay-at-home-mom. Or she might've wanted to keep working at Stormcloud, too. Either way, he would've been happy. She might've even returned to Koongarra Station, where the community of local Djungan indigenous people ran a successful pastoral lease. Bring up her daughter surrounded by her own culture, show her the ways of living on the land. It was less than an hour's drive away from Stormcloud, on a neighboring property, and Wazza would've been happy moving there, as well. Or at least, that's what he told himself.

All this could've been possible if she hadn't been brutally murdered, taking their unborn child with her. Taking *his* daughter with her. Wazza still didn't like to go back to that section of the creek, it reminded him of finding the body. He could still see her. A dark, amorphous lump caught at the edge of the fast-flowing stream. It wasn't until he turned her over and saw her eyes, open and vacant, staring back at him, that he realized it was Karri. At least, Steve seemed to have worked out Wazza's aversion to that area of the creek now, and always sent Dale or Julie if the cattle needed checking near that spot, for which Wazza was eternally grateful.

He shied away from the image of Karri, floating faceup in the water. Down that path lay darkness and misery. Instead, he let his mind return to the fantasy he'd created. He liked to think the baby would've been a girl. Karri was less than two months pregnant when she died, but Wazza still mourned her death. Mourned the death of what could've been. Would his little girl have been walking yet? She would've tuned one year old a few months ago. Hadn't he heard kids started walking around their first birthday?

In his mind, he'd named her Ava. It was a nice name; sweet and innocent and wholesome. Would she have had dark hair, like his? Or a blonde tinge, like Karri's? Would her skin have been dusky, inherited from her mother's indigenous lineage? Eyes dark, or blue as the sky? The possibilities were endless.

Sometimes, he'd have quiet conversation with his little girl, usually while he was lying in his single dorm room, unable to sleep. They'd talk about silly things like the pretty pink-and-gray birds in the eucalyptus tree this morning, and how balloons frightened her, but not if they were purple. That always made him smile.

But it was all in his head. Sometimes he had to remind himself of that fact. Funny, it'd been nearly two years since Karri had passed, but in all that time, the solid stone of melancholy had sat heavy and cold in the pit of his stomach. He'd thought it might get easier as time rolled by, but so far, it hadn't. Most of the time, he managed to keep his despondency hidden behind his smile and his Akubra hat. Few people understood how deeply Karri's death had affected him. They'd only been seeing each other for three months, or so, when she died. And it'd been a mainly physical relationship; both in it for the fun and the sex. It wasn't until after her murder, that he'd realized what he'd lost.

Perhaps it was time to move on. A change of scenery might do him good. His guts lurched as he thought about the email he'd sent yesterday, applying for the job at the Gondwana Pastoral Company. Was he doing the right thing? It would be a big change to his work as leading hand at Stormcloud, but perhaps that was what he needed to get him out of this funk.

Too late to contemplate that now. The watering point appeared through the glare across the windshield, and he slowed. Wazza stopped the four-wheel-drive next to the concrete trough. There were no cattle around, which was a little surprising. But the ground was churned up, covered with hoof prints, so they must've been here recently. He cut the engine and got out to stand next to the car, eyes searching the surrounding bushland. He always felt like a speck of dust in this vast land, totally alone and insignificant. The quiet of isolation was emphasized by the call of a single bird floating on the hot breeze high above. A flurry of flies encircled him, and he wished he'd brought the insect repellent; they were always worse out here where the cattle congregated.

Time to check the trough. He strode over and examined the long concrete gutter. It was full to the brim with sparkling water, and Wazza let out a relieved sigh. At least the cattle still had access to plenty of life-giving liquid. This watering point was fed from a bore over two kilometers away. Wazza gazed in the direction of the main bore, where a diesel pump ran twenty-four hours a day, keeping the storage tank full. But it was too far away to see much of anything, and he couldn't even hear the faint hum of the pump that sometimes drifted over on the breeze. That particular bore fed three other watering points in this area. It was the reason they employed a full-time bore runner. The job of checking all the bores on this large station every other day kept Tad a busy man.

Looking up, he spied the little solar-powered camera

mounted atop a metal pole, pointed at the trough. They used them to monitor stock health, to detect any leaks or problems with the water, as well as site security. It was state-of-the-art equipment, using satellite links to send a series of still photos back to Steve's computer in the office.

Something was covering the camera. A piece of clothing, if he wasn't mistaken. And it looked like it'd been draped there on purpose.

Wazza stepped onto the edge of the trough and reached up to drag the material off the camera. It was a light blue shirt, the type a woman might wear, and he crumpled it into a ball in his fist. His height made the job easy, but he wondered who had covered the camera, and why? Jumping down onto the ground, he bent his head to study the churned-up dust. There. A footprint amongst the cloven hooves of the cattle. He got down on one knee and studied it. The print was as clear as day, and it overlaid the cattle marks. Which meant it must've been made today. More footprints encircled the trough. Most of them were scuffed and muddled, but he could make out the shoe size. They were small, the size of a woman's shoe, or a small man. He gazed at the shirt in his hand and then back at the shoe print. Something odd was going on here.

The bore runner hadn't been out to this trough in three days. Who else would be out here, then? There was nothing for hundreds of kilometers around, besides cattle and flies. Wazza looked up, a puzzled frown creasing his brow, a sudden prickle of unease running down his spine. As he stood, he felt the back of his neck tingle, like he was being watched. He spun around in a full circle, but there was nothing to be seen. The area was mostly cleared, just a dry, dusty plain, with a few patches of acacia trees huddled together, and a couple of large bottle trees standing tall and aloof, their branches breaking up the unadulterated blue sky.

"Hello." His voice sounded inadequate in the vast expanse of desert, so he drew a deep breath and called out again. "Hello. Is anyone out there?" Nothing moved, and no one answered, but his feeling of disquiet grew.

Wazza sidled closer to the car. Should he call this in? There was a satellite phone mounted on the dash. He could call someone at the lodge and let them know. But what would he tell them? That he had a feeling? They'd laugh him all the way back to the lodge. As he stood next to his vehicle, pondering his next move, something moved in his peripheral vision. He whirled to face a figure emerging from behind a small stand of ironbark eucalyptus trees, around twenty meters away.

A woman regarded him warily. Dark eyes fixed on him, she balanced on the balls of her feet, as if one wrong move from him would send her running. She was petite; the top of her head wouldn't even come to the middle of his chest. Wearing denim shorts and a slim-fitting T-shirt which exposed supple legs and graceful arms, her skin was the color of mocha. A long, dark braid fell over her shoulder, a few strands of limp hair, damp with sweat, hanging around her face.

"Hello," he said again, raising his hands, palm forward to show he meant no harm. "My name is Warwick. I work for the owner of this property, Steve Williams. Who are you? And what are you doing out here?" he added as an afterthought.

She ignored him, gaze darting from his face to his vehicle and back again. He guessed she was assessing the risk he posed, because she still looked as if she might run at any second. What in hell was a young woman doing alone out here?

"Have you got any water?" she asked, in a tightly controlled voice.

Before he could answer, a child's voice emanated from

farther behind the woman, in a clump of wattle bushes. "Mummy. Is the man going to give us some water?"

Wazza leaned sideways so he could look around the woman. Sure enough, a little girl, perhaps three or four years old, was peering out from between two low branches, dark eyes full of hesitant watchfulness. She had the same mocha skin and soft features as her mother. Not just a woman on her own, but a woman and a small child. This was going from bewildering to all-out-crazy.

"I told you to stay hidden." There was quiet exasperation in the woman's voice.

"But I'm thirsty, Mummy." Tears tracked down the little girl's face.

"All right. Come here, then." She held out her hand, and the girl ran to her mother's side. The woman kept one eye on Wazza the whole time. She held the little girl's hand tightly, tucking the child partway behind her legs and staying next to the tree, as if it could somehow shield them from harm, glaring at him suspiciously. It was only now he noticed the state of the woman's clothes. They were filthy, as if she'd been wearing them for days, covered in dust and streaks of grease and red dirt. The same for the girl.

It suddenly dawned on him. "Have you been drinking the bore water?" Wazza tried to hide his alarm. God, how long had they been here?

"It's all we had," the woman replied, meeting his gaze with a defiant raise of her dark eyebrow.

"You can get sick if you drink that." He tilted his chin toward the trough. It wasn't safe to drink the same water as the cattle, there could be all sorts of diseases in there, apart from the high salt content and other chemicals found in bore water. "I've got a couple of bottles in my vehicle," he said, striding back toward the Land Cruiser. Reaching in, he fished two bottles from the back seat. Everyone always carried extra water out here.

But as he made his way over to them, the woman held up her hand. "Stay right there," she commanded. When he halted in his tracks, she said, "Put them down there and back away." She directed her dark stare at him as he did what she asked, returning to the side of his vehicle.

Wow, this woman had a whole shitpile of trust issues. But who was he to judge?

When she was sure he was well out of range, she walked forward, grabbed the bottles, and took them back to the tree, where her little girl was waiting, casting worried glances back toward Wazza over her shoulder as she went. As if she expected him to charge at her and tackle her to the ground at any moment. More than just trust issues, then. She looked downright scared of him.

He watched as she unscrewed the lid and handed the bottle to her daughter, who gulped it greedily, some of the liquid spilling down her chin and making dark splotches on her pink T-shirt. The little girl drank her fill until she finally tipped the bottle back and smacked her lips. "That tastes good." She gave Wazza a cautious smile. "That other stuff was yucky."

Wazza could well imagine. Bore water often had a metallic taste, and smelled even worse. The poor little thing, having to drink contaminated water. Which made him wonder again, how long had they been out here? He was still trying to get his head around this shocking turn of events. What was this woman and her child doing here? How had they got here? There was no vehicle nearby. And they surely hadn't walked. It was over twenty kilometers to the nearest main road, let alone a township. There was a definite puzzle here that needed to be solved. But the way the woman was glaring at him with barely concealed animosity—or was that fear?—he didn't think the answers were going to be easily discovered.

CHAPTER TWO

Kee Singh watched the man out of the corner of her eye as she tipped her own bottle back and sucked down the sweet liquid without letting go of Benni's hand. It was lukewarm, but that didn't matter, it was wet and didn't taste like rotten eggs.

The man took a step toward her, and she startled, almost dropping the precious water bottle. "Stay there," she warned, holding out the plastic container as if to ward him off. It was a stupid command, because the man didn't have any reason to obey her. An instinctive demand, more to protect Benni than herself. He was twice her size and could do whatever he wanted, and there probably wasn't much she could do to stop him. Most men liked to throw their weight around, use it to dominate and intimidate those smaller than them. She flinched, her hand pushing Benni farther behind her legs.

Surprisingly, however, he did as she asked, and stopped walking, holding his hands up in placation again. "Okay, I'm not going to hurt you," he reiterated. He removed his sunglasses, hooking them into the front of his shirt, revealing blue eyes. "But can you at least tell me your name?"

The guy was tall, much taller than her. Big and broad-shouldered, dressed in dark jeans, and a blue shirt, with a

9

brown hat on his head. He looked like one of those cowboys on the front of the magazine she'd spied on the table at the roadside diner a few days ago.

Kee had studied him from her hiding spot behind the tree trunk as he got out of his car to investigate the trough and its surrounds. At first, she'd been determined not to reveal herself, praying that Benni would do as she was told and stay safely in her hidey-hole. It was too risky. She had to protect Benni. Her daughter was the only thing that mattered.

But she also knew they couldn't stay out here forever. They'd been here for two days already, and he was the first person they'd seen. Which was admittedly her fault, she'd intentionally covered the camera, but that was back when she'd been naïve enough to believe she could fix her car.

It was his kind face that finally made the decision for her. Even though his features were often hidden by the shadow of his big, brown hat, she caught enough glimpses to see it was open and friendly, giving her a feeling of certainty that he wouldn't hurt her. So, she'd drawn in a deep, fortifying breath, and stepped out from her hiding place.

Now she appraised him again. He had a nice face. A handsome face, if you liked them a little rugged. Which she didn't. Then again, all the men she'd dated had been clean-shaven and smartly dressed, and look where that had got her.

What other choice did she have?

While she and Benni were standing in the shade of the sweeping eucalyptus tree, the man was out in the blazing sun. Large sweat stains marked his shirt under his arms and formed down the line of his buttons.

"Warwick, is that your name?" she asked with a heavy sigh.

"Yes, ma'am, Warwick Nobles. But you can call me Wazza." His pale, blue eyes lit with contemplation.

She winced at the name. Such an Australian term of

phrase, to shorten everything and put an A on the end. But the name suited him in a way, he looked like an Aussie bloke through and through.

"Why don't you join us over here in the shade?" She beckoned him over, but backed around the tree trunk, keeping a good distance between them. He ambled over, booted feet kicking up small puffs of dust. This place was ridiculously dry. She'd never been anywhere this…barren before. It was like a wasteland straight out of that terrible movie Mad Max she'd watched once with Jakov. Why had she ever thought it was a good idea to head to North Queensland?

Because no one would find her up here, that's why. And because nothing up here could be as bad as what was following her.

Warwick stopped at the edge of the shade, as if respecting her need to keep a distance between them. He was even taller up close, strong looking, with long legs slightly akimbo, and large hands, which he kept held out in front of him in a pacifying gesture.

"My name is Kee," she offered. "And this is my daughter, Benni."

Until now, Benni had remained quiet and withdrawn, hiding behind her legs, taking a sip from her water bottle now and then. "My real name is Benita," her daughter said defiantly, poking her head around from behind Kee. "And I don't like it out here. I want to go home."

"That's enough, Benni," Kee said sharply. It would do them no good, if Benni revealed all their troubles to this man. Kind face or not, he was still a stranger. And going home wasn't an option. Home was no longer a place of safety. But Benni was too young to understand, and it broke Kee's heart to hear her say such things.

Warwick glanced at Benni, pursing his lips. She could see

many questions hovering in the depths of his eyes, and she squared her shoulders. She wasn't about to be bullied into revealing the truth; she'd had enough of that from Jakov. If need be, she would take Benni by the hand and march out of here. Find some other way to rescue herself.

But his face suddenly cleared, and he said, "Kee, that's an interesting name. Is it short for something, as well?"

Yes, it was. Her family called her Keiyona. Kee was a nickname her workmates at the animal shelter had given her. But telling him her true name might give away too much, so she merely shook her head and looked him in the eye. "No. Just Kee."

"Hmm," was all he said in reply. But those light blue eyes were fixed on her face, as if he knew she was hiding something.

"Do you know anything about repairing cars?" she asked. Time to get this conversation onto the important stuff. If this man could help her, she might be back on the road and headed north again sooner than she thought.

"You have a car?" Surprise showed in the lift of his mouth, and his gaze searched the flat land around them. Which gave her a certain pleasure; it meant she'd chosen a good spot to hide it. "I can take a look, if you like. But where is it?" he asked.

"It's a little farther down the road." She lifted a hand and pointed toward the large stand of trees over half a kilometer away, where she'd stashed her car when it started to make noises like a dying gorilla, sputtering and coughing, then losing power, until she had no choice but to pull over. "It just sort of stopped. And I couldn't get it started again." She got the car to limp behind the cover of the trees before it died completely.

Kee knew she was lost even before she'd passed the water trough that morning, two days ago. Knew she must've taken a wrong turn somewhere back down the road—more like a goat track, really. But her only real choice was to keep going forward, hoping that eventually, she'd come out on a better road again. Benni had wanted to stop and look at the strange watering contraption, and Kee didn't blame her, there was nothing else of interest to look at in this strange, flat country. But she'd been determined to keep going, and so placated her daughter by saying they'd stop at the next one they saw. Little did she know that water trough was going to be her saving grace. And the bane of her life.

Wazza squinted down the track from beneath the brim of his hat. If you knew where to look, you could just make out the glint of the faded white rear bumper of her old four-wheel-drive. She saw the second Wazza spotted it, he stood a little straighter and clamped his lips together.

"Right. Come on, then. Let's jump in my car. I'll drive us down there." Wazza strode across the clearing to his vehicle. She shrugged and followed hesitantly. It wasn't until he was almost at the car that he noticed Kee and Benni were hanging back.

"We'll meet you there," Kee called out. There was no way she was getting into his car.

Wazza eyed her skeptically. "It's a long bloody walk. Especially in this heat." That concerned frown was back, puckering the skin of his brow. "It's not good for the little one," he added, glancing down at Benni, who held tight to Kee's hand.

Yes, Kee knew exactly how far away her car was, she and Benni had walked between the water and the vehicle at least eight times over the past few days. And she knew that by the time she and her daughter covered the distance back to her car, they'd be desperately thirsty again. Each time they'd done the trip, they'd drunk their fill of the disgusting water, then filled two water bottles with the stuff to take back to the car with them. How could she not have thought to bring more water with her? It still astounded her every time she thought about it. But how was she to know? A girl brought up in the heart of Sydney, where there were shops and kiosks and cafés on every corner. Finding a drink had never been a problem.

But even so, she was loath to get into his vehicle. If she got in with him, she lost all control over the situation. Effectively became his prisoner. She shot a quick glance up the road and then swung around to face Warwick, indecision keeping her feet planted firmly in the dirt.

"The car's air conditioned. And I've got more bottles of water in the back," he said, opening the driver's door and beckoning inside. "It's clean, look," he added.

As if she'd care how dirty the car might be. But his plea touched a chord inside her heart.

"Come on, Mummy." Benni suddenly tugged on her hand, pulling her toward the open door. "I don't want to walk."

Should she trust this man? Her daughter obviously did. Benni was often shy around strangers, but she'd seemed to take an immediate shine to this guy. Or was it just that her little daughter, who'd been so stoic and cool-headed about their situation—lost in the desert without water or proper shelter—was finally tired of the heat and the flies and the dust? Kee had a sudden urge to take Benni into her arms and hold her tight, so she'd know just how much she loved her. Sometimes Benni was wise beyond her years; showed intelligence that scared Kee. Kee's father might've called her an old soul. If he ever met her. Kee tucked that dark thought away for another day.

"Here, you can drive, if you like." Wazza held out a set of keys.

It was this act of careful compassion on his part that finally had her shaking her head in embarrassment. "No, no, it's fine." She led Benni around to the passenger side and boosted her daughter up into the seat. Then she climbed in behind her and placed Benni in her lap, not bothering to put on the seatbelt; they weren't going far. It was much hotter in here, the cab acting like a mini greenhouse, concentrating the sun's heat. Wazza started the engine, but it took a minute for the air inside the cab to cool. Kee directed a vent on to her daughter's face, and Benni laughed with glee.

"It's colder than ice cream," she said, with a giggle that made Kee want to smile along with her. It was often the simple things that made Benni happiest. Kee drew in large gulps of the cool air, letting the gusts dry the sweat off her skin, the relief from the searing heat a godsend.

Wazza steered the vehicle carefully over the bumpy track. His big hands rested lightly on the wheel as his blue eyes studied the ground ahead. Kee was suddenly acutely aware of the large man sitting beside her. Of his physicality. Of his solid male presence. He exuded an air of attentiveness, as well as an aura of calm. Completely different to Jakov's manner of restrained violence, as if he might explode at any second. When Kee had first met Jakov, she'd been attracted to his vitality and strength. But over time, it'd morphed into something uglier and meaner. Wazza's air of calm was a soothing balm to her soul. She just wished she wasn't so *aware* of him.

The drive seemed to take an eternity, even with the cooling cabin and Benni bouncing on her lap with excitement, pointing out little things of interest as they passed by, like the pile of brown cow dung by the side of the road, or the pockmarked trunk of the old bottle tree growing all alone and lonely farther out into the plain. At one point, Benni stared at the man next to her intently, glancing from his large hat right down to his boots, before she finally asked in a slightly breathless voice, "Are you a cowboy?"

He laughed, and said, "Yes, I guess you could call me a cowboy. But out here we're called station hands, or a ringers."

"Oh." Benni seemed to consider his answer, but by the way she puckered her lips, she wasn't that enamored with it.

At last, Wazza drove up behind her car, tucking it into the shade behind it, and pulled on the handbrake.

Trying to see their little campsite through a stranger's eyes, Kee scrutinized her attempt at making them both as comfortable as she could out in the middle of the desert. Her four-wheel-drive was old and rusty in some places, but her friend Leni from the animal shelter had assured her it still had plenty of miles left in it. She wished she could tell him now that he'd been wrong. But she had no one else she trusted to help her. And Leni's heart had been in the right place. Perhaps whatever was wrong with her car was something that even a trained mechanic might not have been able to spot. Cars broke down all the time, for no reason that she could see. It was all Kee could afford, anyway, and at least it blended in well with all the other vehicles out on the country roads. Both doors on the side nearest the clump of trees stood open, and she'd rigged up an old sheet to form a sort of roof, strung between the car and the branches a little higher up. Underneath her rustic tent, she'd spread out a couple of beach towels to keep them off the red dirt. At night, they slept in the back seat of the vehicle, Benni wrapped carefully in her arms, despite the heat. Kee had hardly slept during the two nights they'd spent out here, too scared of the nightly noises—at one stage she'd heard a dog howling and had shut the car door until the stifling air had forced her to open it again—and too hot, her daughter's sweaty little body acting like a furnace. During the day, when she wasn't tinkering uselessly under the hood of her car, they spent most of their time stretched out in the shade. It was too searing to do anything else. Except when they made their trips to the water trough.

"Jesus…" Wazza seemed to bite back any further words, but he glanced at her sideways, as if reassessing her character. Was that admiration she saw in his eyes? "How long have you been here?"

"Two days and two nights," she replied. There was no point in lying about that part. It was pretty obvious they'd been here for a while.

"Jesus," he said again, adding a low whistle. "Right, let's take a look, then." He jumped out of the driver's seat and headed to the front of her car. The hood was already propped up. She'd peered into that engine so many times over the last few days. Prodded and poked and yelled in frustration. But she had no idea about anything mechanical. That'd been Jakov's thing. And her father had never encouraged her to learn anything about looking after a car. It was expected that her husband would do all that for her. She didn't even know how to check her engine oil. Which was one more thing she'd beaten herself up about over the past days. Self-flagellation wasn't normally her thing, but with so much time on her hands to dissect everything she'd done wrong over the past two months, she'd pretty much covered every aspect of her life. How had it all become so mixed up?

Wazza had his head down in the engine bay, and she couldn't see his expression because of his large hat. Then he lifted his head, and with a frown of consternation he went around to the driver's seat and turned the key in the ignition. The motor whirred for a second, then nothing. Exactly like it'd done every time she'd tried to start it. He came back to the front and stared into the engine, using his long fingers to gently prod at something.

"Come and sit in the shade," she said quietly to Benni, taking her hand and crouching down to lead her into their makeshift tent. When Benni was settled with more water and her dolly—thank the lord she'd remembered to snatch up some of her daughter's toys before they'd left—Kee went back to watching Wazza examine the engine.

Finally, he looked up at her. "It looks like the fuel pump is gone. It's either that, or a clogged fuel line. How old is this car?" He leaned over the engine, rubbing a finger over some writing scrawled at the back of the engine bay.

"I don't know," she answered in a hurry. She didn't care how old the car was, there was only one question on her mind. "Can you fix it?" she asked, trying, but failing, to keep the hope out of her voice.

Her heart sank at the shake of his head. "No, sorry. You'll need a replacement part. This'll have to get towed into town. But don't worry, I know a great mechanic…"

The rest of his words were lost in a fog of despair. She knew she shouldn't have, but she'd pinned all her hopes on this man. She needed her car fixed. Now. Not in town, and not in a few days' time.

"*Jebi ga,*" she spat the word at the sky.

"Excuse me?"

"What? Oh, sorry. It's Croatian." It took her a second to regain her composure. There was no point in showing this man her desperation. She angled her head slightly in Benni's direction. "So she doesn't know I'm swearing," she added quietly.

A large grin split Warwick's face. "Nice," he said, one eyebrow raised in amusement. "Are you Croatian, then?"

"No, my husband is…was…" Oh, now she'd said too much; hadn't meant to reveal even that much about her life. This man was making her too relaxed, too easy in his presence. She needed to remember to keep her guard up. "Whatever, it doesn't matter. What does matter is that you can't fix my car."

His curiosity must've finally got the better of him, because he took off his hat, ran a distracted hand through his damp hair, fixed her with his baby-blue gaze, and said, "Do you mind if I ask just what you're doing out here? I mean, you seem woefully under-prepared for a trip into the Queensland outback. You have no camping gear, no water, nothing at all that might help you survive in the desert."

"I have extra fuel," she said, pursing her lips at him. Which was true, she at least knew she didn't want to run out of fuel all the way out here. But she was only half focussing on her reply. It was the first time she'd seen him without the shade of his hat covering his face. Sunlight played over the planes of his cheekbones and brought the true color of his eyes to the fore. They were so pale, they were almost gray, like the morning mist lifting from Pushkar Lake back in India. She'd never been to the sacred lake herself, but her mother had shown her photos, and she'd loved to stare at them endlessly as a child.

Kee shook her head. What *was* she doing? Drooling over the color of a stranger's eyes, like a lovesick teenager?

Wazza was still waiting for an answer. What should she tell him? It was obvious she wasn't a tourist. All the travellers she'd seen in the past few towns had new, four-wheel-drives, stacked to the roof with camping gear, and often towing a caravan or trailer. She certainly didn't fit into that category.

"I'm on my way to..." she scrambled for one of the township names she remembered from the maps she'd studied as she planned her hasty drive away from Sydney. "Cooktown," she said, hoping her hesitation didn't come through in her words. "I'm going to visit my aunty."

"Cooktown?" She didn't need to look at his face to see his confusion. "Yes, but I think I took a wrong turn somewhere," she added hurriedly.

"A pretty big wrong turn. You should've turned north when you hit Mareeba. Headed back toward the coast."

She knew that. But she was staying as far away from the major roads and big towns as she could possibly get. This road was supposed to take her deeper into Queensland. Away from the coast and toward the Northern Territory. Even though she'd thought she'd been prepared for the back roads, she now knew how woefully ignorant her knowledge of life in the desert was. How long might she have been stuck out here, before anyone else came along? It was a hard lesson to learn. Kee didn't want to die out here, and next time she'd make sure she was much better prepared. Eventually, she would've removed the cover from the camera and hoped someone at the other end noticed her waving madly. But that'd been her last resort. She hated being reliant on the kindness of strangers. And the fewer people who knew where she was, the better.

Kee pursed her lips and widened her eyes in mock surprise. "Really? Is that where I went wrong?"

"That's not the only place you went wrong." Wazza's frown was almost comical, and it was all Kee could do not to laugh. She needed to keep up the dumb-woman façade if he were to believe her, however, so she smoothed out her complexion, lowering her eyes and demurring. Something she'd become extremely good at while she'd been Jakov's wife. And at the moment, it wasn't that far from the truth, either. It had been pretty dumb to get lost in the middle of the desert.

CHAPTER THREE

Wazza hoped his mouth wasn't hanging open. This woman's sheer lack of knowledge about driving in the outback, her lack of common sense appalled him. Were all city people like this? Woefully unprepared, thinking that driving into the desert was the same as going to your local park for a picnic? Because it wasn't. Didn't she realize people died out here? This land was a harsh and unforgiving mistress. The fact that she and her daughter were in relatively good shape after two days in this heat was a miracle. Thank God she'd stayed with her vehicle and not tried to walk back to civilization. That was a sure path to death by heat stroke and dehydration.

Wazza mentally shook himself. There was no point in lecturing her now. They were just lucky they'd broken down where they had, and that he'd come out to investigate the blocked camera. Which raised another question. Why *had* she blocked the camera? Did she not want to be rescued? Too many questions and not enough answers. He tucked that away in the growing list of issues he needed to discuss with her.

"Anyway, it doesn't matter now. I can show you the correct road later. We need to get your car fixed, first." Wazza turned toward to his vehicle. "I've got a sat phone. I'll see if Lefty can come out to tow your vehicle back to Dimbulah for you." Although Lefty wouldn't be pleased about having to come all the way out here, he'd charge a hefty bill for this recovery effort. What had Kee been thinking when she took this road? It wasn't signposted, and probably wasn't even on Google Maps.

"Can't you get someone out here to fix it? I'll wait here with the car until they come," she asked, as if it were the easiest thing in the world.

Was this woman for real? A mechanic coming to her? That might've worked if you lived in the city. But not out here. They were over a hundred kilometers from the nearest town.

"I don't want to go to town," she added. Her voice was subdued, but there was a steel running through it, like she wasn't going to take no for an answer.

"What do you mean? Where else are you going to go while you wait for your car to be fixed? It will most likely take days; they'll have to order the part in." Was it a matter of money? Could Kee not afford a few nights' accommodation while she waited for her car to be repaired? Perhaps he could organize a lift back to Cairns for her. But then, he didn't even know where she'd come from. That might be just as bad, and accommodation was certainly more expensive in the coastal tourist town.

"I don't know," she answered with a belligerent jut of her chin. "But I'm not going into that town. Not any town," she added hastily.

"Well, you can't stay here." Even as he said the words, he knew how absurd they sounded. But a little voice told him that was exactly what this woman might do.

"Why not?" she retorted, confirming his worst fears.

"Mummy, I'm hungry." Wazza spun around to see the little girl staring up at them with beseeching eyes. Benni's presence surprised them both; they'd been so caught up in their conversation that for a moment he'd forgotten she was there.

"Oh…I'm sorry, bunny." Kee brushed past him as she hurried over to the makeshift tent and got down on her knees in front of the child. "Can you wait until I've finished talking to Warwick? Then I'll get you something to eat." There was a strange hesitancy in Kee's voice that Wazza didn't understand.

"But I'm hungry now," the little girl sniffled. "I want some cornflakes."

"I don't have any cornflakes, my bunny." Kee's shoulders visibly sagged, and she hugged her girl to her chest.

Sudden realization hit Wazza. They didn't have any food. No water and no food. This woman was either breathtakingly stupid…or something else was going on here that he couldn't figure out. "I've got some apples in the car," he volunteered.

Benni's eyes brightened at the mention of fruit. Kee didn't say a word.

"I'll get them for you." He strode around to the rear door and pulled out his little cooler bag. It was only on a whim that he'd grabbed the bag and the fruit as he strode through the kitchen on his way out the door. Now, he wished he'd asked Skylar for a sandwich to add to his haul. He handed the apples to Kee. They both heard her stomach growl loudly at the sight of food. But she ignored it and handed both pieces of fruit to her daughter.

"Here you go." Then she watched with satisfaction as Benni bit hungrily into the fruit. An apple in each hand, Benni went and re-took her seat in the shade of the tent.

Wazza watched the whole scene play out with growing certainty. There was something wrong here. And he needed to find out what it was.

Kee didn't look at him, but murmured, "Thank you, that was a nice thing to do."

They needed to talk. He went to take her by the arm, but

she flinched away from him. "Sorry," he apologized. He'd forgotten how distrustful she was. Was it just him? Or all men? Another thing to add to the growing list. "Come over here." He beckoned her to the front of the vehicle that was still partially in the shade. Far enough away for Benni not to overhear what they were saying.

He stood with his hands on his hips, staring down at the petite woman in front of him. She finally returned his stare, her big, brown eyes watchful and guarded. Beads of perspiration had formed on her brow and on her top lip. They glistened like jewels against her brown skin, and for a second, he forgot where he was. Forgot what he wanted to ask her. Instead, wanted to run his thumb over her lip, taste her skin. With a flick of her wrist, she swiped at her forehead, and his daydream was broken. What had he been thinking?

He sucked in a lungful of hot, desert air. "I'm sorry, but I can't help you if you won't tell me what you're running from."

Her brown eyes filled with fear at his words, and she took a step away from him.

"What are you so frightened of?" he demanded.

"I don't know what you're talking about." She flipped her long braid over her shoulder with a disdainful grimace. "I told you. We're on our way to see my aunty. We just got a little lost, that's all."

Bullshit. He wanted to say, *never bullshit a bullshitter*, but instead, he asked, "Oh yeah, what's her name, this aunty of yours?"

"Her name? Oh. Ah…" Kee's eyes widened, and put her hands on her hips, mimicking his pose. "It's…ah…Beryl. Yes, Aunty Beryl, that's it."

Bullshit. Again, he only just stopped himself from saying the word. "Hey, Benni," he called out. "Are you looking forward to seeing Aunty Beryl?"

"Don't," she spat, dark eyes flashing. Then she turned and said in a saccharine voice, "Don't worry, bunny, you go back to your apples."

Turning back to face him, Kee shot daggers at him, crossing her arms over her pert breasts. "Don't you dare involve my daughter in this."

Wazza stared at her thoughtfully. She certainly was protective when it came to Benni. Overprotective, even. But enough was enough. "Perhaps I should call the police," he said quietly. "They can sort out this mess you've gotten yourself into."

"No!" Her voice was like the clang of a bell in the quiet desert.

"No? Why not?" He knew he probably wasn't being completely fair, but she wasn't leaving him with many choices. He was hot and thirsty—they'd drunk his last two bottles of water—and this stalemate needed to come to some sort of resolution.

Suddenly, all the fight seemed to drain right out of her. Her hands fell to her sides, and she hung her head. "Fine, I'll tell you. But please keep your voice down. I don't want Benni to hear."

She looked so pathetic, he wanted to reach out and touch her, but she'd only flinch away, so he merely stood, watching her carefully.

"My ex-husband and his family are trying to take Benni away from me."

"What? Why?"

"It's complicated. But the reason I don't want you to call the police is that my ex is…was a cop. He has contacts everywhere in the force. If they report my whereabouts… Then he'll find me."

"Wow. Okay." Wazza digested her story, turning it over in his head. This felt like she was telling the truth, for once, but it was a hell of a story, if it were true. He could also feel there was more, but it seemed like all he was going to get out of her for now. One thing was for sure; he suddenly understood her overprotectiveness of her child. Hell, he suddenly felt just as overprotective. "So, you're what…? On the run after a messy divorce? And he wants the child?" He closed his mouth with a snap. Those were a whole shitpile of questions, but only one was really important right now, and that was getting Kee and her daughter somewhere safe and out of this heat. He could find out the full truth later.

"Like I said, it's complicated." She stared up at him, eyes almost as beseeching as her daughter's had been. "I just need to get somewhere where he can't find me for a little while. Then I can fight this ridiculous custody battle. But they were going to take Benni away from me. And I couldn't…" She stumbled to a halt, her lower lip trembling. God, he was such a sucker for dark-brown eyes. And hers were as deep and beguiling as warm chocolate. Add to that a woman on the verge of tears, and he was a definite goner.

He held up a hand to forestall any more speech. "Let me think for a second."

Could he take her back to Stormcloud? Daniella wouldn't be happy with him bringing in a stray woman and her child. But she also wouldn't turn them away. Daniella might run the lodge with a resolute hand, but even she would only need to take one look at that little girl for her heart to melt. But that'd involve having to make up a story to keep Kee and her daughter safe. And Daniella had a knack for finagling out the truth of things.

Where else could he take her? If he took her to the motel in Dimbulah, even if she kept a low profile and never went out, word would get around. People in small country towns *always* knew everything that was going on.

Daniella's daughter, and head chef at the lodge, Skylar, and her fiancé, Nash, owned a property halfway between Dimbulah and Stormcloud. They had plenty of room in their rambling, colonial home. So much space that her half-sister Julie and new boyfriend Aaron were renting out one of the larger old barns until they could afford a place of their own. But Nash was the local senior constable, and if Kee's story was true about not wanting to get other cops involved, then he couldn't ask them to hide her.

Then a thought struck him. He turned it over and over, dissecting the pros and cons. It wasn't the best idea, but it was all he could come up with right now.

"I know a place you can stay for a few days. Come on, bring your belongings, and hop in my car."

"Really? Where?" she asked suspiciously.

"The boss's stepson, Dale, has a fiancée, Daisy, who lives out in a small outstation a few miles down the road from Stormcloud lodge. She's over in Perth visiting her family for a few weeks. Dale's going to move in with her when they get married in December, but for now, he still lives at the lodge. So, the place will be empty." He'd just have to hope that Daisy hadn't asked Dale to pop over and check on her place while she was away. It was a busy time of the year, with another late-season muster being planned for a few weeks' time. So hopefully Dale would have his hands too full to worry about Daisy's place.

"Are you sure? When is this Daisy due back? And won't she know someone's been staying in her house? I'm not sure I'd like a stranger gate-crashing my house without my knowledge."

"It's all I've got." Wazza held up his hands in defeat. "If you have a better plan, I'd love to hear it. And no, you can't stay out here," he added, as the light of rebellion entered her eyes, and she opened her mouth to speak. "So, come and help me pack up your stuff."

Kee stood, frozen, biting her bottom lip. What the hell? He was trying to help her. Offering her a sanctuary for the next few days. Why was she waiting? Kee turned to study her daughter, who was noisily sucking on the apple core and playing with her doll, and he suddenly understood her hesitancy. It wasn't just her she had to think about. It was her child's welfare that was utmost in her mind. What would he do in her situation? Would he trust a stranger with the safety of his child? His mind flicked back to his imagined images of little Ava. He knew what he'd do if it came down to protecting his daughter. Anything that it took. But she wasn't real. She only existed in his mind. It was easy to make a decision when the stakes weren't tangible.

Kee finally lifted her wretched gaze to his. "I'm not sure why you're doing this. Helping me, that is. But I guess I have no choice. And I guess I owe you a debt of gratitude."

"You don't owe me anything." He waved away her concern. Was that what she was afraid of? Of owing him something? Well, he wasn't that sort of guy. He'd never ask for anything in return. He was doing this as much for the little girl as he was for the mother. Even if there was something about Kee. An air of fragility. A sensuality that affected him like few other women had. Let alone that the graceful tilt of her long neck, or the way she walked, the hedonistic sway of her hips, lit off sparks deep in his belly.

He tried to tell himself he would've done the same for anyone he'd found stranded out here.

It didn't take them long to dismantle the makeshift tent. Wazza folded the sheet and towels, while Kee grabbed a few things scattered throughout the car and rammed them into two small bags she'd kept in the trunk. Then she unfastened the child's booster seat and took it to the rear of his car. He helped transfer everything to the back seat of his Land Cruiser, but she waved him away when he offered to help her install the booster. Which was probably a good thing, he had no idea where to start with one of those. That thought set his heart to aching before he could rein in his thoughts. If Ava had been born, he'd be all over installing child seats. No point in mulling over things that'd never happened. Instead, he started the engine to get the air conditioning going, while Kee went back to make sure she hadn't left anything behind. Benni stood by, not asking questions, as some children might, but content to watch everything they did with an eagle eye, holding her doll tightly to her chest.

At last, she asked, "Are we going with the cowboy man, Mummy?"

"Yes. He's taking us to a friend's place. We can stay there for a little while." She hunkered down in front of Benni. "Is that okay?"

"Oh, yes," she answered with delight. "I don't like it here. It's too hot."

Wazza had to hold in a laugh. She had that one right, it sure was hot, and getting hotter. The dial on the dash now read thirty-six degrees. The temperature had gone up even in the hour or so he'd spent with Kee. It'd probably hit forty by midday. Way too hot to be sitting under a sheet, trying to survive.

"I agree," Kee replied with a relieved grin.

It was the first time Wazza had seen her smile, and it drove home to him how terrified she must've been. How much resolve did it take to pack your car with the bare essentials and drive your child into the unknown? Leave your life behind to save the one thing you loved? She was certainly a brave, courageous woman.

Kee helped Benni into the rear seat, which was a long way off the ground. After buckling her into her booster and making sure she was happy, she drew a deep breath and swung up into the passenger seat beside Wazza.

"Ready?" he asked.

"Ready as we'll ever be," both Kee and Benni chimed together, and Wazza gave her a curious glance. "Sorry," she said, chuckling. "It's a thing we always do when someone asks us if we're ready."

"Yes." Benni was bouncing in her seat. "We did it with Daddy all the time."

Kee's face blanched.

"Didn't we, Mummy? Daddy was the best at saying it."

"Yes, bunny, he was," Kee replied, but her mouth puckered up like she'd sucked on a lemon.

"I miss Daddy. When are we going to see him again?"

Kee cast an unhappy glance at Wazza, but kept her voice bright and cheery, as she said, "I'm not sure, Benni Bunny. You know he had to go away. I'm not sure when he's coming back."

"But soon, Mummy. We'll see him soon," Benni continued, a determined tilt to her chin, making her look like a mini version of Kee. Wazza took his eyes off the track for a second to glance back at the little girl, and she had her doll clutched tightly to her chest again, as if the toy would make it come true.

"Yes, soon."

"Okay." Benni settled back in her chair.

Wazza wondered exactly where her ex-husband had gone. And for how long. How could he be conducting a custody battle if he wasn't even in the same state, or perhaps not even in the same country? But he let none of the worry he felt reach his face. She'd called him her ex more than once. He hoped she was telling the truth about them being divorced. There was no ring on her finger—he'd already scoped that out earlier. He wondered idly how old she was. Her brown skin was smooth and supple, no signs of wrinkles. She looked young, especially to have a four-year-old daughter, but he probably wasn't much of a judge. His thirtieth birthday a few months ago had come and gone without much fanfare. Of course, Skylar had baked him one of her amazing cakes and all the staff at Stormcloud had sung "Happy Birthday" at the top of their lungs. But Wazza had really only wanted to forget he'd turned another year older. Thirty might be a milestone for some, but for him, with nothing new on the horizon, no real ambitions or goals, he felt like he was merely drifting through life.

Conversation inside the cabin was kept to general topics as they drove. Of course, Kee didn't want to tell him more in front of Benni, and he had to respect that. But he itched to ask the questions burning in his brain.

It took around twenty minutes to travel the track from the water trough, to the larger dirt road that'd eventually take him out to the highway. Once he was on the wider road, he lifted the sat phone from its cradle on the dash. "I'll tell Lefty you're a friend of Daisy's, come to visit her, but you arrived a few days early. I'll ask him to keep it quiet, as you want to surprise Daisy when she gets back. How does that sound?"

CHAPTER FOUR

Kee forced her gaze from the road in front. Her eyelids had been about to drift shut. Lord, she was tired. The heat and the flies and the lack of sleep were finally getting to her. And now, encased in Wazza's car with the cooling air flowing around, she finally felt almost...safe. Almost as if she could let go, for a few minutes at least. For the first time in nearly a month, since she'd left Sydney, she thought she might've found someone who she could trust.

What had Wazza asked her? Something about telling the man towing her car that she was a friend of this Daisy woman. "Oh, yes, that sounds fine." Did it? She wasn't sure, but she was so worn out, she couldn't find the energy to care. For this moment in time, she was happy to go with his proposal. It was so nice not to have to be responsible for every tiny detail for once.

Kee had been brought up to believe that the men in her life would take care of her. That her husband would shoulder the burden of worry and responsibility. Her strictly Hindu parents had immigrated from India when Kee had been only four and her sister Pooja only two, bringing their culture and traditions with them. After growing up in Sydney's outer suburbs, Kee now had a good grasp on western culture and modern feminism, but she still found it hard to completely let go of her parents' ideals. Even though she thought she'd understood what kind of man she was marrying when she agreed to Jakov's proposal, a tiny part of her still believed he'd look after her right up into her old age. That she'd never have to fend for herself again. How wrong had that ideal turned out to be? She'd had to learn the hard way over the past year, during the divorce, and then when Jakov's family tried to take Benni away, to find a grit and determination inside that she hadn't been sure existed.

She needed to make sure she didn't lose that hard-won independence. Sitting up straighter in the seat, she rubbed her eyes. Now wasn't the time to become complacent.

Wazza was talking to someone on his radio and so Kee glanced into the back seat and saw that Benni was fast asleep. Poor baby. She was just as haggard and weary as Kee. How could she ever have even contemplated staying out in that blasted place for even one more hour? She barely listened as Wazza made arrangements for her car and then ended the call.

"You want to fill me in on some more details, now?" Wazza kept his voice low, so as not to waken Benni, but his mouth was set in a firm line that said he wanted answers. Which she probably owed him, seeing as how he was helping her when he didn't need to.

When they'd first got into the vehicle, he'd removed his hat and placed on the console between the two front seats. His short, dark hair stood up in tufts, where he dragged a hand through the sweaty locks. It was an interesting combination, his dark hair—almost black—and those pale, blue eyes that reminded her of her the sacred lake. Not something you often saw, especially in a man.

She nodded, but her fingers gripped the edge of her seat tightly in anticipation. She wasn't sure she was ready for this.

"Why did you cover the camera? You clearly knew that someone would see you. Didn't you want to be rescued?" he asked.

It took her a second to grasp his meaning. He was talking about her covering the camera with her shirt. She'd seen the device the moment they'd walked back to the water trough, and it'd been instinct for her to strip off her shirt and throw it over the lens. Not having any knowledge about how these things worked, she didn't know if she'd already been videoed, or if it was perhaps driven by movement. Did the camera feed only go back to the owners of the cattle, or did the police see it, too? When no one arrived in a fit of rage that someone had tampered with their camera after that first night, she assumed she hadn't been spotted.

"Not at first," Kee admitted. "I thought that if I could get the car started again, no one need even know we'd been there. But this place is so different from anywhere else I've ever been. I didn't understand how dangerous it was. I never knew it got so dry out here, like it might never rain again."

"Ah, but you wait. Because when it rains up here, boy, does it rain. All the rivers overflow, and the pastures become like an inland sea. They don't call them floodplains for nothing. Everything gets green and lush. The colors can be so bright they almost hurt your eyes." He gave her a quick sideways glance. "Actually, I'm not sure which is worse. To get lost during the dry season or the wet. They both have their challenges."

Kee didn't really understand what he meant by dry and wet season, so she just nodded.

"I'm thinking that you weren't really headed to Cooktown to see Aunty Beryl?"

"No, sorry, I made that up."

Wazza grunted in reply, as if he'd guessed her ploy right from the beginning. "Where were you headed, then? Did you have a plan?"

Kee felt the blood rush to her face, but she pursed her lips and forced herself to look at him. She was not going to let shame take over. Her plan had been to get as far away from Sydney as possible. To stay away from the major cities and roads, to make herself and her daughter invisible. Her plan hadn't included getting lost, or her car breaking down in the most remote part of Australia.

"No, not really. I was trying to get to the Northern Territory border. That was as far as I'd thought ahead. Once I was there…" Kee merely shrugged.

"You were just going to keep driving? Until what? Until you felt safe enough to stop? I don't get it, Kee. This all sounds a little…impractical. Taking on a drive across two states, in an old, unreliable car."

"Maybe it was." Kee jutted out her chin. "Maybe I am stupid for doing all these things."

"More like batshit crazy," Wazza interjected. Then he winced. "Sorry, but it's true. Surely there are better ways to resolve a custody battle?"

She didn't need to be lectured to by this man. Perhaps she had made mistakes, but it was better than the alternative.

"All I wanted was to get Benni away from those people. Jakov's parents." She couldn't even bring herself to say their names. They had betrayed her, betrayed her trust. "After the divorce, I decided Benni should still see her grandparents. They are her family and she loved her *baba* and *dida*." Wazza glanced at her with a lift of his eyebrow. "It's Croatian for Nana and Poppa," she said by way of explanation. When he nodded, she went on. "I let them take Benni one day every week. She always came back from her stay as happy as a clam, so I thought I was doing the right thing. But then one weekend, they refused to return her to me." Her chest tightened at the memory. She'd stood on the steps to the

Babić house staring at the closed front door, after they'd slammed it in her face, telling her she'd never see Benita again. Her heart had literally stopped beating in that instant. That'd been two months ago, and she still remembered it so clearly, like it was mere seconds ago. "They had her hidden away in their house and weren't even letting me see her. Said they'd put in a petition with the Family Court, saying I was an unfit mother." Kee held in a sob. How dare they say such untruths? How dare they try to take her daughter away from her? Her light. Her life.

Kee was staring straight ahead, not even seeing the road unfurling before them. Her mind was back in those terrible days she'd spent without Benni by her side. A warm hand landed softly on her knee, bringing her back to the present. This time, she didn't flinch away from his touch. It offered compassion and caring. And something more that Kee didn't want to explore. A spark of heat travelled up her leg and settled low in her belly.

"I'm sorry, Kee, that sounds awful. What a horrible thing to do to you," Wazza said softly.

"It was horrible," she agreed. "For days, I didn't know what to do. I went to the Family Court, and they told me I needed to get a lawyer. That I needed to prove I wasn't an unfit mother. His parents were lying about me, said I was a drug addict and I was out of it so often that I forgot to feed Benni. That I was neglectful." She'd had to force herself to read the document the man at the Family Court had given her. It was hard to believe, but those black and white words on the page had driven it home; this was all really happening. "But none of that's true. It's all lies." This time, the sob that'd been building in her throat broke free. Quickly, she glanced back at Benni, but she was mercifully still fast asleep. She took a deep breath, and then another. No tears in front of Benni, she'd promised herself.

"But what about your husband? What role does he have to play in this? You haven't mentioned him yet."

"My ex-husband, you mean," she snapped. At least she'd done something right. Divorcing Jakov had been the best thing she'd ever done.

Wazza merely inclined his head.

"Jakov is in jail."

"What?" The car veered across the road as Wazza turned to her in disbelief. He quickly had it back under control, but the look on his face said it all.

"My ex is a corrupt cop; he's in jail for the next ten years. The reason his family is trying to take Benni away is because they want to punish me. Because I put him there. I testified against him, so he'd go to prison." There, she'd said it. It was out in the open. This was the first time she'd told anyone about the sordid details of her life. That she'd been married to a dirty, unscrupulous man, and was tainted by association.

"Oh. Holy. Jesus." Wazza gave a low whistle. "That's... Wow, that's mind-blowing stuff. I can hardly get my head around it." He gave her another long glance. So long that she almost told him to keep his eyes on the road. Evaluating her. "That must've taken a helluva lot of courage," he said quietly.

She liked the edge of respect in his voice. At least he could see how much it cost her to do such a thing. Most men might only see the faults in what she'd done, see that she'd stolen her child and was now evading the law. Perhaps wanted to turn her in. But he didn't seem to be condemning her or judging her. It was almost like he supported her frantic decision.

"And Benni knows nothing about all this? What does she think about this little trip you're both on?"

"No. I told her Daddy had to go away for a while. I said he was in another country." She hung her head at this admission. She hated to lie to her daughter, but how else could she explain her father's disappearance? "And I told her we're going on an adventure. To find a new place to live for a little while."

"And what about your ex's parents? Did they not tell her where Jakov was? What he'd done?"

"I don't really know, but I don't think so. Otherwise, she would've mentioned something. Perhaps they asked her what she thought had happened to him and went with that. I guess I'll never know."

"How did you manage to snatch Benni from the grandparents? You said they were keeping her locked up in their house. Not letting you see her."

"Yes, that's right. And the lawyer I talked to told me they had the law on their side and there was nothing I could do unless I fought it in court." Kee had only seen the lawyer once, a rotund man with buttons that strained over a large belly. He'd smirked at her from behind his desk. Fat lot of good he'd done; he hadn't been able to tell her anything that the man at the Family Court hadn't already said. His fee had been preposterous, and Kee knew she could never afford to pay him. Then he'd told her it might take months or even years for the court case to be scheduled and she knew she couldn't be without Benni for that long.

"I began to stake out their house. I already knew a lot of their habits and timetables from when we were...more of a family. They had a big, old house, only a few blocks away from where we lived, with a big, rambling back garden." In her mind's eye, Kee could picture the yard, with its large fruit trees and vegetable garden, taking up most of one side. "I knew Marta went out to do the grocery shopping at the local farmer's market every Saturday morning. And I knew Ivan liked to spend that time in his shed—he's very old school, he likes to fix things like a broken lampshade, instead of buying a new one—and Benni would play in the garden. I climbed over the gate and snuck down the side of the house. Benni was right there, playing in the sandpit and when she saw me, she squealed so loud, I was sure Ivan would come out of his shed to investigate. I hugged her so tight." Tears pricked the back of her eyelids at the memory. "As quick as I could, I bundled her back over the gate and into the car, which I parked a few houses down, out of sight. Then we got out of there as fast as we could and have been driving ever since."

"Wow. That's almost cloak-and-dagger kind of stuff." Again, she thought she caught the hint of admiration in his tone. "So, it's not just that your husband has friends in the force out looking for you? Do you think they'll have reported her missing? That the police are on the lookout for you? Issued a warrant for your arrest?"

Kee licked her lips and made a noise in the affirmative.

Wazza's eyebrows drew together as he contemplated her answer. A small furrow appeared right between his eyes, and she couldn't drag her gaze away. This was the second time she'd noticed that crease; it must be a sign of whenever he was in deep thought. It was appealing, in a strange way that he was that worried about her. "Are you sure, though? Is there some way you can find out if the police really have issued a warrant?"

Yes, she knew without a doubt that the police were looking for her. But that wasn't the worst of it.

"Oh, I'm sure. The texts Jakov's parents sent me—before I turned my cell phone off—made it very clear they were going to bring the full force of the law down onto me. But Jakov has an older brother, Bruno, who also used to be a cop. I think the parents have sent him after me. I've seen him. He's following me. Trying to track me down."

"What?" For the second time that day, Wazza let the car drift to the middle of the road as he stared in bewilderment at her. "Holy shitpile." Wazza's knuckles were white on the steering wheel as he directed the vehicle onto the correct side of the road.

He didn't know the half of it. Bruno wasn't a man to be messed with. He was very good at holding a grudge, and he had a violent streak, much the same as Jakov. Kee had seen it all firsthand over the years she'd been part of the family. So far, no one had been able to link Bruno to any of Jakov's dirty deals, but Kee had no doubt he would've been involved, somehow.

"I saw him a couple of weeks back. Benni and I stayed the night in a little motel on the outskirts of Beaudesert, just this side of the Queensland border. We were packing up to leave, and I saw him through the window. He got out of his car and went into the hotel reception. I don't know how he found us. I paid cash for the room and gave a false name, but I knew without a doubt he was there for me. It was more than a coincidence." From that night on, Kee and Benni had slept either in the car or in an out-of-the-way campsite. She was taking no more chances. Which was why she didn't want to stay at the hotel in Dimbulah.

Wazza suddenly slowed the vehicle, and for a second, Kee thought he was going to stop and make her, and her daughter, get out of the car; that he wanted nothing more to do with them. But no, there was an intersection coming up. And miracle upon miracle, it was a bitumen road.

"The turnoff to Daisy's place is farther down this road," he said, guiding the car skilfully onto the bitumen and accelerating.

Kee checked on Benni, but she was still fast asleep, her chin resting on her chest, dolly still resting in the crook of her elbow. So sweet. So innocent.

"Daisy lives on what we call the outstation," Wazza said, dragging her attention back to him. "It's situated on the Koongarra Station, which is owned by a community of indigenous people, and run by the Kuku Corporation as a pastoral lease. But they're also branching out into other more sustainable agriculture, growing bush foods and the like."

"Right," Kee said when he looked at her expectantly.

"The old outstation was set up as a temporary residence while the main house was built. There's a good twenty kilometers between it and manager's place. And the community is situated farther north again, so no one should bother you out there."

That was good. No neighbors for miles and miles suited her just fine.

The low drone of the wheels on the road and the gentle rocking of the vehicle became too much and Kee's eyelids drifted closed of their own accord. She awoke with a start around half an hour later, as Wazza slowed the car again and took a right-hand turn onto yet another dirt road. So much for the small luxury of bitumen. The car bumped along at a slower pace as Wazza negotiated potholes and deep ruts. "Daisy needs to get Bryan out here with his dozer," Wazza mumbled to himself.

Benni gave a yawn from the back seat, and Kee turned to put her hand on her child's knee. The bumpy road must've woken her up. "Did you have a good sleep, my love?"

"Mm-hm." Benni rubbed her sleepy eyes. "I'm hungry."

"There'll be food at the house. We'll be there soon," she promised. Although she had no idea if that was true. Wazza hadn't mentioned anything about what sort of rations she might find out there. She hoped Daisy kept a well-stocked pantry.

Kee sat back and was content to soak in the scenery and let Wazza drive unhindered. She could ask about food later. She stared through the sparse scrubland, which opened up as they came over a small rise. Tall, spindly, eucalyptus trees were scattered randomly across an open savannah of brown tussock grassland. Now and then, one of those huge trees with spider-like branches reaching for the sky was dotted in between the eucalypts. Wazza had called it a bottle tree, from memory. He'd also said that when the rain came, there would be green grass as far as the eye could see. But now, they were surrounded by dead, brown clumps, and the desiccated skeletons of weeds rustling in the dry wind.

Squinting through the trees, she thought she could make out a flash of dull red and a square shape at odds with the native vegetation. As they got closer, she could see the faded, red metal side of what looked to be shipping containers.

"Over there," Wazza indicated with his chin toward the buildings.

"I see it."

They followed the road through a thick copse of trees and then emerged into a cleared area around the buildings. Wazza pulled up in the middle of the gravel clearing. Kee tried to take everything in at once. Four containers were set up onto high concrete pads, and it took a second for Kee to decide this was probably to keep them away from any flooding damage.

This strange-looking homestead consisted of two shipping containers, adjoined end-to-end to make one long, thin room, and two more at right angles, forming two wings that jutted out on either side.

"This place was pretty run-down when Daisy first moved here," Wazza said.

Kee raised her eyebrows but said nothing. It still looked pretty run-down to her.

"Daisy works for Angel Gold Corp, a Queensland-based, gold-mining company, finding more sustainable methods of rejuvenating old mine sites, as well as discovering ways to help to give back to remote communities." Wazza' voice held a touch of pride and Kee suddenly decided she'd like to meet Daisy one day. She sounded like a special person. And if

Wazza liked her, then she must be nice.

"They added these two sea containers to the main structure, one at each end," he said, undoing his seatbelt. "There's now a whole new bedroom, and a modern bathroom in the wing on that side of the building. You'll like it, I think."

Kee found it hard to stop the skeptical lift of her mouth. But beggars couldn't be choosers, and at least this would be a roof over their heads.

"Where are we?" Benni's voice came from the back seat, reminding Kee of her duties. Quickly, she unbuckled her own seatbelt and jumped down onto the dry earth. The scorching heat hit her as soon as she opened the door. She'd never experienced such dry, unrelenting heat as this. It was enough to suck the moisture straight out of your skin. She reached in and freed Benni from her booster, holding her on her hip so they could both survey the place they might call home.

"This is where we're going to stay for a few days," Kee replied. "It looks like fun, hey? A new adventure."

"Yeah." Benni's eyes lit up and Kee smiled. It didn't take much to ignite Benni's delight. Sometimes she wished she could hold on to such childish optimism. She made a decision that she was going to like this place, no matter what. She was going to look at things through Benni's eyes, for once.

"Wait here." Wazza disappeared around the side of the building, leaving her and Benni standing in the hot sun. Now she understood why Wazza wore that big, wide-brimmed hat, to keep the sun off his face. A cowboy hat. She needed to get them both one of those.

A large, covered patio jutted out from the front door, with a set of out outdoor furniture scattered under the iron roof. It might be a nice place to sit and enjoy a leisurely dinner, once the fierce sun had disappeared. Kee walked over to stand in the shade, Benni still balanced on her hip, her daughter's eyes wide as she took everything in.

"Found it." Wazza held up a key as he jogged around the side of the structure. "I'll show you where it's kept before I go." He slipped the key into the lock and opened the metal door wide, waving for Kee to precede him.

It was even hotter inside, almost like an oven, and Kee hesitated on the threshold.

"Don't worry, I'll get the air con going," Wazza said, hovering behind her until Kee stepped into the room. A kitchenette took up most of the far wall directly ahead, with a small, round table and four chairs to be able to sit and eat. Farther down the long room was a living area, with a couch, and two winged chairs, a television mounted on the wall, and a small stereo set. It all looked surprisingly fresh and modern, with floorboards, a brand-new gas stovetop, a microwave, and a gleaming, stainless-steel sink.

Wazza brushed past her shoulder and flicked a button on the wall. "It'll take a few minutes to cool the place down, but I can vouch for how well it works. When the mining company updated the place, they made sure Daisy had the best of everything. They even installed a brand-new block of storage batteries, and new solar panels on the roof. The system supplies more than enough electricity to run everything."

Kee looked up at Wazza. He was so tall, he seemed to dwarf the room, the roof almost brushing the top of his head. It made her suddenly aware of how close he was standing to her. A shiver of awareness ran down her spine and settled low in her belly. To cover her reaction, she made a show of turning to her daughter and placing her gently on the ground. But she kept a tight hold of her hand. Had he felt it, too? She dared not look at him to find out.

"There's also a backup generator if you ever need it. I'll show you how to work that before I leave. It's easy," he added as he caught her look of dismay.

Kee wasn't convinced. She was the opposite of a handywoman. She wouldn't know the first thing about generators or batteries. This Daisy woman must be terribly self-sufficient to live out here on her own. Kee was starting to see it took a certain type of person to exist in the outback. Back in the city, these sorts of things never bothered her. She never had to think twice about where her electricity came from, she just flicked a switch.

"Why don't you take a look around and I'll bring in your bags." Wazza disappeared out the door, before she had a chance to comment.

"Oooh, look, a TV." Benni ran up and touched the screen. "And the couch is blue, my favorite color." Benni climbed up on the couch and settled in with her dolly. Cool air began to flow past Kee's face as the air con finally kicked in.

Hesitantly, Kee made her way toward a doorway at the end. It led to a bedroom, which was small, but had a queen-size bed, a closet, and a bedside table. The bedroom was neat and tidy, done up in soft blues and grays. A pile of books dominated the small table. This lady must read a lot. A couple of shirts were draped over a small chair in the corner and a pair of cowboy boots took pride of place at the foot of the bed.

She suddenly realized she was intruding on someone else's life. Her palms began to itch, and an uncomfortable knot lodged in her chest. Not only was Wazza going out of his way to help her, but this other woman was unknowingly doing the same. It was too much. Kee couldn't do this.

Wazza came in at that moment, carrying both of their bags.

"We can't stay here," she said, gathering Benni up from the couch. "This isn't right. We have to go."

CHAPTER FIVE

Wazza clenched his jaw until his teeth ached in an attempt to keep a blank face. Why on earth would she refuse this? He was offering her sanctuary, a place to hide for a few days. "Why don't you want to stay?" he asked, trying to keep his exasperation under wraps.

"This is someone else's house. I'm a stranger. If it were my place, I wouldn't want someone I didn't know staying here."

Why were women so hard to figure out sometimes? She was on the run, desperate to protect her little daughter. Had admitted that her ex-husband's brother was looking for her. And she was worried about upsetting a woman she'd never met? He wanted to throw his hands in the air.

Instead, he sat down on the couch next to Benni and removed his hat. Benni stared up at him with wide, dark eyes. The cool air conditioning felt nice on his feverish head. Daniella hated it when he wore his hat inside the lodge, she was constantly berating him for forgetting he had it on. Like most men out here, his Akubra was an extension of himself, part of the image he projected, as well as an important piece of safety equipment. But he was trying to do better. Trying to follow Daniella's rules.

"Sit down," he said, pointing to one of the wing chairs.

But Kee refused, standing near the doorway, tapping her sandaled foot in agitation. From this angle he could see the curve of her hips beneath her shorts, her T-shirt stretched taut against her breasts. Mocha skin, warm and inviting. Just to look at her made him want to lick his lips. He couldn't say that she wasn't his type. He'd dated all sorts of women. Karri had been indigenous. He'd also dated a Malaysian backpacker when he'd still worked on the family stone-fruit orchard in Goulburn, and a German student studying agriculture with him for over a year while he'd attended Uni. There had been others as well, one or two of the jillaroos he'd worked with on the first station that'd employed him up in the Northern Territory, and a local lady in Dimbulah for a while, but they were all as different to each other as could be. None of the women he'd ever dated had had a child, however. That made everything so much more complicated. Impossible, really. So why was he even looking at her?

Because he couldn't keep his eyes off her, that's why.

"Look," he said, as patiently as he could. "I know Daisy. She's a wonderful woman. Very determined, very strong willed, but also sweet and generous. She's got an…interesting past and has had a lot of hurdles to overcome. When she first arrived at Stormcloud, she was also running from something. It took a lot for her to finally trust Dale, but in the end, he helped her overcome her problems." He shook his head. This wasn't coming out properly. He didn't want Kee to think he was her savior, nothing like that. All he wanted was for her to accept his help and move on. "What I'm trying to say is that Daisy knows what it's like to need help. She perhaps understands what you're going through better than most. And I know she'd want to help another woman in need." This was all true, but Wazza didn't want to say too much, because the story wasn't his to tell. He hoped it was enough to convince Kee that she'd be safe here for a few days. To take the time to regroup and, perhaps, with his help—although he kept that thought to himself—time to come up with a better plan.

Her foot stopped tapping as she listened to him. Dark eyes roamed over the inside of the small house. What was she thinking?

At last, she said, "What do you want to do, Benni Bunny? Stay here? Only for a little while, mind you."

"Yes, please." Benni moved closer to Wazza and lay a soft hand on his arm. "Mr. Cowboy says we should." Her serious gaze almost had Wazza smiling, but he held it in. Such solemn earnestness from one so young. She really was a sweet little thing.

"Okay, then, we'll stay."

"Great." Wazza jumped up and took two strides toward the small kitchenette. "I'm pretty sure Daisy keeps this place well stocked. We all do out here; it's a necessity when you live in such isolation."

"I want to repay her everything that we use," Kee said, nearly as earnestly as her daughter. "We don't steal," she said, tilting her chin until she could look him in the eye.

He held in a sigh. He clearly wasn't going to convince her it wasn't stealing; it was just what you did in the bush. Help a friend in need. "Sure thing," he replied. "Why don't you keep a list of everything you eat, and I'll restock it next time I'm in town."

Kee eyed him suspiciously but nodded her agreement.

Wazza got down on his knees and searched through one of the low cupboards. He'd been out to Daisy's a few times over the past year. Usually, to join a few of the Stormcloud staff for a drink with Dale and Daisy. But he knew his way around the place enough to find the food. "Ah-ha." He held up a tin of spaghetti. "Will this do?"

"Yummy," Benni squealed, bouncing on the couch.

"That couch is not a trampoline." Kee frowned at her daughter until she sat down again, but the radiant smile remained on her face.

Wazza took another quick look into the pantry. Tins of beans and corn and vegetables filled the shelves, next to cartons of long-life milk, and plenty of dry ingredients like flour, sugar, oats, and rice.

"Perhaps you could find a saucepan to heat this?" he directed Kee over his shoulder. There should be bread in the freezer, if he wasn't mistaken. Yep, a full loaf of white bread was tucked into the small freezer at the bottom of the fridge, along with half a dozen packages of frozen meat and poultry. There was plenty of food here to keep Kee and her daughter going for the next few days, at least.

"Sorry, there won't be much fresh stuff. Daisy wouldn't have left anything perishable." He opened the fridge to make sure he was correct. Nothing in there but a few cans of beer, a jug of cold water, and jars of condiments, pickles, jam, olives, and a block of chocolate. Daisy hadn't been sure how long she'd been gone. Dale had said probably a month. It'd been only two weeks since she left, so Wazza was hoping he had at least another week to let Kee stay here. If she wanted to, of course.

Kee had found a pan and put the spaghetti on to heat on the stove, while Wazza put two pieces of bread into the toaster. They both leaned against the small counter and watched the spaghetti begin to bubble. The scene felt altogether domestic, and Wazza suddenly had to clear his throat.

"Hey, Benni," he called out. "Want to help me set the table?"

"Yes." She jumped off the couch and took out two plates from the low cupboard where he was pointing.

"Careful, now," Kee warned.

"I am." Benni pouted but concentrated on carrying the plates to the table as carefully as possible.

"Are you not eating with us?" Kee asked, noticing the number of plates her daughter was putting out.

"No, I'll eat when I get back to the lodge." His stomach grumbled to itself because he hadn't eaten anything since an early breakfast this morning. But he wasn't about to eat their precious supplies. Going hungry for a while never killed anyone.

The toast popped up, and he put a piece on each plate. "Sorry, no butter," he told them.

Kee spooned the spaghetti over the toast, and Benni scrambled up in her chair, fork held in her chubby little hand, eyes alight with hunger.

"Let me cut it out for you," Kee said, when Benni looked like she was about to shovel the whole thing into her mouth.

Wazza watched mother and daughter as Kee hovered over the table, cutting the toast into bite-size pieces, while Benni tried to steal some from the side. It struck him again at the domesticity of the scene. The simple act of a mother feeding her child. It twisted something into a knot deep inside him, and he had to turn away. An image of what Ava and Karri might have been like if they lived. Busying himself, he found three glasses and filled them with water from the jug in the fridge. He placed a glass in front of each of them, and drank his own in three large gulps, leaning up against the kitchen countertop.

Kee drank her water as well, watching him thoughtfully over the rim of the glass.

"The water from the tap is safe to drink," Wazza told her.

Then he ran through some of the things she needed to know about living out here, while Benni slurped her lunch noisily. Kee merely nodded and continued to watch him, eating a lot more daintily than her daughter.

"Can I have some more toast, please?" Benni said.

"What beautiful manners," Kee replied, touching her daughter lightly on the head.

"I'll get it." Wazza got out some more bread, thankful for something to keep his mind off those dark eyes watching him.

Benni ate two more pieces of toast with jam, and drank two full glasses of water, before finally giving a large sigh. He'd been trying to ignore the clock on the wall. He really needed to get back to the station before Steve wondered where he was. It'd be easy enough to get Steve to believe that an old plastic bag had become stuck on the camera, covering the lens. Odd pieces of litter could be found blowing around in the wind, even that far from civilization. But Steve would know how long the trip should take, and he'd be expecting Wazza back by now.

"Full now, Mummy," Benni said, hopping down from her chair.

"Good girl. You can sit on the couch again."

Wazza glanced at Kee just in time to see the look of utter love cross her face. Like she would give anything to make a daughter happy, to see her content. A muscle jumped in his cheek, and he pursed his lips.

"I can turn the TV on for her if you like," he offered. "It runs off a satellite dish on the roof. You won't get all the stations you're used to in the city, but I should be able to find something suitable to watch."

"Yes, please," Benni said loudly, and then wilted slightly under her mother's glare.

"All right," Kee finally agreed. "Just for a little while."

"Yay." Benni clapped her hands.

Wazza found the remote and switched on the TV. It didn't take him long to find the ABC station, which was playing a kid's cartoon. Something about Dot and a kangaroo. He raised eyebrow in Kee's direction, and she nodded. It would do.

"I need to show you a few things outside," he said.

Kee's gaze slipped between him and Benni. She really was reluctant to leave her child alone.

"We'll only be five minutes," he told her.

"Sure." Kee squared her shoulders. "You stay here, Benni Bunny. I'm going to look at something outside."

Benni's eyes never left the screen, but she murmured, "Mm-hm."

Wazza snagged his hat and sunglasses off the table and held the door open. The heat outside was palpable as it blasted past them into the cool interior.

It looked like a huge effort for Kee to tear her gaze from her daughter. "Poor little thing," Kee said when she was standing beneath the patio outside. "She hasn't had much normality in the last month. Just doing something simple, like watching TV, is the highlight of her day. I know she's missed it. But she hardly ever complains."

"She's a great kid," Wazza said, meaning it. There was so much more he wanted to say. That he could see why she was doing what she was doing. That if he were in the same situation, he'd do exactly the same. He didn't blame her one little bit for doing everything in her power to keep her daughter safe. Even if it was the wrong thing in the eyes of the law. Some things that were wrong were also right.

Instead, he said, "Follow me. I'll show you how to prime the generator and start it, if for any reason, the solar stops working." Which it wouldn't, not in the next few days, anyway, not with the cloudless skies of the dry season and the never-ending sunshine to keep the batteries full. But it was important she know how to do this. She seemed to have a lack of faith in herself, lack of faith in her abilities. But she'd got this far on her own. She needed to see how much of an achievement that was.

As he strode around the side of the building, he replaced his hat and put on his sunglasses, but he noticed Kee shielding her eyes from the blazing sun with her hand. "The generator is housed here," he said, bending one knee so he could reach the latch on a small wooden lean-to. "It's never locked. And you shouldn't need to use it. This is all just a precaution."

"Okay," she said doubtfully.

Kee peered intently into the wooden structure, absently waving away the innumerable flies from her face. Her shoulder brushed against his as she got down lower so she could see the priming mechanism he was pointing out. The air between them went static, crackling with something unnamed, and he suddenly held his breath, wanting her to touch him again. He closed his eyes for the briefest of seconds. Did she feel that, too? Like a stroke of lightning against his skin. Her face was only inches from his, he could smell the heat emanating off her skin. Perspiration and something else...spicy and enticing. He turned to look at her, saw the shine of sweat on her top lip, mouth slightly parted as she returned his stare. Rosy and plump, her lips tempted him. She regarded him from beneath long, dark lashes. So long they seemed almost unreal, made her eyes look wide and unguarded for a second.

This was a bad time for him to get an erection. But the way his jeans tightened uncomfortably made him thankful he was crouching down, so hopefully his reaction to her was hidden. A crazy urge took him to lean in and take those lips. Would she moan, deep in her throat, at his touch? He inclined his head toward her.

Kee suddenly straightened and took a step back, breaking the spell. Leaving him blinking like an owl in a bright light. What had he been about to do?

"Right. So, have you got that?" He tried to go for an officious tone to cover the slight crack in his voice. Had she noticed? He straightened as well, keeping his body angled away from her.

"I'll show you the water tank. It works on a pump system, which you need to keep an eye on." He led the way around the back of the building, up the slight slope to where a large, green water tank sat on a concrete slab. Out of the corner of his eye, he saw Kee hesitate for a millisecond before following him. Oh yeah, she'd noticed, all right. Wazza hid a grimace. She was out of bounds, he just needed to keep reminding himself of that.

"Gosh, there's so much to learn. So much to do out here. How do people cope?" She spoke to his back.

Wazza stopped and turned around. "You'll get used to it."

"Seems like there are a lot of things I need to get used to." She snorted. "The heat, for one."

"Yeah, well, no one really gets used to that. If you don't need to be out, then it's better to stay inside during the middle of the day when it's hottest."

"We already figured that one out the hard way," she said with a wry grin, and he was reminded they'd just spent two days camping out in this interminable heat. "It'll be nice to have somewhere cool to stay."

She waved at more flies trying to settle on her face. "And these blasted little insects."

He held in a laugh. Lots of city folks couldn't believe how damn annoying and unceasing the flies were at this time of year. Some of them even resorted to wearing fly nets over their hats. But you got to the stage where you could almost ignore them. Almost.

It felt like they were back on solid ground again. She wasn't going to hold his split second of insanity against him.

For the next ten minutes, Wazza led her around the

outstation, showing her how the water pump worked, where the machinery shed was situated, if she needed any tools, or the like. It was only when Kee's gaze repeatedly slid toward the main building that he remembered Benni. She wanted to get back to her daughter. But there was one more thing he needed to give her. He headed back to where his vehicle was parked beneath the sparse shade of an acacia tree, he reached in and removed his sat phone from the dash.

"Say goodbye to Benni for me," he said, handing her the phone. "My number is third on the list of buttons." He pointed to the pre-programmed buttons on the handset. With one hand resting on the steering wheel, ready to step into his car, he added, "I really have to get going. But if there is anything else you need, you just call me, okay?"

She nodded, but he could see a question in her eyes. Her lips remained firmly together, however, as if she was afraid to ask.

"What?" he asked gently. "You can ask me anything, you know."

"Do you have a spare one of those?" she asked, pointing to his hat, surprising him. Of course, why hadn't he thought of that? Everyone needed protection from the sun and the flies.

"I'll see what I can find."

"For Benni, too?" The way she bit her lip and said she thought she might be asking too much of him. "She loves your hat."

"For Benni, too," he replied. That might be harder, finding an Akubra her size, but he'd certainly try. There might be an old one of Skylar's or Julie's still left at the back of the tack room, or perhaps in the shed where they kept all the old pairs of boots discarded by previous staff and family, and sometimes even left by guests.

"I'll come back tomorrow and make sure you're okay." He wasn't sure how he might work it into his schedule, but he knew he'd do it, somehow. "And fill you in on how your car is going." He hopped into the four-wheel-drive and wound down his window.

"Thank you, Wazza," she replied. Her obsidian gaze sought his. "I don't know how I'll ever repay you."

"Don't you worry about that." Wazza waved a hand out the window and accelerated down the track. Glancing in the rear vision mirror, he saw the figure of Kee fading to a light blue blur in the dust from his tires. God, he hoped they'd be okay out here alone.

CHAPTER SIX

Kee woke with a start. Where was she? It took a second for the room to come into focus. She was in a large double bed, Benni curled up beside her. An extremely comfortable bed it was, too. That's right, the outstation. Daisy's place. She touched her daughter's hair lightly, satisfying herself that she was safe and well, and fast asleep. She rubbed the sleep from her eyes and rolled over, careful not to wake Benni.

They'd made it through the night without incident. Actually, it was the best night's sleep Kee had had in months. Which surprised her. When she'd crawled into bed next to her daughter to sing her to sleep, Kee had been wide awake, still on edge and wary. Worried that perhaps Daisy might return early. Worried that Bruno might find her. Worried about how long it would take to fix her car. Desperate to get back on the road.

With a good night's sleep, came clarity. Nothing seemed quite so desperate now. They had a roof over their heads out of the heat—Kee had left the air conditioning running all night, pure bliss, they even needed to pull the blankets up at one stage—a place to hunker down for a few days and rest and recuperate. Her fears from last night seemed silly now. Bruno would never find her here.

Slipping out of bed, she tiptoed barefoot across the floor, closing the bedroom door behind her. Filling the kettle with water, she turned it on, then padded quietly to the door, pulling it open to stare outside. It was still early, the sun barely above the horizon, and the world was painted in pink and gold hues. The air was still, not a breath of wind. Trees formed a curtain around the outstation, fringing it with green, branches reaching for the indigo sky. And while it wasn't exactly cold, there was certainly a cool ambience, as if the day were holding its breath, revelling in the dawn before the heat of the sun came to turn everything into a furnace again.

The sound of birdsong hit her. So many birds. Kee knew enough to understand they must be near a water source somewhere. And it was attracting the birds in their hundreds, thousands, even. They wheeled in great flocks above her, then headed out over the treetops and disappeared into the veil of trees. Brightly colored parakeets, large, white cockatoos, and hundreds of small, brown birds hopping from branch to branch between the leaves. Even at the concrete water trough, the birds had flocked to drink in the early morning, delighting Benni with their squawks and flapping. But this was something else again.

Kee was suddenly, deliriously happy that she and Benni hadn't had to spend another night camped out in her car. She stood on the wooden platform of the outdoor patio and breathed deeply. In and out. In and out, until a blanket of peace descended over her.

"Mummy, where are you?" Benni's voice sounded from inside. The hint of concern in a daughter's voice had her hurrying back up the steps to the door.

"Good morning, my darling." She scooped her daughter up into her arms and kissed her sleepy face. Benni wrapped her skinny arms around Kee's neck, and she drew in her child's warm, sleepy scent. They were safe. At least, for a little while.

The morning slipped by easily. Kee found a washing machine in the bathroom and put on a load of clothes. Washing was a luxury she could barely afford while they'd been on the road. Most of it done by hand in the hotel bathroom sink. Then, after she'd seen Bruno and they stayed away from hotels and people, it'd been in a gas station bathroom sink, sometimes dirty and cracked. She and Benni had been living in the same outfits for the past three days. While Benni watched another of her favorite shows on the TV, Kee hung their clothes out on the line beside the house. They'd dry quickly, the heat was already building, even this early in the morning.

Kee kept one eye on the satellite phone Wazza had given her as she went about the chores, trying not to hope too hard that he would call soon. Hoping for news of her car. Not wanting to admit that she missed his soothing voice, his take-charge attitude. His quiet presence that made her feel somehow safe. But the phone never rang. Perhaps she should call him. But no, she would wait at least until lunchtime, even though her fingers itched to push the button.

There was no bath for Benni, but her little girl had gotten used to getting clean in a shower on their travels. Kee unwound her daughter's long braid and washed her hair quickly under the spray of water, Benni giggling and telling her she liked the smell of this shampoo. Daisy had good taste in toiletries, it seemed. After drying Benni, she let her sit on the bathmat, wrapped in a towel, while Kee showered. She would've liked to take her time, luxuriate in the warm streams running over shoulders, but Wazza had mentioned how precious water was out here and so she was as quick as could be.

Then she and Benni had a breakfast of toast and jam and

tea, still wrapped in their towels, while they waited for their clothes to dry. Kee took a chance, when she ducked out to the washing line, clad only in her towel. But there was no one around to see her. It was heaven to slip into clean clothes and she was reminded that the simple things in life often gave the most pleasure. Jean shorts and a T-shirt for both of them, with sneakers on their feet. There was no need for anything fancy. Kee had only packed practical clothes for herself and her daughter. But at the last minute, Kee had slipped one of her summer dresses in on top. It might come in handy if she ever needed to dress up for an occasion, although what that occasion might be was beyond Kee's imagination.

Benni wanted to go exploring, and so, as soon as they were dressed, they went outside before the midday heat really settled in, the sat phone tucked into the back pocket of her shorts. Kee wouldn't go any farther than the first ring of trees, wanting to always keep the house in her line of sight.

Benni handed Kee another leaf to add to her collection, and Kee dropped it into Benni's backpack, which contained all sorts of offerings. Large nuts, fallen from the trees above, bits of bark run through with shades of red and ochre, a fossilized insect husk Kee had refused to touch, some oddly shaped seedpods, and a large, red rock. Benni was a collector. Back at home, she had shelves full of things she thought were beautiful. Colorful bird feathers. Stones of all shapes and sizes stored in little piles, or left individually in-between more collections of shells, both large and small. Benni always came back from the beach laden down with so many treasures that often had to be washed in fresh water to get rid of the smell. Sometimes, when Benni wasn't watching, Kee might even threw away some of the dried seaweed and bits of sponge that retained a fishy aroma. Kee was interested to see what Benni would pick up here. Back at the water trough, Benni had half-heartedly collected some of the sharp rocks from beside the edge of the road. But after the first day, she'd lost interest and stopped handing her mum things to keep.

"This is fun," Benni crowed. "A better adventure than sleeping in the car."

"Yes, it is, my bunny." Kee watched her daughter fondly. The little girl was hunkered down next to a large tree trunk, poking at the bark with a stick. Kee often wondered where her child's interest in nature had come from. Certainly not from her. Not from Jakov, either. Jakov showed absolutely no interest in the garden, and refused to let them have a pet, no matter how hard Benni had begged. Kee loved animals, of course. She worked in a shelter, helping to save the discarded cats and dogs people no longer loved. Benni loved animals, too. But her fascination went much deeper than that. She liked to get down on her belly and prod and poke at the small insects in the grass. To dissect each flower, pull its petals off one by one and then document their exact coloration and number. Perhaps she was going to be a scientist when she grew up.

Kee hoped she was around to see that day.

Some of her trepidation returned and her anxiety ramped up at that thought. Bruno wouldn't give up looking for her. Not with Jakov urging him on. Why hadn't she listened to her parents? Followed their wishes and married Reyansh, like they wanted, then none of this would be happening. Her marriage had been decided ever since Kee had turned ten. Her parents had made an agreement with Reyansh's parents that it would be so. An arranged marriage. It was more common than people realized in Indian culture. People still clung to the old ways and traditions, her parents especially, wanting to keep their customs alive, even though they'd moved to a different country. Reyansh didn't want it, either. He was a nice enough man; they'd grown up together, the two families united in friendship. But Kee didn't love him.

And she'd been determined to marry for love.

So, when Jakov had come along, she'd jumped in with both feet, without testing the waters first. He was exciting, good looking, seductive, a diamond in the rough. All the things that Reyansh wasn't.

Her parents refused to see it her way, however. She had shamed them, let them down in front of their friends. No amount of arguing would get them to see that Reyansh felt the same way, that he didn't want to marry her, either. By the time she met Jakov, her father had stopped speaking to her, and her mother would turn sad, brown eyes in her direction whenever she entered the room and shake her head slowly. But Jakov had been an answer to her problems. A way to get out of from beneath her parents' control.

When she announced she was going to get married to this Croatian man she had met only a few months prior, her parents had taken the news badly, banishing her from the house, her father going as far as disowning her. Kee thought they were being melodramatic and overly harsh, and so she'd stuck to her guns, believing they would come around in the end.

But they hadn't. Poor little Benni had never met her maternal grandparents. They refused to have anything to do with her. Which made her increasingly sad. Made her rely more and more on Jakov's family for help with the new baby.

Kee wondered how Pooja was doing. Her sister had stood by Kee in the beginning, arguing against their parents, saying Kee had every right to choose who she wanted to marry. But in the end, they'd threatened to disown her, as well, and Pooja wasn't that strong. Her sister was a stickler for the rules. She was daddy's girl and liked the comforts of living at home. Pooja was no rebel like Kee. Would Pooja go ahead and wed the man her parents had picked out for her? Only time would tell.

"Look, Mummy, look," Benni squealed. "It's so pretty." Benni was poking at a brightly colored beetle, clambering up the bark in a hasty retreat away from Benni's stick. It was the color of a red ruby, bright as a jewel, and Kee leaned in for a closer look.

"Leave it, honey. It belongs in the bush. Shall we take all your treasures back to the house? We can sort through them on the kitchen table." It'd be nice to get back into the air conditioning. Still only mid-morning, and the temperature must be hovering over thirty degrees.

Suddenly, the sound of the vehicle brought Kee's head up. A dust plume rose above the trees behind the outstation. "Quick, get inside," she ordered. They both scampered toward the house. Kee shut and locked the door behind her, breathing heavily. Was it Wazza? Or someone else coming down the track? She wavered between wanting to make a run for it—but where would she run to?—and wanting to hide in the bedroom, wait for whoever it was to go away.

"Who is it?" Benni was staring at her wide-eyed, and Kee knew she needed to stop being afraid. If only for her daughter's sake.

"I'm not sure," she admitted. "Let's look out the window." Kee lifted Benni up and then stood on tiptoe, so they could both peer out the small window in the back wall of the shipping container. All the windows were small in this house, and this one in particular was up high, meant to let in light more than afford a view.

A glint of white flashed between the trees as the vehicle approached. Wazza drove a white, four-wheel-drive. But then again, so did most people out here. She couldn't count how many white vehicles she'd passed on the road to Dimbulah.

"It's the nice Mr. Cowboy," Benni said with delight.

"Oh? How can you tell?"

"I can see his hat. I like his hat." Benni squirmed to be let down and Kee put her on the floor, but continued to stare out the window. Sure enough, she glimpsed Wazza's big, brown hat as the vehicle got closer. Other people might well have a similar hat, but it was more than that. The way he held his shoulders back, how his hands gripped the wheel, sure and strong.

Benni was already at the door, waiting for Kee to unbolt it, bouncing up and down on her toes. Benni had certainly taken a liking to Wazza.

They stepped out onto the covered patio just as Wazza pulled the vehicle up in the shade of the acacia tree.

"Wait till he's turned the car off," Kee warned, keeping a hand on her child's shoulder as she tried to surge forward to go and greet Wazza. The car door opened and Wazza stepped out, grinning at them both. "Right, off you go." Kee watched Benni run to Wazza, her little legs pumping up and down, small puffs of dust rising at each step. She stopped right in front of him and held up something for him to see.

Wazza knelt down, so he was at Benni's eye level, and she waved a black and red feather in his face, talking excitedly about where she found her *treasure*. Wazza's face remained serious as he examined her find. Then he said something in a low voice that Kee couldn't catch, but Benni smiled as if he'd told her something wonderful.

Kee was spellbound by the tableau before her. Wazza was a big man, tall and rugged. Strength coursed through him; she could feel it whenever he was close. But he had such a gentleness when he was around Benni. It made her heart ache just watching them. She'd made so many stupid decisions in her life. Picked the wrong man to marry. Picked the wrong family to pin her hopes and dreams on. Now the malicious Bruno was hunting her, trying to take her only daughter away. But watching Wazza with her daughter, a little of her faith in men was restored.

Wazza raised his eyes, and his gaze found hers. His eyes were the color of blue stones. He smiled and something fluttered in her chest, and her insides felt liquid. She tamped down on the emotion. Benni's safety was the only thing that mattered to her right now. Not some man she barely knew who made her insides go to mush. That was a frivolous thought. Lust was a frivolous emotion, and she had no time for frivolous at the moment.

"Hi," he said, standing and removing his hat.

"Hi," she replied, unable to tear her gaze away from his. The silence drew out until it became uncomfortable.

"I've brought you some supplies." He reached across the driver's seat and retrieved a bag. "Some milk, butter, and fresh fruit. I know how much Benni loves an apple." He grinned down at the girl hovering around his knees. Kee wanted to believe that Wazza was doing this to impress her. Make a show that he was thinking about Benni. Get her on his good side. But she knew that she shouldn't be so ungracious. She'd become bitter and scarred by her years spent with Jakov. There were still some truly good people in the world, she reminded herself. And Wazza might well be one of those people.

"Thank you." She strolled toward the car to help him as he grabbed another bag, bursting with foodstuffs. Where had he got all this? Surely, he hadn't had time to drive into town this morning. She hoped he hadn't stolen it from this place where he worked. Stormcloud Lodge, he called it.

He handed her the two bags. "Oh, I almost forgot." His upper body disappeared inside the cab for a second, and when he re-emerged, he had a hat in each hand. "This one is for you, young lady." Wazza carefully placed the smaller one on Benni's head. It was a pale blue, and suited Benni's coloring perfectly. "This was an old one of Skylar's, I think. It was in the tack shed, underneath a pile of burlap sacks. It's still in pretty good condition."

Benni took it off and turned it around in her hands, lips pursed as she considered her gift. "I love it," she said at last, putting it back on her head, and turned toward Kee.

"It's very pretty," Kee said, holding in a smile. A tad too big, but that didn't matter. It would keep the fierce sun off her face.

"And this one's for you." Wazza came forward and placed a tan hat on her head. "It's supposed to be a snug fit." He fiddled with the hat, pulling the brim down and working the hat onto her head until he was satisfied. "So they don't blow off when you're galloping after a runaway cow," he added.

Wazza had come through. For both of them. Words suddenly failed her.

"They're called Akubras by the way," he said, as if trying to fill the silence.

"I knew that," Benni piped up.

Kee was pretty sure she hadn't known that, but she smiled and said, "Come inside, I'll put the kettle on."

For some reason, she felt flustered once they got inside. While the house was small, it was cozy and practical, and Kee had quickly gotten used to the layout. But Wazza seemed to fill the room, his presence distracting her, so she was only half-concentrating on emptying the contents of his two bags into the refrigerator. He stood awkwardly by the door before finally taking a seat at the small table. But his gaze never left her, she could feel it, like a laser beam attached to her back, following her around the small kitchen.

Kee sat next to Wazza, placing her hat neatly on the table beside her, exactly like Wazza had done. She'd noticed a container of what looked like homemade cookies in one of the bags, and she put some on a plate on the table. Benni immediately went to reach for one until Kee's stern gaze stopped her. "Remember your manners, please," Kee said.

"May I please have a cookie?" Benni said, eyes wide and a look on her face like butter wouldn't melt in her mouth.

"Yes, you may." Kee turned to pour the hot water into the cups, removed the teabags and added milk to both.

"I swiped those while they were still hot from the tray," Wazza said, as Kee placed the tea in front of him, and a glass of cold water for Benni. "Skylar's going to kill me when I get back, but it's worth it. You wait until you taste them. She's the best cook this side of Brisbane." His handsome face split into a grin. It was the second time Wazza had mentioned this Skylar today, and Kee's interest was piqued. "Skylar is the owner's daughter," he said in response to Kee's raised eyebrow. "She's also the chef at the lodge, does the cooking for all the guests and staff, alike." "She's a good friend. You'd like Skylar," he added quietly.

A good friend, huh? For a second, Kee wondered how far the connection went, before she realized what she was doing and shut that train of thought down. She had absolutely no right to be jealous of this man. He had every right to date whomever he wanted. Hell, he might even be married or in a long-term affair, for all she knew. The subject of his relationship status had never come up. And now that Kee though about it, Wazza might have mentioned that Skylar had a fiancé. He'd mentioned so many names that she was having a hard time keeping track of them all.

"Actually, you'd like everyone at Stormcloud," he added, almost as an afterthought.

Be that as it may, she was never going to Stormcloud, so that would never happen.

"Have you heard anything about my car?" she asked, changing the subject.

His face fell ever so slightly. "Yeah, I had a call from Lefty this morning. He, ah…"

This didn't sound like good news. Kee put her cup down

slowly and stared at him.

"It was the fuel pump, like we thought."

Like *he'd* thought. She hadn't had a clue what was wrong with her own car.

"Lefty doesn't have one for your model vehicle in stock, so he's ordered one from Sydney." Wazza hesitated. "But it could take up to a week to get here." He winced as he noticed her frown. "Sorry, there's not a lot we can do. I asked if he could put an urgent request in, and he said he already had."

Kee dropped her gaze to the tabletop, her hand going to cover her heart, which was beating erratically.

"The cookies are yummy. Can I have another one, please?" Benni asked, unaware of the tense silence that'd fallen around the table.

"Mummy? Can I?"

Kee didn't answer; couldn't answer. This was terrible news. Horrible. The worst. What was she going to do for a whole week? She needed to be moving on. A week in one place might give Bruno the time he needed to track her down.

"I can't stay here that long," she said, hating the sudden wobble in her chin. "I need to leave, or he'll find us."

CHAPTER SEVEN

The two-way radio crackled to life in Wazza's shoulder holster. "Warwick, are you there?" It was Steve. His boss hardly ever called him Warwick.

He let go of the wire strainer, laying it carefully on the ground, before he tilted his chin toward the radio and pushed the button. "Yep, almost finished the second post. What's up?"

"We…ah…need you back at the lodge, asap."

"Okay." Wazza left the silence hanging for a few seconds, giving Steve time to explain this sudden urgency. He trusted his boss implicitly. Steve was solid and reliable and always treated his staff fairly. Wazza often felt more part of the family than a hired hand. Steve was always blunt and to the point. This vague demand wasn't like him.

Eventually, after continued radio silence, Wazza asked, "Do I have time to finish up first? It'll only take me another fifteen minutes, tops." This job had taken him most of the morning. It'd be a shame to leave it now. A few of the posts holding up the fence around Steamers Paddock were leaning at a precarious angle. They needed to have new metal posts rammed in to replace the old ones and new wires strung along their length, otherwise the feisty bush cattle would find the weakness and delight in pushing their way through.

"Ah…no, you should come back straight away. One of us can finish that up this afternoon." Wazza thought he heard Daniella's voice in the background, which was unusual. She always left the running of the cattle side of the resort strictly in Steve's hands.

Wazza was becoming irritated. What could be so important that he had to leave a job half-finished? And why was Steve not telling him what was going on?

"Sure," he said curtly into the radio. "On my way now." He loaded his tools up into the rear bed of the ATV. Steamers Paddock was close to the lodge, and so he'd chosen one of the special-built, four-wheel-drive, all-terrain vehicles, taking it across country to get where he needed to go.

This minor hiccup wasn't going to help his plans to get over to the outstation today. He'd been hoping to finish work a little early and tell Steve he wanted to head into town for a few hours, to catch up with some mates at the pub. But really, he'd go over to see how Kee was coping. She hadn't taken the news of the delay in fixing her car well yesterday. She'd almost broken down in a hysterical mess. He suspected that the only thing keeping her together was her daughter, staring at her with increasingly wide-eyed worry.

Wazza had talked her down, eventually. Because there was no other choice. She'd looked so forlorn as she'd walked him to his car that he'd nearly handed over the keys and told her to take his car. If he'd owned the vehicle, he might well have gone through with it, but the Land Cruiser belonged to Stormcloud, and there was no way he'd steal from his boss. He was itching to get back there to make sure they were both okay. She'd asked him again yesterday why he was helping them, and he'd given her some rote answer that it was the right thing to do. But he knew there was more to it than that. And by the way she looked at him from beneath lowered eyelashes, she did, too.

His mind lost in thoughts of how else he might help Kee, Wazza came around the last bend of the driveway to find a strange tableau of people waiting for him at the top of the steps to the main entrance of the lodge. Steve and Daniella stood slightly to the left of a larger group, Daniella shading her eyes to watch as he approached. Both looked serious, and an ominous tickle slid down his spine. Skylar and a man who looked vaguely familiar were also there, hovering at the back. What…? It took him a second to recognize the two figures in the center of the huddle, and his heart leapt into his throat. Kee and Benni, Kee holding tight to her daughter's hand. Benni was wearing the light-blue hat Wazza had given her. What were they doing here? Then he spotted Daisy and Dale flanking them, and his heart fell like a stone all the way to his feet.

Oh, shit. Daisy was home early.

But he'd checked with Dale last night. Casually asked him over dinner how Daisy was enjoying her stay with her family. And Dale had replied with an equally casual wave of his hand that he never really knew what Daisy was up to, but it sounded like she was having fun. Wazza had taken that to mean Daisy wouldn't be home anytime soon. Shit, he should've dug a little deeper. But Skylar and Julie, who'd been sharing the table, burst into peals of laughter at something they were discussing, then Dale asked them what they found so funny, and the moment was lost. Julie was always making people laugh, she had that way about her. She even managed to get her big, serious boyfriend, Aaron, to lighten up sometimes. The two stepsisters were as close as could be, and Dale was equally fond of both of them. As the youngest brother, Dale was often the brunt of their jokes, but he took it all with a cool head and a smile.

Wazza pulled the ATV to stop with a spray of gravel in

front of the steps and leaped out. But then he stood mute at the bottom of the stairs, unable to form the words, wondering where in hell to start. It was the accusation in Kee's eyes finally pushed him to say something.

"I can explain everything. It's not their fault. It was all my idea. I'm sorry Daisy, I really am," he babbled until finally coming to a stumbling halt as Daisy glared at him.

"Why don't we take this inside?" Daniella said smoothly. "Let's all go to the boardroom, where we can discuss this away from prying eyes." Wazza knew that she meant out of sight of the guests. With Daniella, the guests always came first, she'd never allow an in-house scandal to be revealed, if she could help it.

He nodded and hung his head, following the group through the large, glass doorway, into the cool great room of the lodge. Wazza felt like a condemned man being led to the gallows. Was Steve going to fire him? Would he lose his job over this? He lifted his chin. None of that mattered. He'd do the same again to keep Kee and Benni safe.

He tried to see over the top of everyone else's heads to where Kee was walking with her daughter. But Daniella had steered her right to the front, and there was no chance to even say sorry with his eyes. What was she thinking? Did she blame him?

Wazza nodded to Sasha, who was watching them all file past the reception desk with a question hovering on her lips. But Sasha was the epitome of a professional, so she didn't ask. Sasha was the newest member of the Stormcloud staff, having arrived a little over eight months ago, but she fitted into the team seamlessly. Dark-haired, with dark eyes, she was small and petite, and people often misjudged her on her size. She was a pocket dynamo, ready to take on any challenge. She was attractive, bubbly, but also not afraid to take control of a situation. Alek, Stormcloud's activities manager, had confided in Wazza that he found her extremely attractive, but he still hadn't worked up the courage to ask her out yet. The Polish man was the most straitlaced man Wazza had ever met. But Alek liked to think he lived life on the edge. He was the only one in his family to have travelled, and he thought that taking a job in outback Queensland was the most extreme thing anyone could ever do. He and Wazza got on well.

Alek and Julie had taken a small group of guests to the gold mine this morning. They would be back for lunch in around half an hour. So at least they wouldn't be included in this meeting.

Daisy dropped back and took him by the arm as they turned down the hallway. "It's okay Wazza, I'm not mad at you."

He let out a gust of air. He'd always known Daisy was one cool chick, but this just cemented the fact in his mind. "Thank you," he answered quietly.

"Yes, well, when we arrived home to find a strange woman and her child living in my house, let's just say I was a little shocked. She wouldn't tell me why she was there, kept saying that she needed to talk to Wazza, so I decided the best thing was to bring them both here. I don't want to get you in trouble, but this woman obviously needs help."

Trust Daisy to understand. And he didn't blame her for bringing Kee here. He probably would've done the same thing. Then he fully digested her words. She'd said *when we arrived home*. Who did she mean by *we*? Wazza sought the other guy who'd been standing at the rear of the group. Comprehension suddenly hit. He *did* recognize him. It was River, Daisy's brother. She must've brought him home with her. Perhaps that was why she was home early.

Bindi glanced at him through the doorway to the kitchen as they passed by. Skylar's assistant cook stopped what she was doing and gave the group curious stare. Then it was too late to ask Daisy any more questions, because they'd arrived at the boardroom door. Wazza avoided everyone's stares as he filed in with the rest of them. Everybody pulled up a seat around the large table that took up most of the room. This board room was mainly for the guests' use; they had plenty of high-flyers staying with them, some of whom couldn't seem to leave work behind. It was set up like a second office, with a fax machine, printer, and computer monitors arranged on a counter at the back of the room. But it'd also seen many a staff meeting called, as it was the only room big enough to house them all away from the guests' prying eyes.

Wazza took a seat opposite Kee, placing his hat carefully on the table in front of him. She wouldn't look at him. Benni did, however, and gave him a tremulous smile. Then she carefully took her hat off and laid it on the table, mimicking Wazza's actions. She seemed so out of place amongst all these adults, small and lost, but bravely held onto her mother's hand, Dolly clutched tightly in the other.

As usual, Daniella took the lead once everyone had found their seat.

"Right," she said, clapping hands for quiet. "First, I hope you all remember River, Daisy's brother."

The look some of the staff flicked his way seemed to say, how could they not? River had been involved in the scandalous incident surrounding Karris' murder. Wazza still wasn't sure how he felt about the other man. Karri had stopped seeing Wazza to start an affair with River when he and Daisy had first arrived in the area, and before she knew she was pregnant with Wazza's baby. Wazza would never know what she'd intended to do, because she'd been killed before a choice needed to be made. It was never clear whether she knew she was pregnant or not, either. Would she have chosen Wazza as the father of her baby? He liked to think so.

But he could be wrong. She might well have chosen River, his indigenous heritage, a closer match to her own. But would River have accepted someone else's baby? River would never need to answer that question, but Wazza had his doubts.

Daisy had been helping River run from the police over a crime he'd committed back in Perth. At the time, she'd thought he was innocent. But River had spent time in jail for his crimes after the law finally caught up with him. Dale had helped Daisy, even though he was unsure of the truth, much as Wazza was helping Kee now. Which was why Wazza knew Daisy would understand. But River was out of jail and, according to Daisy, on the path to redemption. Wazza still viewed him with suspicion.

"It seems we have a little mystery here," Daniella continued, after everyone had acknowledged River. "I'd like to introduce you to Kee and her daughter, Benni." Daniella inclined her head in their direction. "Daisy arrived half an hour ago with these two in tow, and…"

Daniella's words trailed off as Wazza stood, hands splayed on the table for support.

His gaze sought out Skylar, sitting to the left of her mother. "Before we go any farther, Skylar, you may want to leave."

"What? Why?" Her blue eyes flashed with surprise.

Wazza gritted his teeth. He hated to do this, but it was the only way to keep Kee safe. "Because Nash can't know about this."

Skylar narrowed her eyes at him, her lips going thin, as realization hit her. If Wazza didn't want the police involved, then there was something decidedly shady going on.

"I mean, you can stay if you want to. But you can't tell Nash what was said in here."

Skylar considered him for many long moments as a hush descended over the table, while she considered how much of a compromise she was prepared to make.

"No, you're right, Wazza," she said, putting her hands on the table and rising from her chair. "I don't keep secrets from Nash, and I don't need to hear anything that'd compromise Nash's job, either." She glowered at Wazza; Skylar didn't take kindly to not being in full control. She was a perfectionist in the kitchen, and in her own life, as well. Although, being with Nash had begun to soften her hard edges. Skylar's gaze flicked to Kee and her daughter and rested there, her mouth forming a speculative quirk.

"It seems these two have one helluva story to tell. But if you really don't want Nash involved, then I guess I have no choice. I'm sure Bindi probably needs my help in the kitchen, anyway." Skylar opened the door, her long, blonde braid slung down her back, shoulders tight with indignation. "It just so happens that Nash is out of town for the next few days, on a training course in Brisbane. But do let me know what story you've concocted, because I'll need to tell him something about the strange woman and her child who've been staying at Daisy's house when he returns. He will find out the truth eventually, you know." She speared him with her sapphire gaze, and a stab of guilt roiled in his stomach. But he was prepared to deal with Nash's reproach later, as long as Kee and Benni were safely out of harm's way by then. With one last look at Wazza, Skylar shut the door quietly behind her.

Wazza breathed out the sigh of relief. He hadn't been sure which way Skylar was going to go. And he still wasn't sure if they could keep the truth away from Nash. But they now had some breathing room.

"Sorry, boss," he apologized in advance for what he was about to say next, but this needed to be sorted out now, before things went any further. "But if Kee is to tell you the truth, I need everyone else to agree not to mention this to Nash, or Constable Willow. If you can't agree, then I need to take Kee and her daughter out of here, right now." Wazza could hardly believe he was standing there, demanding that his boss and the rest of the family and staff keep this from the police.

"How much trouble is she in?" Daniella was the first to speak. "Has she murdered someone? Can we all go to jail as accessories for aiding and abetting a murderer?"

It was a fair question.

Just as Wazza was about to answer, Kee rose from her chair. "Thank you, Wazza. But I'd like to speak for myself." She kept her chin up, dark eyes fixed on him, as if drawing courage from him. "No, I haven't murdered anyone. But I do believe there is a warrant out for my arrest, however, I'm not completely sure, because I don't know how these things work. But that's only part of the issue. My fear is that the police will betray me to my true enemy."

Benni stirred beside Kee, and she placed a protective hand on her child's head, stroking her hair in an unconscious bid to calm her. What did Benni think of all this? How much did she understand? Kee had told him that Benni didn't know her father was in jail, and that this trip north was merely an adventure.

"Are you saying you think there's corruption in the police force? Surely, you're not implying that Nash is dishonest?" Dale said, the scorn evident in his tone.

"No, she's not implying that Nash is in any way unethical," Wazza butted in. "Nash is the most honorable man we know. But this is complicated. And if he found out Kee and her daughter were here, he'd be duty-bound to report it, and others in the force who are less scrupulous may share that information. We don't need to put him in that position."

Daisy lay a hand over Dale's, stopping his fingers tapping on the tabletop. "None of us would willingly ask Nash to compromise his job," she said. "So, I can see why this is so hard for you." She looked pointedly at Wazza. "But I, for one, would like to hear her story. I'm staying." Daisy's brown eyes fell on Kee's face and Wazza could see the compassion she had for the other woman. "It seems the outstation is becoming a bit of a sanctuary for lost souls," she added quietly, almost as if to herself.

Dale added his agreement with a nod of his head, although there was a twist to his mouth that said he wasn't completely happy with the situation. Wazza knew Dale and Nash had become close friends; he obviously didn't want to betray that friendship. But his love for Daisy was far stronger and Dale would also understand the connection she felt to a fellow woman in need.

Daisy skewered River with her gaze, and he held up his hands in surrender.

"You know me, sis," he said. "I ain't got no love for the coppers. I won't spill a word."

She nodded her consent and then returned her gaze to Wazza, happy that River would also hold his tongue.

Neither Daniella nor Steve had uttered a word during this exchange, but now Daniella gave a large sigh. Her eyes fell on the little girl sitting next to Kee and something in her face softened. Wazza sympathized with Daniella, no one with a heart beating in their chest could resist those liquid brown eyes, filled with such innocence.

"You know I don't like…secrets. And I certainly don't condone lying to the police. But where need necessitates, I'm willing to make an exception."

Steve looked from his wife, to Benni, and back again. "I'm not sure I like this position you've put us in, Warwick."

Wazza winced. There was his full name again.

"But I'll go along with it for the child's sake, for now. As long as you can promise me there will be no danger to any of us, or to the station."

"No, it's us they're after. Bruno won't bother any of you," Kee said, then sat back as if she might've said too much.

"Great," Wazza said, retaking his seat.

But before he could decide where to start, Kee asked, "Is there somewhere that Benni might be able to watch some TV?" She raised her eyebrow in Wazza's direction. Of course, she was hinting that she didn't want Benni to overhear what they were about to discuss.

"Skylar would be more than happy to look after her," Daniella offered, catching on straight away. "There's a small television in the kitchen. Benni could sit in the corner and watch that." Wazza doubted Daniella's claim; Skylar was busy prepping meals for the dinner time rush. And Skylar wasn't the most motherly type, either. But he couldn't come up with an alternative, so he held his tongue. One thing he knew; Skylar would allow no harm to befall the child.

"Will you come with me, my love?" Daniella offered her hand to Benni, who looked at her mother for permission.

Kee nodded and said, "We won't be long, Benni Bunny. I wonder if Peppa Pig might be on TV."

Benni calmly placed her hat back on her head and reached for Daniella. One corner of Wazza's mouth lifted in surprise as he watched Daniella and Benni walk out, her small hand tucked safely into the older woman's. There was something so endearing about the way Daniella led the young girl, almost as if she were her own granddaughter, not some stranger's child.

Steve watched the pair go with an odd tilt to his head, that made Wazza think that perhaps Dale and Daisy better get married and start having kids sooner rather than later. But then Steve sat forward again and said, "Let's start. Daniella can catch up when she returns. We've got a busload of guests arriving straight after lunch, and we all have things to do."

That's right, Wazza remembered Aaron had driven the four-wheel-drive bus to Cairns this morning to pick up eight new guests, all coming as one large party to stay for the next week. Aaron was employed as the new helicopter pilot among some of his other duties, and he often ferried the guests in on the new chopper. But it only had room for four extra people, and so the station also had a specially-kitted-out bus to make the four-hour round trip as comfortable as possible for the customers.

Kee glanced at Wazza, then took a deep breath. "If it hadn't been for Wazza, Benni and I might've died out there." That had everyone sitting forward in their chairs, as Kee went on to detail how her car had broken down by the water trough and how she'd been too silly to understand that she needed help until it was almost too late. Wazza sat lower in his chair, avoiding Steve's gaze. He'd outright lied to his boss about what he'd found at the bore, and it didn't sit well with him.

Then Kee went on to tell everyone why Wazza had found her where he had and what she was running from. Daniella returned, and quietly took her seat without interrupting.

Even though Wazza had already heard the story, he learned a few more things about Kee in the next half hour. That she'd been avoiding an arranged marriage. Her parents had tried to push her to marry a man from another Indian family who they'd been friends with for years. But Kee wanted more, she wanted to be allowed to marry under her own volition. Which perhaps explained why she'd jumped into the arms of the first man who came along. Kee admitted that she knew it was a mistake early on in the marriage. But then she became pregnant with Benni, and she couldn't leave.

When Kee finally stopped talking, Wazza was brought back to himself with a start. He was embarrassed to discover he'd been staring at her. Sketching her profile with his eyes, drinking in the soft, ski-jump curve of her nose and how pink and rosy her lips were. How her tongue darted out to touch her top teeth when she was nervous. Today, she was wearing a light-pink tank top that bared her brown shoulders and clung to the curve of her small breasts. A couple of soft tendrils of hair had escaped her long braid and fell heedlessly around her face. She was an amazingly beautiful woman. Exotic and alluring. And he had to admit he was desperately attracted to her. What a shitpile of luck that was. That he was attracted to the only woman he couldn't have.

Daisy and Daniella seemed to especially sympathize with Kee, and they took turns asking her questions, probing for the truth amongst Kee's sometimes scattered story. They comforted her when she told them of her complete shock and horror at how Jakov's parents had stolen Benni from her, to get revenge on her for what she'd done to their son, and refused to see that Jakov was the one who'd been in the wrong, wouldn't believe that he was as corrupt as everyone was saying. The grandfather had flatly denied that Jakov would ever take money for stolen drugs, said that he was a *good boy*.

It was Steve and Dale who wanted more information on why Jakov was in jail. On the court case and how Kee had stood up in the witness box and told the jury what she'd seen. How she'd overheard some of Jakov's phone conversations, and had answered the door to strange men demanding to see her husband in the middle of the night, seen Jakov's ego slowly inflate, and his love for expensive things, like watches and designer clothes outstrip their meager income.

She answered all the questions as well as she could. Looking each of them in the eye and holding her chin up high. But Wazza could tell this whole thing was taking a toll on her. She would probably be mortified all these people now knew her intimate business.

Finally, Daniella held up a hand. He'd seen her getting

more and more on edge as the time slipped away. She clearly wanted to get back to business. "I think we've heard enough for now. This lady and her child deserve our protection. I'm happy for her to stay here until the car is fixed, at the very least. She can't keep staying at Daisy's, not with River staying there, too. We've got a spare cabin she can use. Do you agree Steve?"

"Yes, she needs to stay here. Where we can help her," Steve agreed.

"Wait. What?" Kee looked shocked. "I don't want to stay here. I don't want to put you out like that."

"Well, it's too late, my dear. It's already been decided."

Kee opened her mouth to argue, and Daniella held up a hand. Kee was about to find out that when Daniella made up her mind, it was like trying to argue with a brick wall.

CHAPTER EIGHT

They were finally alone. The rest of the Stormcloud family had left to go about the duties. Daisy was the last to leave, and she'd stared at Kee long and hard before finally shutting the boardroom door behind her. But Kee had kept her chin up, returning her stare. She knew Daisy was still trying to figure out the best way to help Kee. Problem was, none of them could give her what she wanted. A life where she was free to live with her daughter without fear or prejudice.

Kee blew out a long breath between pursed lips, lifting a few stray wisps of hair off her brow that'd come loose from her braid. "Holy cow. Daniella sure doesn't like to take no for an answer, does she?" That woman was a force to be reckoned with. It was no wonder this luxury ranch ran like clockwork, with a woman like her at the wheel. But Kee wasn't sure she wanted Daniella meddling in her life, even if it was with the best of intentions.

"No, she doesn't. She might come across as a hard-headed woman, but don't get her wrong, her heart's in the right place." Wazza pulled out his chair and sat down heavily. He ran a hand distractedly through his hair, and for a moment Kee couldn't take her eyes off the way short tufts stood out at all angles. It made him endearing. And sexy. Who would've thought a man running his hand through his hair could be sexy? It was doing all sorts of strange things to her insides. "But it was one of the reasons why I took you to Daisy's place, instead of bringing you here. I knew they'd ask too many questions," he added.

Tearing her gaze from his beguiling hairstyle, she pulled out the chair next to him. "Well, you made the right choice. But with Daisy bringing me here, it feels like the choice was taken out of our hands. Out of my hands. I feel like I've lost all control. All my plans have been derailed." She understood that she probably sounded a little unhinged. Because she had no real plan. And no real destination. She had no control over the fact that her car had broken down. But at least it had been her making all the decisions, both good and bad. Now this family had taken her under their wing, treating her like a wounded animal who needed their help. It was all completely overwhelming.

"I feel like I'm being coerced to stay here. What am I going to do now?" Her question was almost a wail of despair. She was close to losing it, tears once more threatening to break free, holding in all that tension so no one saw how scared and frightened she'd been was taxing. And now all she wanted was to take Benni somewhere safe. Just her and her daughter. It was all about Benni, in the end. She was so confused.

The whole morning had been one big whirlwind. Starting from the moment she'd heard the hum of a vehicle coming down the track and being unable to stop Benni from running out to greet the car, thinking it was Wazza arriving. Only for Benni to stop short when a dark-haired woman and a young man stepped out to the gravel. Kee pulled her daughter to safety behind her legs and stared at the two strangers, heart racing wildly. There'd been no doubt in her mind this was Daisy returned home early, and she'd wanted to swear and curse at Wazza for getting it so wrong.

Kee had remained frozen, standing like a statue, unsure whether to run and hide, or welcome the woman and her friend—she later found out it was her brother—inside. Daisy had solved the problem for her by holding the door open and suggesting they all have a cup of tea and a quiet chat out of the heat. Daisy had been cool and calm, as if finding a strange woman and child living in her house was nothing to be worried about. She'd been genuine and friendly, just like Wazza said. Even getting down on one knee to speak to Benni, telling her how much she liked her hat, and offering her a cookie from the bag of groceries her brother had carried in.

River had been far more reserved. Watching Kee warily out of the corner of his eye. But at least he kept his thoughts to himself and let Daisy do the talking.

"They're only trying to help," Wazza replied, failing to keep the defensiveness out of his tone.

"I know that," she snapped. "But maybe it's not the sort of help I want." She could feel the anger starting to rise, a reaction to all her surging emotions. Unable to sit still, she got to her feet and began pacing up and down the length of the enormous table.

Wazza watched her for a few moments, then he also stood, his large frame barring her way and she pulled up short before she ran into his chest. "What do *you* want, then?" His light-blue eyes searched her face. "Tell me, and I'll try and help. If you want to leave, I'll take you wherever you want to go." His hand came up to rest on her shoulder. His touch ignited flames of sensation on her bare skin that flowed through her like lightning flashes.

They were standing so close she could feel the heat emanating from his body. And she suddenly, stupidly, wanted to lean her cheek against that hand resting on her shoulder. She hadn't given her brain permission to think about how Wazza affected her. How her body lit up when he was around. In fact, she thought she'd expressly forbidden it to remember how he set the blood beating through her veins, how her limbs felt suddenly wobbly when he touched her. Like he was now. As if her muscles turned to hot liquid and that molten heat was all pooling in between her legs, even now as she stared up at him.

"Thank you," she whispered. It seemed like the appropriate answer, but she could no longer recall exactly what it was she was thanking him for.

"I need you to understand that you're not trapped here. This isn't a jail, you're free to go whenever you want." His voice was deep and unhurried, oozing like warm honey. He lifted a finger to stroke her cheek. She almost closed her eyes at the sheer intimacy and pleasure of it. Today, Wazza's sleeves were rolled up to his elbows, revealing strong, tanned forearms. She stared at the perfection out of the corner of her eye. Nicely honed and well-built from long hours of physical labor. A man with nice arms was such a turn on. She'd always thought that.

"Mm-hmm," she murmured. He was staring at her lips. Which unexpectedly felt so dry that her tongue came out in an unconscious act to moisten them. Uh-oh. That was the completely wrong thing to do, because now his eyes were laser-focussed on her mouth, irises going dark and unpredictable. He took a step closer, his body crowding hers, and her nipples tightened to sharp points. His aroma surrounded her. She'd expected him to smell like cattle and dirt. But he smelled like crisp hay and leather.

She was about to take a step back, away from this aching awareness of how close they were standing, when his other hand slid to the small of her back, pulling her gently into him.

Instead of swaying backward, Kee found herself standing straddling Wazza's thigh. Something hot and urgent tingled between her own thighs. It'd been a long while since she'd had a man that made her feel this way between her legs. Sure, Jakov had wanted her, had wanted to have sex with her, but it was always done his way. Often rough and unsatisfying. This was something altogether more powerful and heady. Jakov had never looked at her with such tender desire.

His lips found the side of her neck and she didn't stop him, as his mouth buzzed down her soft skin. Warm and wet. His kiss ignited all sorts of feelings in her breasts, and stomach... and down lower. She was powerless to resist and turned her lips to seek the heat of his. His mouth claimed hers, slow and sweet, gentle, and forgiving. Something in him must've understood not to push her too hard, or she'd run like a startled rabbit.

Their kiss deepened, and he slotted himself into her thighs, so she could feel his erection pounding between them. He groaned deep in his throat, but didn't break their kiss, as her hand slid over his chest, feeling all those delicious muscles underneath. As though a switch had been tripped inside, and a goddess of sexual abandonment had been released, she shivered and pulled him tighter. She ran a hand through his deliciously tousled hair, pulling his mouth down harder onto hers, wanting him closer, wanting him to devour her. Wanting them to become one, his skin on hers, his hands all over her body.

If anyone had told Kee two days ago that she'd be kissing a cowboy with reckless abandon, she'd have waved them off as belonging in the lunatic asylum.

But maybe she was the one who needed to go into an asylum. Because what was she doing kissing a cowboy in a luxury lodge in the middle of Queensland? And what would happen if her daughter suddenly walked through that door and caught her doing...this with Wazza? It was this thought that finally brought her to her senses. She tipped her head back, breaking his hold on her lips. Instead of withdrawing, his mouth moved once more to the soft skin at the base of her clavicle, and she drew in a shuddering breath. Oh. My. God. She was pure sensation and light. And need. She wanted this man with an intense longing she'd never felt before.

Benni. She needed to think about Benni. Not about what she wanted.

"Wazza." She gently pushed on his shoulders, and he reluctantly removed his lips from her neck.

"Hmm," he grunted against her skin, but she could feel him tensing, withdrawing from her.

She held him at arm's length, letting her breathing come back to something resembling normalcy. Letting her pounding heart stop trying to beat out of her chest. "We shouldn't have done that. I don't do this sort of thing. With other men," she added, dropping her gaze. "I haven't even known you for two days, and look at us."

"Yes, but it feels like we've known each other for weeks, months. We have...chemistry." His voice was still low and throaty, his hand remaining in the small of her back, as if he were unwilling to break their connection completely.

"Maybe we do," she admitted. For a crazy second, she'd forgotten her troubles, forgotten the reality of needing to protect her daughter against her psychotic paternal family. But chemistry wasn't any kind of excuse to forget her responsibilities.

Wazza regarded her silently. She felt her cheeks turn pink. She owed him an apology. A big one. She'd come across as ungracious and churlish before, and he deserved better. He'd been willing to help her. Had even suggested he'd take her away from the station, to wherever she wanted to go, against his boss's wishes.

"Sorry. I need to thank you for everything you've done. I've been so...ungrateful." She hadn't done anything to deserve this man's empathy. His kindness. All he'd ever done was offer her his generous heart. Found her a place to hide out. Brought her food and organized to fix her car. Right down to bringing them both Akubras yesterday.

Which reminded her. "You know, Benni won't take off that damn hat you gave her." She laughed lightly, and stepped away from his embrace, putting a chair between them, needing something to stop her from reaching out to touch him again. "She even wanted to wear it in the shower this morning."

A grin lit up his face. "Really?"

"Yes. She wants to be a cowboy when she grows up."

"Nothing wrong with that."

No, she guessed there probably wasn't. Certainly, if Benni grew up to be half as compassionate and honest as Wazza, there was no harm in it at all.

"I'll be happy to teach her the rules, if you like. No wearing hats at the dinner table, that sort of thing. I did notice she took hers off when I removed mine earlier."

"Yes, she thinks you're the stars and the moon. You can do no wrong in her eyes."

"It's nice to know I have at least one admirer." His mouth tilted up in a quirky smile that she hadn't seen before. Amusement, with a hint of a challenge. But she wasn't prepared to accept that challenge right now. Wasn't prepared to admit that she admired him also, possibly as much as Benni did.

There was a brisk knock at the door, and then Daniella entered. Kee's hand flew up to cover her heart. What if Daniella had a walked in on them only a few minutes before? She shuddered to think.

"Right then. I've got Sasha opening cabin three for you. It's closest to the lodge, as well as the staff quarters, in case you need us." Daniella shot Wazza an unreadable glance. Her straight, short bob swung around her face as she turned toward him, absentmindedly tucking the strands behind one ear. Daniella looked exactly like what Kee would've picked for farming aristocracy. If there was such a thing. Neatly dressed in white jodhpurs and a light-blue, button-up shirt, done up to the neck, there wasn't a speck of dirt to be found. Unlike Wazza and Steve, whose clothes were well-worn and covered in dust. "Why don't we get you settled? Wazza, I think Steve needs you at the stables," she added, effectively dismissing him. Making it clear that Wazza had a job to do.

Guilt swirled suddenly in Kee's stomach, for taking up Wazza's time. For taking everyone's time. And she felt an apology forming on her lips. But her friend Levi's words came back to her. *"You need to stand up for yourself more. Stopping being everybody's doormat."* His comment had stung at the time, even though he said it half in jest, after she'd deferred yet again to Clarice's request that Kee bring her a nice cup of tea and biscuit. Clarice was one of the animal shelter's vets, and Kee thought she was wonderful. She had said please after all, Kee had replied to Levi, her feet already making a beeline for the kitchen. But it was on that day Kee finally realized that Clarice didn't ask anyone else to make her a cup of tea. It was the reason Jakov thought he could treat her like he had. But then she'd shown him, hadn't she? By taking the stand and testifying against him. He hadn't seen that one coming. It'd shocked him to the core, the fact that she'd finally gained enough courage to take him on. But it was also the reason he thought he could take her daughter away from her.

But Wazza didn't jump up to obey Daniella's command straight away.

"Will you be okay?" he asked, blue eyes hovering on her face. He would come with her if she asked, she could see it in the tilt of his head. She wanted to say no. Ask him to stay. To have his solid, unwavering presence around. Because her mind wanted to dwell on that kiss. Hungered for his touch.

"Of course," she answered, with more confidence than she felt. He needed to get back to work, and she needed to get back to her daughter. No more thinking about Wazza kissing her. "Thank you again for everything." The smile she offered was for him alone.

Wazza snagged his Akubra from the table and put his hand on the doorknob when Daniella's voice stopped him.

"Oh, Wazza," she called. "Steve and I had a quick chat. We think we should keep Julie and Aaron, and Bindi and Alek, in the loop, too. I don't like secrets between the staff. I think we should all be on the same page. Do you agree?" She glanced between Wazza and Kee, including her in the question.

Kee had no real idea who these people were. Wazza had mentioned Julie and Aaron before, and she thought Julie might be part of the family. Kee looked to Wazza for guidance.

"Yes, it's probably for the best. As long as they know not to mention anything to Skylar or Nash."

"She's still quite annoyed about that. I'd stay out of her way if I were you. But I'll make sure they know."

"Good. See you later." Wazza turned his blue gaze to Kee for a second, and then he was gone.

"Right then. Come along," Daniella directed. "Let's go and find Benni. Lunch service will be up soon. Skylar and Bindi are in the kitchen getting the meal ready. Are you hungry?"

Kee stifled a sigh and turned to follow Daniella out of the room.

CHAPTER NINE

Wazza knocked on the door and waited. Bare feet padded across the wooden floor inside, and then the door opened. Kee stood there, long hair tumbling over her shoulders, down over her breasts. Curly and slightly wild, it was a shock to see it out of the normal long braid she always wore. Holy shitpile, she looked gorgeous, in a just-got-out-of-bed, casual sort of way. He let his gaze linger, but that was a mistake. He felt his cock begin to stand to attention. Not a good way to start the morning. And not a good thing with a small child around.

He cleared his throat. "Good morning. How did you sleep?"

"Great, thank you. This place is amazing. Absolutely... amazing."

Sometimes he forgot he lived on a luxury resort. People paid shitloads of money to come and stay here. And these cabins were the epitome of opulence. His own dorm room in the staff quarters was well laid out, large, with plenty of space, solid wooden furniture, and air conditioning, much nicer than other places he'd worked. But nothing like these cabins, that had a rustic luxury renowned throughout the country. Kee probably had never stayed anywhere quite like this before.

"Yes, they are," he agreed.

A face appeared around the side of Kee's legs, Akubra already on her head. "Hello, Mr. Cowboy."

"His name is Wazza," Kee reminded her.

"I know," Benni replied with a giggle.

"I've got something Benni might like to see." Wazza said, meeting Kee's gaze and holding his breath, hoping she'd come with him.

"Don't you have work to do? I don't want to intrude or get in the way." Kee's eyes became shuttered, and he knew what she really meant was that she didn't want to get him in trouble with the boss. More trouble with his boss.

"You won't," he assured her. "The thing I want to show you is in the shed, where I'm working today."

"We'll need to get our shoes on." Kee still seemed hesitant.

"I don't mind waiting." Taking a chance, he mouthed the word, "Puppies," over the top of Benni's head. Kee's eyes widened, and a smile lit up her lips. Who didn't like puppies? They were a winner every time. He took a step back, ready to sit on one of the cane chairs on the front porch until they were ready.

"Come in." She held the door open wider. His gut fluttered as he squeezed past her, brushing her shoulder. That was mistake number two. She smelled wonderful, like she'd just stepped out of the shower, and he wanted to lean in and taste her. Run his hands through all that glorious, dark hair. Quickly, he took a seat at the end of the couch, putting distance between them. And hopefully hiding his reaction, at least from Benni.

Benni bounced around like the proverbial bunny Kee had nicknamed her after. "Look, Wazza," she said, handing him a gum leaf. "I found this on the back step this morning." She peered down at the leaf in his hand and then back up at his face, sheer delight in her eyes.

"It's beautiful," he agreed.

"Get your shoes from under the bed, missy," Kee commanded. Then, when Benni disappeared into the main bedroom, she said, "Sorry. Benni loves to collect things from nature."

"Not a problem. I'm a nature lover myself. Among other things." His gaze rested on her slim, brown legs, enjoying the view, and letting her know exactly what he was thinking. The tips of her ears turned pink, and she puckered her lips, frowning at him. She might've intended it as a form of rebuff at the obvious lechery in his smile, but to Wazza it made her lips look all the more like a rosebud. Plump and inviting. *Oh shit.* He needed to stop thinking like this; there was a young girl in the house.

Kee turned and marched into the bedroom, saying, "What is keeping you, young lady?" And he blew out on a breath of relief. He sat back on the plush, leather couch, glancing around at the living room. Kee and her daughter had made themselves at home. Well, at least Benni had. There were toys all over the rug, and a couple of half-dressed Barbie dolls on the opposite couch with tiny clothing scattered all around; there was even a set of small, plastic farm animals arranged up on top of the bookshelf in a circle, as if they were all having an intimate conversation. Wazza smiled to himself. So, this was what it was like to have a small girl around.

He hadn't had much time to see Kee or Benni yesterday afternoon. The lodge was almost full with the eight newly arrived guests, and only two cabins left unoccupied. Which wasn't unusual, this was the busiest time of the year, but it meant the staff were often run off their feet, having to multi-task and multi-skill. Steve had needed him in the stables—the farrier was shoeing some horses—while his boss and Dale took the guests on a hike up the escarpment. Then later that afternoon, Skylar had Wazza helping her with the trimmer around her orchard and veggie patch, keeping the weeds down. Her kitchen garden was an important part of the station, it provided many of the fresh ingredients she needed to produce her extraordinary food creations. But it was all part of the job, and Wazza enjoyed the fact that each day was different. No humdrum, nine-to-five job for him. It meant he only had time to quickly poke his head in the cabin door to make sure Kee had everything she needed, before he had to help Alek set up tables and chairs on the grass by the billabong, so the guests could dine outside in the wonderfully balmy air that night. The guests always raved about the outdoor dinner, said it was one of the most special experiences. Strings of fairy lights were strung up between eucalyptus trees, and the tables were lit with flaming torches surrounding them. With the stars twinkling in the crystal skies above, Wazza agreed it was a pretty remarkable thing to do, and one of the many reasons Stormcloud was so extraordinary. He'd asked Kee to join them, but she'd politely declined, saying that she and Benni were going to have a quiet night in the cabin together. It'd been a hectic day, and she needed time to think. Which he guessed was fair enough. And he thought he'd hidden his disappointment perfectly well behind his smile. Because he would've liked to spend more time with Kee. As much time as she'd give him. And she would've absolutely loved eating out under the stars.

Kee and Benni returned to the living room, breaking Wazza out of his musing. Wazza was glad to see Kee wearing the tan hat he'd given her the other day, her hair tied back in its usual braid. And of course, Benni still wore her blue one with pride.

"We're ready," Kee said.

"Great." Wazza sprang from the couch and opened the door. "I can give you a tour around the rest of the lodge on the way, if you like?"

Again, Kee hesitated. Wazza wished she'd just get over whatever it was that made her not want to be seen to be taking advantage of him. As if she didn't deserve his help. He wouldn't have offered if he hadn't meant it.

"Sure," she said eventually. "Benni's been nagging me to take her down to that beautiful lake all morning. But I wasn't sure if we were allowed."

"Well, that's the first place we're going," he said gallantly.

"Yippee," Benni squealed. The sound was bright and happy and shocked Wazza for a second. Stormcloud was an adults only resort, so it wasn't often that children's voices were heard around the lodge. It was one more thing that'd surprised Wazza, just how readily Daniella had let the two strangers stay, even though having a child on the property went against her strict policies. Either Daniella was suffering an episode, or she might finally be starting to soften her principles. With age came wisdom, wasn't that what they said? Perhaps Daniella secretly wanted grandchildren, and this was her way of scratching that itch.

"This way," Wazza directed them down the slope and across the lush grass in front of the lodge toward the billabong lower down. Kee took Benni's hand, and they walked along beside him. Then Benni slipped her hand into his. It was done unconsciously, without guile or any thought of consequence, but Wazza's heart skipped a beat. Her hand was small and warm, and oh, so terribly innocent. She skipped along beside him, heedless of what was going on inside his chest, the upheaval of emotions. It brought thoughts of Karri and little Ava to the front of his mind. Would he have made a good father?

He glanced over at Kee, wondering what she thought of her daughter's action. Benni's trust in him was implicit. But Kee was still holding back. Kee caught his eye from beneath the brim of her hat, her gaze unreadable, leaving him unsure what she felt about it all. Even after that kiss that'd nearly scorched his brain yesterday in the meeting room, Kee seemed to have withdrawn into herself again.

He suddenly didn't care. Today was a good day. The sun was shining; the sky was blue. A kookaburra began its throaty, laughing call from somewhere high in the branches above. He began to whistle.

"What's that song?" Benni asked excitedly. "Will you teach it to me?"

"What? Do you mean you've never heard 'Kookaburra Sits in the Old Gumtree' before?" he asked. Most Aussie kids knew that song, it was sung around campfires, at pre-school, at Girl Guides and in most homes across the country.

"No. Sing it. Sing it," Benni said, swinging on his hand and looking up into his face.

"You forgot to say please," Kee admonished. "And perhaps Wazza doesn't want to sing right now."

"Not a problem," he answered. And then he began to sing the children's song he'd learned so long ago. After a while, Benni joined in with the chorus, adding a little giggle when she got the words wrong.

They arrived at the edge of the billabong, breathless from singing. Wazza hoped Daniella didn't come charging out onto the veranda to find out what all the noise was about, who was disturbing the peace and quiet of this adult retreat. But no such apparition appeared.

"Such a pretty pond," Benni exclaimed.

"Out here, we call it a billabong," Wazza corrected gently. "There's lots of fish swimming in there. If you watch closely, you might see one jump out of the water to catch an insect."

"Really?" Benni breathed in disbelief.

"Really." Wazza kept his face solemn. "Steve, the boss, he grows barramundi in here. They can get really big, and they're delicious to eat."

"I don't like fish." Benni screwed up her nose.

"Oh, look at that beautiful bird, Benni," Kee called. "It's got metallic feathers." She hunkered down on the grass next to her daughter and pointed to a kingfisher skimming along the surface of the water, chasing down insects. "Don't go too near the water," Kee admonished as she let go of Benni's hand. "It looks deep," she said, eyeing the water warily.

"It can be deep in the middle, but it's really shallow around the edges," Wazza replied. Of course, she was probably worried about Benni falling in. The kid was only four, she probably couldn't swim well. "She's quite safe," he said, hoping to calm her fears. "The water only goes up to my knees for a long way out. I'll keep an eagle eye on her."

"Oh, okay." Kee seemed to accept his explanation.

They both stood back and watched Benni hunt around at the edge of the tall sedge grass, exclaiming in delight as she discovered a slimy snail, or a bit of bright-green algae. Wazza made sure he kept an eye on Benni, not letting her go into the high grass farther around the slope. He didn't want to scare Benni, she was having so much fun. But later, Wazza would have a conversation with Kee about the danger of snakes, even this close to the lodge.

"I never realized there were so many creatures out in the desert," Kee said.

"Yeah, the diversity is amazing."

They stood close, but not quite touching. Then, he made the mistake of looking directly into her dark, fathomless eyes, and for uncounted seconds he was lost.

Like she'd said last night, they'd only known each other for a few days, but he felt as if it'd been much longer. There was a connection between them that couldn't be explained. Couldn't be denied. But his connection to this woman was complicated. Because it was mixed in with his connection with Benni. You couldn't have one without the other. And he had growing feelings for both. The feelings were different, but entwined, nonetheless.

What the hell was he getting himself into?

"Show me the thing?" Benni interrupted his thoughts and broke his contact with Kee. "You know, the thing you were going to show me."

"Right. This way." Wazza started back up the grassy hill, taking them past the infinity swimming pool—which had no one in it this morning—and around the side of the lodge. On the way he pointed out Skylar's kitchen garden, which Kee was most impressed by, gave them a quick run-down of the history of the resort, and how it'd grown, showing them some cabins that could be seen peeking through the trees, explaining that there were now twenty cabins, Steve having added an extra couple last year to keep up with demand. Kee made all the right noises of appreciation in all the right places. But he could see she didn't really understand just how hard Steve and Daniella had had to work to make this place what it was today.

The machinery shed was up the hill, beyond the lodge and behind the stables. Benni wanted to go and see the horses, but Wazza said they'd save that for another day, as he had something really special to show her. It was a huge, square building made from corrugated iron sheets, with a high roof, and a concrete floor. It wasn't too hot in here yet, but during the middle of the day the iron walls concentrated the heat and it became like an oven. Which was why he was hoping to get his job done by smoko time. The tractor needed all the fluids and oils checked, along with the belts and hoses. Not a complicated job. Steve always made sure maintenance was a priority with his vehicles, but he needed it done by this afternoon, so he could grade the dirt driveway; the potholes were becoming a menace.

"Over here." Wazza beckoned them toward a dark corner

at the back. A pair of bright eyes regarded them from out of the gloom.

"What is it?" Benni whispered.

"A mummy dog and her babies," answered Wazza, and right on cue, they all heard the distinctive yipping of young dogs.

Benni's eyes went round, and she gasped, "Puppies?"

"Is she friendly?" Kee hung back, gaze wary, tugging on Benni's hand.

"Yes. Of course."

"Can I see them?" Benni asked, voice full of awe.

"As long as you're quiet and don't scare them," said Kee.

"It's fine," Wazza assured her, and leaned into the dim corner, then returned with a puppy in each hand. He put them on the floor next to Benni, who got down on her hands and knees and cooed at the tiny animals. They were roughly two weeks old, and had just opened their eyes and started to explore their surroundings, crawling around on their bellies. The bitch squirmed out of her den—a pile of hessian sacks beneath a set of metal shelves running along one side of the shed—and yawned and stretched, obviously glad for an excuse to escape her offspring for a few moments.

"Be careful, bunny." Kee made as if to bend down, then laughed as the female dog licked her hand. "Oh, she's gorgeous," she cooed over the kelpie. "I love dogs. It was one of the reasons I took the job at the animal shelter, so I could be around them more. Jakov never allowed us to have any pets."

"Who's dog is she?" Benni asked.

"Kali is Steve's dog," Wazza replied. That was stretching the truth. Steve might've purchased Kali as a puppy, but she belonged to everyone, really. She was one of the many station dogs, although possibly Steve's favorite. They had a few of them to help with the cattle. But more than that, a dog was an everyday part of running a farm. They were part of the culture, as much as the horses, and barbed wire, and dusty boots.

The farm dogs normally slept in a suite of kennels on the other side of the stables. Because there were so many guests around, Daniella didn't want the dogs roaming around at night. Kali had broken away from her kennel and no one could find her for over two days. Then Wazza had heard a noise while he'd been hunting around for the large wrench which normally lived on the shelf at the back of the shed. He'd got down on his hands and knees and found the missing dog, with five gorgeous puppies all suckling noisily. Kali was a black-and-tan kelpie, as was the purebred father from a neighboring property, and so were all her puppies. Steve was delighted when Wazza told him that he'd found her. The puppies would be worth a pretty penny if Steve decided to sell them. Quality working dogs were highly sought after out here, and Kali had impeccable breeding, as well as a friendly nature.

"Are you all right here for a while? I need to get back to fixing the tractor."

"What? Of course," Kee said hastily. "Don't let us take up any more of your time."

Wazza strode down the length of the shed to where the tractor sat waiting for him. But he couldn't help himself, and he turned to stare at the two figures half-hidden in the gloom. Benni was still on her hands and knees, making encouraging noises as she tenderly patted one of the puppies. She was extremely gentle, and Wazza decided that she hadn't needed her mother's words of warning. It was as if she had an affinity with the animals. Much as Kee did. Other kids might've yelled or jumped around, scaring the dogs, but Benni sat calmly, moving with care, and not picking the puppies up, but instead letting them come to her.

Kee's slim figure was silhouetted by a ray of light shining

through a hole in the iron. From this angle, in those tight-fitting shorts and tank top, with the Akubra on her head, he could appreciate her curves, her thin waist and nice legs. She was a damn attractive woman. Then she glanced in his direction, and he was struck by how young and forsaken she looked. Out of place. His heart went out to her, because it was obvious she had no idea what she was doing, or how she was going to solve this shitpile of trouble she'd got herself into.

He wanted to help her. Help them both. Right at that second, he made a vow. He'd do whatever it took to make sure she wasn't in this alone. Whatever it took.

CHAPTER TEN

Kee sat deeper into the sumptuous leather couch and lay her head back so she could stare at the ceiling. It was still searingly hot outside, but inside this wonderful, air-conditioned cabin, it was deliciously cool. Kee let herself wallow in the simple pleasure of being cool on a hot day in a cabin that had every whim catered for. She lifted her head to stare around the room.

The cabin was open plan, with the living room and kitchen combined. The living room was well-appointed with two couches and a matching wing chair, done in the softest tan leather, all the other furniture looked like it was handmade, perhaps from local wood. A modern and stylish TV was affixed to the wall—not so large that it was ostentatious, but bigger than the one Kee used to own—and a large bookshelf sat next to the television, full to the brim of all sorts of books, both old and new. A set of French doors led out to a rear porch, allowing an amazing view of the forest of eucalyptus trees marching off down the slope. On cooler nights, she imagined, you could open the doors and let nature inside.

The kitchen was full of high-end appliances that Kee didn't dare touch. A black and silver coffee machine that looked more suited to serving customers in a ritzy café than here in the outback. The refrigerator was stocked with gourmet foods, bottles of wine and beer, fresh homemade bread and butter replaced every day, snacks such as macadamia nuts and exotic, dried, native fruits. A bowl full of fresh fruit—one of the few things Kee allowed Benni to eat—sat on the countertop. In a normal hotel, you'd have to pay for these items, and Kee could just guess that the prices would be exorbitant. Guests wanted for nothing at Stormcloud.

But she wasn't a guest. Not really. She was an imposter, relying on the goodwill of a cowboy. Kee's head slumped back against the headrest of the couch.

Benni was lying on her stomach on the rug at Kee's feet, surrounded by her toys, reading a book to Dolly. She still had the blue hat firmly planted on her head. Benni had only recently stopped taking a daily nap, but it was still a good idea to have some quiet time in the afternoon, to let her wind down. Especially after the past few days of excitement.

Yesterday had been a flurry of activity, starting with Daisy and her brother discovering her staying at their house, and ending up with her and Benni moving into this cabin. The cabin was gorgeous, but Kee couldn't help but feel she'd been railroaded into something she wasn't really prepared for. Last night, she'd asked if they could have a quiet dinner alone, just her and Benni, she couldn't stomach having to talk and mingle with all those strangers up at the lodge. It'd become her habit to stay away from people as much as possible. It sounded like a cliché, but she saw it as her and Benni against the world. And the truth was, the fewer people who knew she was here, the fewer people could give away her location to Bruno, or one of his corrupt cop mates. It was common sense to stay in the shadows, away from the limelight.

This morning Wazza had called past their cabin and invited her and Benni up to see a litter of puppies. Which Benni had absolutely fallen in love with. Every five minutes after they left the shed, she wanted to go back and play with them. Kee wasn't sure whether to thank Wazza, or murder him. It was a wonderful distraction for her daughter, a little piece of normality in all this craziness. But there was no way they were taking on a puppy; certainly not while they were fleeing Jakov's family. She had no idea how long they'd need to be on the road.

They'd spent the rest of the morning and into lunch time at the lodge, chatting with Skylar and Bindi. Skylar had even let them help pick some vegetables from her kitchen garden to go with the epicurean meal she was preparing. Then Dale had offered to show them around the stables. Benni had jumped at the chance to see the horses, but she'd wanted Wazza to come with them, and pouted when he said he had to help take some of the guests on a horse safari to check on some cattle in a nearby paddock. Kee had secretly wanted Wazza to come as well, but she'd kept her doleful reaction under wraps a little better than her daughter and made Benni apologize for her woeful behavior. Wazza had a job to do, and the last thing she wanted was to jeopardize it. And Dale was lovely, such a gentleman, tall and good-looking. Daisy was a lucky lady.

They'd come back to the cabin to chill out for an hour or so before dinner.

There was a knock at the door, and Kee jumped up to open it.

Wazza stood on the front verandah, looking all dirty and hot from his ride. Cowboy boots covered in dust, jeans slung low over lean hips, blue shirt sleeves rolled up to his elbows again. So damn sexy, Kee had to hide a flush of desire.

"Hi," he said. She'd forgotten how deep and gravely his voice was. It was doing strange things to her heart rate.

"Hi," she said in reply. Then, when she realized she was standing there gaping at him like some half-blind fool, she added, "Come in and get cool. Can I get you a drink or something?"

After a moment's hesitation, he replied, "I wouldn't mind a glass of cold water if you have it." As he stepped through the doorway, he removed his hat, dropping it on the little side-table next to the door.

She was suddenly flustered and flittered around the kitchen like her mother had used to do, fussing over glasses and getting the jug of cold, filtered water out of the fridge.

"It's Mr. Cowboy," Benni crowed with delight. Wazza sat down in the wing chair and Benni nearly leapt into his lap.

"Give Wazza a chance to sit in peace," she said, trying to keep her tone even. But Benni ignored her admonishment, talking a mile a minute, telling Wazza all about her visit with the horses. Kee was going to have to have a word with that child later.

"I don't mind," he said over the top of Benni's head as Kee handed him the tall glass of water. His smile was so dazzling that Kee nearly dropped it.

"I have some good news. Lefty called; he said your fuel pump will be in on Friday. He can have it fitted and ready to go by lunchtime."

Kee let out a whoosh of relief. That *was* good news. Today was Tuesday, which meant only three more days at the station. Finally, something she could grab hold of. This odd sort of limbo she'd found herself in had been driving her crazy. Daniella and Steve were well-meaning, as were the rest of the family and staff at Stormcloud. But it was well beyond time she was gone from here.

Kee glanced up and couldn't stop a flash of sensation burning through her stomach at the way Wazza was looking at her. Definitely time to move on. Not least of all, because of this man.

She could feel connections forming. Friendships. Not just with Wazza, either. Daniella had taken to Benni, almost as if she were her own granddaughter. Which surprised Kee, after the way Wazza had described her as being very driven, an extremely professional woman, with high standards. Like today, right after smoko—a new word that Kee had learned meant morning tea—Kee had been in the kitchen chatting to Skylar and Bindi, when Daniella had stalked in, a frown darkening her brow. But as soon as she saw Benni, the stormy clouds lifted from her face, and she'd pulled up a chair at the countertop next to where Benni was industriously coloring, and asked her what her favorite color was. Then, when Benni had said she could help her color if she liked, Daniella had taken up a pencil and started on a pink flower, chatting with Benni as she did so.

The look that'd passed between Skylar and Bindi had said it all. They were quietly amazed. So, it seemed that Daniella *was* acting out of character.

But she wasn't the only one.

Steve always took the time to stop and get down to Benni's level to have a quick conversation with her. And when he did, he lost that serious, gruff exterior that was his normal persona. Even Skylar was happy to let Benni sit in her kitchen and watch her cook, or play with her dolls. Placing morsels of food in front of her to let her taste. She told Benni that she was her chief taster, and Benni took her job very seriously. Frowning in concentration before making her verdict. Most of the things Skylar cooked, Benni liked. But there were a few times where she'd screwed up her face with distaste. Kee had tried to teach Benni not to spit out food, it wasn't good manners, but Skylar didn't seem to mind.

Kee had *almost* felt like she was beginning to fit in here. Which was another red flag that proved she needed to move on.

But in the meantime… "I'd like to help around here. Earn my keep. I don't like to feel I'm a burden. I'm just not sure what I could do to help. I've never worked on a farm before. I've worked in an animal shelter, but that's about it."

"You don't need to—"

She cut him off. "But I want to."

"Okay," he replied slowly. That little crease was back between his eyebrows, the endearing one that made Kee want to go up and run her thumb over his forehead until it disappeared. "There are a lot of things that need doing around the lodge that don't require too much training." He tipped his head back as he considered the question, revealing the strong, tanned length of his throat. Kee swallowed compulsively. "Skylar might need help with her garden," he mused, then his eyes refocused and gained a sparkle as an idea came to him. "Have you ever driven a ride-on lawnmower?"

"No. But that doesn't sound too difficult."

"It's not. They're easy as pie, you should be fine with a bit of basic training. Benni can even ride along with you."

"Can you show me now?" Kee was suddenly filled with enthusiasm. Something to keep her mind off her problems, something to keep her busy while she waited, would be a good thing. A bit of an adventure, as Benni like to say.

"Sure. I've got time before dinner. Grab your hat and your shoes. Come on Benni, I'll help you put your shoes on."

The lethargy that'd threatened to swallow Kee whole drained from her body. This was good, a way to pay this family back for all their help. She went into the bedroom to put on her shoes and grabbed her hat, and by the time she returned, Wazza and Benni were waiting impatiently by the door.

The heat hit them like a physical blow as they ventured outside, even though it was late afternoon, and she was glad of the hat Wazza had loaned her to keep the sun off her face.

"I'll have to pass it by Daniella, of course," Wazza said, as he swung Benni down the two front steps onto the gravel path. "But if she gives the okay, you can start first thing in the morning."

"Of course." Kee couldn't see why Daniella would disagree. "I'd like to help Skylar in her garden, as well. I used to do some gardening with my dad when I was younger."

"Great." Wazza led them down past the billabong, showing Kee which sections needed to be mowed. It'd never occurred to her that this lush, green lawn wasn't just a natural feature. Which was stupid, really. Because, of course, it was part of the well-manicured, glossy, shine that the resort radiated. Benni pottered along behind them, chattering to herself, and picking up anything that interested her.

"The lawnmower is housed in a small shed at the bottom of the orchard. We call it the yellow devil because it can be a bit temperamental at times. But don't worry, you'll get the hang of it soon." He gave a lopsided grin.

"Right." Kee didn't let his words sour her good mood. It would be fine. She could handle anything. Even something called the yellow devil.

"I'll show you where it's kept."

Making sure that Benni was close behind them, Kee followed Wazza around the side of the lodge and into the kitchen garden. The garden shed was well hidden behind a row of trees that Skylar had told her were Kakadu plums. Which was interesting, because while Kee had heard of them, she never realized they could be cultivated in a normal garden. Skylar had some very interesting ideas about what you could and should eat. It was something Kee would like to learn more about. They wound their way between the trees, Kee ducking to miss some of the branches. She threw a quick glance over her shoulder and saw that Benni was trailing close behind. She'd found a large stick that she was using to draw a line in the dirt and was humming to herself.

Wazza pulled open a sizable roller door in one end of the shed, which, now that she looked at it, was of similar size to a double garage. A gust of scorching air hit them in the face as they stepped inside. It was hotter in here, if that was even possible. A trickle of sweat ran between her shoulder blades.

"It's over here." Wazza pointed to a bulky shape looming in the shadows.

"Wow. It's…bigger than I expected." The machine looked a little intimidating, greasy and dusty, with four wheels and a seat perched up high on top, it was driven by a steering wheel, and reminded her of a tiny tractor. But she wasn't going to back down now. She could do this. It was just an overgrown lawnmower, not a ten-tonne semi-trailer.

Wazza showed her how to use the step and then swing up into the seat. He pointed out the starter button, and outlined a few basic protocols on how to mow the grass—up and down the hill toward the billabong, not side to side across the slope. It was called the yellow devil because it smoked like the devil, was often temperamental, sometimes hard to start, and sometimes refused to turn off. But it was as tough as nails, and just kept going and going, which was why Steve wouldn't get rid of it.

Kee nodded, taking in everything he said, trying to remember it all.

Suddenly, she lifted her head. Where was Benni? She couldn't see her in the shed. She must be still outside, poking at the trees with a stick. Kee's shoulders relaxed. That child couldn't get enough of this place.

But Kee couldn't rid herself of that itch at the back of her neck. "I'm just going to check on Benni," she said, jumping lightly down from the lawnmower.

Stepping outside, she squinted into the orchard, back the way they'd come. "Benni," she called. There was no answer. And no sign of her daughter. A few quick strides took her farther outside. "Benni, where are you?" Still no answer. Her heart rate picked up. She tried to see between the low shrubs that partially hid the billabong from view. Would she have gone that way? Benni had been wearing her purple T-shirt with Minnie Mouse on the front; she loved that T-shirt. The bright color should stand out amongst the browns and dull green of the eucalypts.

Wazza appeared at elbow. "What's wrong?"

"Benni's not here." Her voice took on a high-pitched squeak.

"Well, she can't have gone far." Wazza didn't sound particularly worried. His seeming lack of concern made her heart beat even faster. He didn't understand. Benni never wandered away. She was a good girl and did she was told.

"You don't get it. She knows not to leave my sight. I drummed it into her over and over." Well, she thought she had. Perhaps she'd given her too much credit, because Benni was still only little. Too little to be wandering around a cattle station on her own.

"She's a smart kid, she'll be fine," Wazza replied, taking a few steps so he could look around the other side of the shed.

"She's only four years old," Kee snapped. She didn't care if she sounded desperate and angry, because she was. "How can you downplay this? We need to find her. I need to find her. You're not her mother. You don't care about her, like I do." Kee put her hands on her hat and spun around on the spot, calling out in desperation, "Benni. Benni, where are you? Answer me." Oh God, what if she'd gone down to the billabong? What if she was drowning in the water right now?

"She can't swim," Kee groaned. "What if she fell into the water?"

The thought terrified her, because Kee couldn't swim, either. How would she rescue her little girl if she was in the water? She had to check.

She turned to race in that direction, when Wazza took her by the shoulders and forced her to look at him. "I am worried about her, as well. But before you get hysterical, I have an idea where she might've gone."

"Where? Where is she?" Kee wailed.

Wazza took Kee by the hand and tugged her back up the hill, away from the billabong, through the orchard and past the raised garden beds, going so fast they were almost running.

"Benni. Where are you?" Kee called at the top of her voice, unable to stop the shaking that was taking over her body. Where had she gone? What if Bruno had found her? The thought stopped her dead in her tracks.

"What's wrong?" Wazza had stopped, as well.

"Bruno. What if he's got her?" The thought was too much to bear, and her knees nearly buckled beneath her.

Wazza's face was lined with worry as he considered this scenario. "Come on," he said again. "If she's not in the machinery shed, we'll mount a full-scale search. She won't get far, I promise."

The machinery shed? Why was Wazza taking them to the machinery shed? No. They had to search the billabong. Or the parking lot. The long driveway. If Bruno had her, he could be driving away with her stashed in his car right now. Her heart was torn in a million different directions. She pulled back against him, but he was too strong, towing her along behind him.

The inside of the machinery shed was dim, but Wazza didn't stop and take the time to flick on the bank of fluorescent lights, he stalked toward the rear, intent on his mission, dragging Kee with him.

"There she is." He let go of her hand and dropped to his knees beside Benni. "Hi, honey. Are you playing with the puppies?"

Kee stood frozen, relief flooding her veins, replacing the cold dread with heat.

"*Jebi ga.*" The Croatian curse slipped quietly from her lips. Jesus Christ, the fucking puppies. Why didn't she think of that? Kee landed on the concrete next to Wazza, scooping up her little girl into her arms. "Benni, you scared me. You can't run away. You have to ask me before you see the puppies." She hugged her tight, drawing in her familiar scent. Benni squirmed, wanting to be let down so she could continue to play, but Kee would have none of it. She placed her daughter firmly on her lap and grabbed her chin with one hand, forcing Benni to look into her eyes. "I mean it, Benita. Don't you ever do that again."

Benni finally seemed to grasp the seriousness of the situation, and she stopped squirming. "Sorry, Mummy," she said contritely. "But I wanted to see the puppies. And I knew the way. I'm a big girl now."

Kee drew in a shaky breath. "Yes, maybe you are a big girl. But that doesn't mean you can go off on your own. Do you understand me?"

"Yes." Benni lowered her gaze, her chin giving a telltale wobble. Kee got to her feet, placing Benni on the ground next to her, keeping her hand firmly locked in hers. They should probably continue this conversation back in the cabin. Kee didn't need Benni breaking down in tears right here.

"How did she even find her way up here? I didn't realize she knew how to navigate around the outbuildings," she asked, flapping her hands in the air.

"Like I said, she's a smart girl." Wazza replied. But his answer was too blithe for Kee's liking. He was looking at Benni like she'd just done something amazing. But she hadn't. She'd done the exact opposite, by ignoring her mother's request that she stay close. By causing Kee to panic. The naked fear that'd been turning her legs to jelly now bubbled up and morphed into anger.

"Well, smart or not, a cattle station is no place for a child. It's too dangerous. There's way too many things that can go wrong," she snapped. A part of her knew it was wrong to take her anger out on Wazza. Benni was her responsibility, not his. She'd only let her focus stray from her daughter for a few moments, but that was all it took.

"That's not altogether true. Plenty of kids grow up on cattle stations, and they're all completely fine. Benni just needs to learn the rules, that's all."

"Well, Benni's not like any other kid. And she doesn't just need to *learn the rules*, because we're not staying here. I can't wait to get her away from this place." The unfair words were out of her mouth before she could stop them. It was too late to take them back, and she was too angry to take them back, anyway. She hauled Benni around and stalked out of the shed, ignoring her daughter's cries of protest. Three more days was too long to spend in this godforsaken place.

CHAPTER ELEVEN

Wazza stood at the corner of the cabin and watched Kee as she sat on the veranda, head tilted backward, contemplating the stars hovering above in the night sky. It was nearly ten o'clock. Dinner service was long over, and Wazza had been headed to bed. But his feet had other ideas, and he found himself stalking towards cabin three, instead.

Should he just leave her be? He was conflicted about his feelings for Kee. She'd treated him like it was his fault that Benni had gone missing this afternoon. Which was unfair and upsetting, and made him want to demand an apology, because he'd been right all along. She was safe with the puppies. But he'd also hated the fact she'd stormed off, still angry and upset. Because she had every right; she was Benni's mother, and of course she was worried sick about her. He knew he'd probably come across as unconcerned and perhaps even flippant, but that wasn't the case. He'd merely been trying to soothe her fears. While inside, his guts had churned like a cement mixer, his palms slippery with sweat. Because Benni was important to him. Very important. As was Kee.

He cleared his throat to warn her of his approach and stepped around the corner into the light cast from the porch lamp.

"Evening," he said, a little more gruffly than he intended. "I just wanted to check you were okay before I went to bed."

"Wazza." Kee leapt out of her chair and was halfway across the porch before she stopped. "I'm glad you came," she said after a second's hesitation. "Will you come and join me for a few moments? I have something to say."

Removing his hat, he climbed the two steps and took the chair opposite to the one Kee had been sitting in. She sat also. The sound of frogs from the billabong and night insects chirping filled the air as an awkward silence grew between them. Moths beat their wings fruitlessly at the lamp above their heads, the sound growing louder every second he sat there.

"It's beautiful out here," she said finally. "Benni's been in bed for hours, but I couldn't sleep, so I came out here. I'm finally starting to see what all the fuss is about." A small smile curled her rosebud lips. Under the yellow glow of the porch light, Kee's features were softened, her eyes dark, liquid pools. Skin as smooth as coffee-colored silk. Her neck long and elegant. She tucked her bare feet beneath her as she sat, and she looked like some exotic goddess from some faraway land. A goddess that he wanted to run his hands all over, feel her curves beneath his palms. His breath hitched in his throat, and he crossed his legs, hoping to hide his physical reaction to her beauty.

Kee drew in a deep breath and leaned forward. "I'm sorry, I accused you of not caring. That wasn't fair," she said. Then held up a hand to stop him from speaking as he opened his mouth. "I know you're fond of Benni, and I know you wouldn't let anything bad happen to her. I was out of line."

"You were just being a worried mother," he replied lightly. "How's that old saying go? Never get between a lioness and her cubs." She gave him a warm smile, and he continued.

"There's nothing wrong with wanting to protect your child. And nothing wrong with being a lioness, either," he added, catching her eye.

"I'm no lion," she scoffed lightly. "But you're right, I was only thinking about Benni, nothing else. I should have trusted you more."

Wazza thought about that for a moment. It wasn't just him she should learn to trust. "I know you're scared. Scared to let Benni out of your sight. But don't underestimate her, she might even teach you a thing or two. Like I said, she's a smart kid. I think if there was ever any danger, she'd let you know."

"You think so?" Kee stood, and went to the far end of the porch, her bare toes hanging over the edge. "I'm just so confused. And scared," she added. "Constantly looking over my shoulder, watching for Bruno. And then, sometimes I wonder if I'm doing the right thing. Taking her away. Sometimes I think I'm teaching her bad behavior, running away from my fears. Maybe I'm a bad mother. Perhaps I should stand and fight. Let them take this to court and battle it out, let justice prevail. I know I'm in the right and they're in the wrong. But what if they win? I couldn't bear to lose her."

He understood her confusion because he'd been wondering the exact same thing. Wondering if she should just find herself a good lawyer and let the truth come out.

Wazza left his hat on the small table and went to stand beside Kee. So close, he could feel small tremors running through her. She was humming with built-up anxiety. Instinctively, he draped a protective arm around her shoulders. She leaned into him, pressing her shoulder beneath his armpit. She was so petite.

"You're a good mother. The best mother," he said, putting emphasis on the word best. Because she was. She was doing everything in her power to keep Benni safe. And Benni was a sweet, well-mannered, intelligent little girl. Proving what a good job Kee was doing.

"Thank you," she said, snuggling in even closer under his arm. He knew it was dangerous to touch her. Last time they'd stood this close, it'd ended in a kiss. But that wasn't what this was about. He was offering her comfort, nothing more.

If only he could stop the leap in his pulse whenever she was around. And how excruciatingly conscious he was of the curves of her body where she was pressed into his side. In a surprise move, she snaked an arm around his waist, and a surge of heat shot straight to his cock. His body seemed to come alive, crackling with electricity.

He glanced down, gaze lingering on the swell of her breasts. He had a sudden urge to see her hair loose and tangled around her shoulders again, and wanted to pull it out of its long braid.

"Look," Kee said, suddenly pointing skyward. "A shooting star. Did you see it?"

"No," he sighed. He hadn't seen it because he was too busy watching Kee. "Did you make a wish?"

She turned to face him, as if considering her answer, her arms sliding around to nestle in the small of his back, almost unconsciously. Her lips parted, and she closed her eyes for a second, a dreamy look crossing her face. He was fascinated by the curve of her mouth. It was sexy as hell.

"You know exactly what I wished for," she whispered, opening her eyes.

But the truth was, Wazza had no idea, because she suddenly touched his lips with her fingertips, her eyes never leaving his face. It was the slightest of touches, but his cock was achingly hard in an instant.

"I know I shouldn't," she whispered. Then she stood on tiptoe. "But I can't ever remember wanting to kiss someone this much before." She pulled his mouth down onto hers. Her lips were a salve to the flames burning through his body.

Urgently, his mouth claimed hers, and she made a small noise at the back of her throat. That noise stoked the flames until they were a bonfire threatening to sear his veins. His body was primed to seek pleasure; to give her pleasure in equal parts. He pulled her closer until it felt like they were a single entity, pulsing with passion.

One hand dropped to cup her ass, pulling her reflexively higher against him. Her hips bucked, thrusting her thigh against his erection. She clutched at his shirt, almost like she wanted to push him away, but then her fingers jerked convulsively, and she tore at his buttons, trying to release them. One popped open, then another. And then her hand was inside his shirt, running over his pecs, tangling in the curls of his chest hair.

He pulled the elastic from her braid and ran his fingers through the curls, releasing the heavy, dark strands to fall down her back. Thick and luxurious, just as he'd imagined. This kiss was not like the first one. It was more. Much more. Her urgency and need burned close to the surface, as did his. As if a beast inside him had been watching and waiting all day for this exact thing, and had now exploded out of his chest, wanting to consume her whole.

He picked her up off her feet, not letting his lips leave hers, and backed toward the chair, letting himself down until he was sitting, with Kee straddling his thighs. Leaning over him, hands on his chest, her hair fell like a screen around them. Her low moan as his fingers found the bare skin of her lower back whispered into the surrounding trees.

He located the hem of her T-shirt and tugged it up. "I need to see you." He meant it to be a whisper, but his voice was loud in the night. That was a mistake. Kee sat up straighter, and he could see a swirl of emotions pass over her face. *Shit.* He knew what was coming next. For a second, she dropped her forehead to his, then wordlessly, she dismounted and stood beside him, rearranging her T-shirt, which was rucked up over her bra. Wazza's head spun at this sudden change of gears, and it took his body long seconds to catch up.

"Kee." His voice was a husky rasp, and he had to clear his throat. "Kee?"

"Oh, God." She moved to sit on the other chair, and dropped her head into her hands. "I can't believe I almost..." She looked up and stared directly into his eyes. "I can't have sex with you, Warwick."

He knew that. Of course he did. Well, his head knew it. His body, however, was a completely different thing. She was leaving in a few days. He was staying. A tiny voice asked if perhaps they could use that to their advantage. Have sex for sex's sake. But Kee wasn't that sort of woman. She had a daughter to consider. And while he might have been that sort of guy once or twice, this wasn't one of those times.

"There's all sorts of things we could do that don't include actual sex," he said in a half-suggestive tone. But he knew she wasn't going to be drawn in. Not this time.

"We're not going there," she said, her face regaining a patina of cool composure. "Not least of all because my daughter is sleeping in the next room." She indicated the window to their left and Wazza's guts gave a guilty heave. He hadn't forgotten about Benni, not exactly.

"You're right," he sighed, and shifted uncomfortably in the chair, willing the remains of his erection to disappear. "Of course."

To give his brain something else to think about, other than running his hands over her body, he cleared his throat, and went back to their previous conversation. "Before you interrupted me with that kiss..." He looked down at his shirt, which was now missing more than one button, and then up at her, waggling his eyebrows suggestively. She gave a mortified grimace and had the grace to flush a light pink. "I was going to tell you that Daniella has spoken to a lawyer about your predicament."

"What?" Kee was half out of her chair, a frown marring her beautiful face.

Before she could get herself worked up again, he held up a hand and said, "I know you didn't want anyone getting involved—"

"That's right, this family has done enough for me. When I'm ready to seek the assistance of a lawyer, I'll do it. Not a second earlier."

Wazza had doubts about the reasons Kee was so loath to contact a lawyer. He suspected that money—or her lack of it —had a lot to do with it.

"I know that, and so does Daniella. This is their family lawyer, and she's been through a lot with them over the years. Daniella trusts her implicitly to keep her confidence. And she was very careful with what she said. Everything was made up as a hypothetical scenario."

"Oh, okay." Kee regained her seat, lifting a glass of water from the small table nest to her and taking a large gulp.

Wazza took that as a sign for him to continue. He drew in a breath. Kee wasn't going to like what he had to say. "The lawyer said that she couldn't answer specific questions because she doesn't practice family law, but she did say that the only way the courts would take a mother seriously in a custody case, was if she turned herself and her child in."

He watched her face, looking for clues as to how this news affected her.

"It's what I thought all along," Kee said. Still, it must be a blow to have it confirmed by a legal practitioner and must be disappointing on some level. "I know I'm probably only strengthening Jakovs parent's claims that I'm an unfit mother by taking off like I did. But I had no other choice. I wasn't going to sit around and wait for a court date, which could take years, I've been told, while Benni was kept a prisoner by that family. I wouldn't have survived."

"I know," he soothed. "I'm not debating that. Daniella just wanted to see what your options were, that was all."

"My only option is to take Benni and disappear off the face of the earth," she said quietly.

Wazza was starting to believe that. He needed to know whether her plans had changed at all in the past few days. "I know you were heading for the Northern Territory border when I found you."

She took another sip of water, and watched him over the rim of her glass.

"Have you come up with anything more concrete as to what you might do after that?"

"Not really." She shrugged, her bare shoulders glowing gently in the lamplight. "I've heard Darwin is a bit of a frontier town. Full of misfits and hippies, cowboys and jocks. Maybe I can hide out there for a while. And I'm hoping the cops won't be looking for me all the way up there."

Wazza had heard something similar about the quirky capital city. But he didn't like to think of Kee and Benni alone and struggling to make ends meet in such a town. And he wasn't sure that just by crossing the border, the police would miraculously stop looking for her. While most arrest warrants were issued by state, he'd knew that states shared their information, and if the Northern Territory cops found her, they'd most likely extradite her back to New South Wales to face charges.

"Anyway, it's not really your problem. I'll sort something out," she said quietly, but there was a finality to her tone. She was pushing him away. The tilt of her chin left him in no doubt of her resolute, strong will; she was going to be stubborn about this.

Her comment stung. While technically it was true, she

wasn't his problem, and the second she drove away in her car, he could wash his hands of her. If that's what he wanted. He wanted anything but. He needed to know she was safe. That Benni was safe. That she never allowed Bruno to find her. Aggravation at her complete disregard for his feelings swirled in his guts. But he didn't allow any of his thoughts to show on his face.

He should get up, grab his hat from the table, and walk off to his dorm room. That's what he felt like doing. That's the way he normally handled these kinds of situations. She was right, it was her life, and he should stop trying to interfere. Except he was already neck deep involved.

So, he did something that surprised even himself. Instead of allowing her to push him away, he took a deep breath and said, "You're wrong. It is my problem, and I want to help you, if only you'd let me. I know you need to go, and I wouldn't dream of trying to stop you. But even if you let me pore over a map with you to find the best route to take, the least roads travelled, so you can avoid Bruno. I can tell you where the best roadhouses are to refuel. Find the most out of the way campsites, where you'll be safe to spend a night or two."

It wasn't much, but it was all he could offer. If only he could go with her, protect her, and make sure she got to wherever she needed to go safely. But that wasn't an option. He had a job to do at Stormcloud, and he knew without even having to ask that Kee wouldn't consider taking him as an option, not in a thousand years. She would never want to feel that indebted.

Kee considered him for many long moments, dark eyes glistening in the starlight. "Thank you, Wazza. You're a good man. And I would love your help to work out my next move."

He leaned forward on his elbows and studied her across

the space between them. Her face was open and guileless, and he decided she actually meant what she said. A part of him liked that she'd called him a *good* man. And at least she'd given him this concession, albeit a small one. He'd take whatever he could get right now.

"I'd better head off to bed." He didn't add that secretly he longed to be in her bed. "I've got a long day ahead tomorrow." He got to his feet.

"Me too." She stood to farewell him.

"So, you're going ahead with the lawn mowing, then?"

"Of course, I am."

"Great." There was no need to tell her he thought she might pull out after what happened with Benni this afternoon. Some women would've pouted and sulked and refused to get on with it. But Kee was keeping her word. This was more proof that she was made of stern stuff. When she said she'd do something, she followed through with it.

"I'll meet you at the garden shed straight after breakfast. Say eight-thirty?"

"See you then."

Wazza leaned down to retrieve his hat and when he straightened, Kee was standing in front of him. She reached up on tiptoe and lightly kissed him on the cheek. A chaste kiss. But it told him everything he needed to know. She was grateful for his help. And she thought he was a good man. Both of those things were enough for him tonight. His skin buzzed with the memory of her butterfly-light touch all the way back to the staff quarters.

CHAPTER TWELVE

A bead of sweat ran from beneath Kee's hat and slid down the curve of her jaw. How did anyone get used to this heat? She'd been helping Skylar and Julie in the garden all morning. Julie was crouched over a nearby raised vegetable bed, pulling weeds from between the bush tomato plants. Kee was tying up the snake beans to a latticework, to stop them trailing on the ground. Skylar had gone inside half an hour ago to prepare smoko, and she'd taken Benni with her. This was harder than she expected, especially working in the hot sun, but it was also strangely gratifying. She was starting to see why Skylar took such pride in her garden. It was an integral part of her artful, creative dishes. Skylar told her she used her bush foods as the inspiration for a lot of her signature dishes.

Wiping the sweat away with a gloved hand, Kee desperately hoped for the call to down tools and head inside for a cuppa and something to eat soon. She took a swig of water from the bottle beside her; she'd learned to keep one on hand at all times when she was working outside in this heat, just like everyone else.

Of course, Benni spent every moment she could with the puppies, begging Kee to take her up to see them four and five times a day. And when Kee was busy, Benni would work on Wazza, Dale, or Sasha, instead. The child was incorrigible.

Kee felt bad that she was taking up one of the guest cabins. She could tell the resort was nearly fully booked, and she hoped Daniella hadn't had to turn away prospective customers just to keep Kee with the roof over her head. So, she'd offered her services wherever they were needed, to try and make up for her board and keep. Daniella seemed to respect Kee's need not to be a freeloader and let Wazza find her jobs she could do while keeping an eye on Benni.

Like riding the yellow devil the other day. It had taken Kee two hours to mow the large expanse of green lawn. By the end of it, she was sweaty and dusty and really, really hot, but she felt that she'd tamed the ornery machine. And as she'd stood back and admired her handiwork, she decided she'd not only tamed it, but done a good job, as well. Benni had enjoyed riding along on the mower beside her for the first little while, but in the end, Sasha had come to her rescue and asked if Benni wanted to help her fold napkins inside, much to Kee's relief, as Benni had lost interest and kept wanting to get down. Everyone at Stormcloud seemed to accept having a small child in their midst, and they all pitched in to keep Benni occupied. People in the city would never have been this tolerant and accepting. They were all too busy with their own lives to see what was going on with other people. Always rushing here and there. Kee was learning that living in the country meant living as part of a tight-knit community. Kee would never have been able to ask the next-door neighbor to mind Benni. Her neighbors were strangers to whom she might have given a passing wave when they pulled out of the driveway, but rarely stopped to speak to, or even shout a greeting over the fence. Living in the city could be isolating.

This morning, she was helping in the kitchen garden, and

this afternoon she'd offered to help Sasha turn around some cabins before the next guests arrived this evening, as the cleaning lady who normally came from town was sick.

Out of the corner of her eye, Kee noticed Julie stop work to take a drink from her bottle, as well. Kee liked Julie, she was funny, kept things light-hearted. She'd been through a bit of a rough patch recently, Wazza had told her. A crazed stalker had taken her hostage, planning to kill her over some delusional, self-obsessed idea. But Aaron had saved her. And now she and Aaron were together. It was a story straight out of a romance book, but Kee was intrigued. She'd met Aaron for the first time the other day, just after she'd finished mowing the lawn. He was the station chopper pilot, and he'd seen her admiring her handiwork, and stopped to introduce himself on his way down the path to the helicopter pad to drop off some guests to Cairns. He was tall and muscular, and a little gruff, but as long as he was in love with Julie, he was all right in Kee's book.

Her mind drifted back to her conversation with Wazza the other night. His words had hit home. She needed to learn to trust people again. Including her own daughter. At first, the idea of letting Benni out of her sight had filled her with dread. But with Wazza's words rolling around in her brain, she forced herself to accept Sasha's offer of help the other morning. It was nice to know she could rely on other people to help her with Benni.

But, as usual, whenever she thought about Wazza, her mind drifted to that kiss. Two kisses, actually. But the one on her back veranda had been especially hot. So hot she'd nearly forgotten where she was. Had nearly forgotten she had responsibilities, such as a daughter sleeping nearby. Wazza was a bad influence on her, a little like an illicit drug. And every time she saw him, her body would lurch in his direction, hungry for another hit. If Benni hadn't been there,

Kee knew she would've made love with Wazza. It'd been a close thing, her brain so addled by the feel of his big hands on her body, the taste of his lips, the way he clearly wanted her, and how his sensual, earthy aura surrounded her that she'd nearly let him undress her right there on the back porch. Heaven forbid, she'd never done anything like that before in her life. Her and Jakov's love life had been played out strictly between the sheets.

"Time for smoko." Wazza's deep voice shook her from her reverie. She glanced up to see him standing over her, grinning down at her as her fingers fumbled with the plant tie. The tight stretch of his blue shirt over shoulders so broad made all sane thoughts go straight out of her head. *Oh. Dear. God.* He looked good enough to eat, standing there in the sunlight, smirking at her as if he knew exactly what kind of thoughts were running through her head.

"Great." She got off her knees, turning away from his smile, pretending to finish the last knot on her string, but in reality, composing her features into a bland smile. But when she turned around, he was still staring at her with that knowing smile, and a surge of heat that had nothing to do with the bright sunshine flushed her face.

Julie joined them, and Kee lowered the brim of the hat, so Julie wouldn't see her pink cheeks. But it was too late. Julie was already narrowing her eyes at Wazza, a question in their brown depths.

"What has Skyler made for smoko today?" Kee asked, desperate to distract Julie. Kee had learned quickly that all of Skylar's cooking was amazing, even something as simple as chocolate chip-cookies took on a whole new meaning when Skylar dragged them from her oven. Without waiting for an answer, she picked up her water bottle and took the lead, heading up the hill toward the rear entrance of the lodge, which led directly into the kitchen.

"Not sure," Wazza answered. "It looked like a lemon cake and some finger sandwiches."

"That'll be her chia and finger lime cake," Julie pronounced, from where she was bringing up the rear. Skyler had proudly showed Kee the bush food version of the citrus orchard this morning, so she knew exactly what Julie meant. The finger limes were slightly different from normal lemons, in that they contained hundreds of tiny beads with a fresh citrus flavor. The plant itself was a lot smaller than a lemon, more like a dense shrub, and it was covered in the small, green fruit. Skylar always made double, so the staff usually ate the same as the guests were being dished up. Kee's mouth began to water at the mere thought of it.

Inside, she remembered to remove her hat and hung it on a hook next to Benni's now familiar small blue one. Then she and Julie washed their hands at the small basin in a separate mud room off the side of the entrance hallway.

Benni was sitting on a high stool at the end of the countertop, and she jumped down and raced over to Kee as she entered the enormous kitchen. "Mummy." She wrapped her little arms around Kee's legs, then looked up into her face. "I've been helping Skylar make the sandwiches," she announced proudly. "I was in charge of buttering the bread."

"I'm glad to hear that you were being helpful," Kee lifted her head and caught Skylar's eye.

"She was a big help," Skylar replied, without a hint of sarcasm. It made Kee wonder if perhaps it was time she let Benni help her more when cooking. She'd always been so busy, needing to get things done in a hurry, that she'd always shooed Benni out of the kitchen, afraid she'd make a mess. But there was more to it than that, she realized. She'd been brought up to believe it was her job as a mother, to cook and clean for her family. Her own father had never lifted a finger to help around the house. And so, she had pandered to Benni, making sure she always got her favorite foods. That'd gone out the window when she'd stolen Benni, and they'd gone on the run. But still, perhaps it was time to start letting Benni do more around the house when they finally settled down in one place, trust in her daughter's abilities, like Wazza said.

More people began to file into the kitchen. Dale and Steve arrived together, laughing and joking over something one of the guests had done while out horse riding this morning. Daniella appeared through the hallway from the entrance to the main lodge, with Alek on her heels, frowning down at his clipboard. Julie and Bindi were helping Skylar put out the plates and cut the cake into slices, and Sasha was getting a raft of mugs out of the cupboard and filling them with hot tea. It was nice that all the staff gathered in the kitchen to eat, it felt like one big family, but she could hardly hear what Benni was saying over the buzz of conversation. Kee knelt so she could be at eye level with her daughter.

"What did you say, my bunny?" she asked, tucking a strand of dark hair behind her daughter's ear.

"Can we stay here, Mummy? I like living with Wazza and Skylar and everyone."

Her surprising words tugged at Kee's heartstrings. "Oh, hunny bunny. I like living here, too." It was the truth, but it caught Kee off guard. She did like living here. Even though, only two days ago, she'd said she hated it, that it was no place to bring up a child. Not wanting to crush Benni's hopes, Kee decided not to mention that they'd be leaving tomorrow. The car would be ready, and they could continue on their mad dash North.

She caught Wazza staring at them, a strange look on his face. His features quickly cleared when he realized she was looking. Lifting a plate, he beckoned to them, then put a piece of cake and two sandwiches on the dish and handed it to Benni.

"Thank you, Mr. Cowboy," she said, as he swung her up onto her stool so she could eat at the countertop.

"I can ask her to stop calling you that, if you like," Kee murmured quietly into Wazza's ear.

"No, don't. I like it," he replied, brushing his shoulder against hers, causing a spike of heat to course through her. Had he done that on purpose?

Before she could do more than narrow her eyes at him, Daniella was suddenly standing by her shoulder. "Have you got a couple of minutes for a chat?"

As usual, Daniella's clothing was as neat as a pin, not a hair out of place, the epitome of country gentry. Kee nodded and followed her into the hallway, first checking over her shoulder to make sure Benni was okay. Dale had pulled up a stool next to her and was earnestly listening to her tale about helping mummy pull out all the nasty weeds this morning. Kee couldn't suppress a smile.

It was quiet in the hallway and Daniella led her a few steps toward the meeting room before she stopped and turned to face her. "I'll get right to the point." No messing around where Daniella was concerned. "I know you asked us not to interfere. And not to get the police involved."

A chill of foreboding slid down Kee's spine. Where was this going? Whatever had Daniella done this time?

As if reading her mind, Daniella jumped in. "I know Wazza said you weren't happy about me contacting the lawyer. But I promise you haven't been compromised in any way."

It wasn't just her fear of being found by Bruno because someone had let something slip to the wrong person that irritated her. It was also that this family had done more than their fair share to help her already. She didn't think she could ever repay them. And she hated to be indebted to anyone.

Daniella went on without waiting for a reply, "But I didn't

want you to leave tomorrow without at least having information that might keep you…safe."

Kee ground her teeth together. And it seemed Daniella was doing it again. Making her more beholden to her than ever.

Daniella continued, oblivious to Kee's growing agitation. "So, I got Aaron to use his contacts—he used to be in the protection agency business—to ask a private detective mate of his to do some digging. Strictly on the down-low, though. I made sure he didn't go through the police to get any of his information." Daniella said this all so seriously that Kee suddenly had to suppress a giggle. *Strictly on the down-low?* Did Daniella realize how cliched and straight out of a B-grade movie she sounded? And just like that, her mood lifted. Daniella was only trying to help, and perhaps Kee should stop being so doubtful. Like Wazza kept telling her, perhaps she needed to trust a little more. If Daniella could give her some vital information, then why would she argue?

"Okay," Kee answered slowly. "What did he find? This detective guy of yours?"

"Not a lot, I'm afraid," Daniella replied in a clipped tone, as if she were displeased that the poor guy hadn't been able to find out more. "You were right, the Queensland police do have an arrest warrant out for you and Benni. They're saying you kidnapped a child, which is quite serious, I'm afraid." Daniella tapped her lip thoughtfully.

"Oh, God," Kee said quietly. Her heart lurched in her chest. It was one thing to suspect the police were looking for her, but the reality of the fact that her face might appear on every police station wall made her shudder with fear.

"I know. It's not the best news." Daniella touched Kee's shoulder lightly, her version of a soothing contact. "But you made the right decision to stay away from the cops. Poor Nash, he's going to be upset when he finds out what we were doing behind his back. And rightfully so," Daniella said the last part almost as if to herself. Kee hadn't met Nash, but Wazza had called him a stand-up guy. "Skylar has just warned me Nash will be home tomorrow afternoon, so maybe it's a good thing you're leaving. Skylar is worried that she might not be able to keep the truth from him once she sees him face to face, even though she has the best of intentions. And I don't blame her. It's very hard to lie to the man you love." Daniella pursed her lips together, her face pinched in concern.

It shocked Kee a little, that this straitlaced woman was prepared to turn a blind eye to the fact that Kee was breaking the law, and that she—and Skylar, and the rest of her family —could also be dragged into this whole mess if they weren't careful. But then again, you could never judge a book by its cover. Wazza had told her a little of the problems the family had encountered over the last few years, and this wasn't the first time Daniella had stretched the boundaries of the law to suit herself, or to save her family. So perhaps she shouldn't be so surprised.

"The rest of the detective's information was sketchy, to say the least." Daniella huffed out a breath. She clearly had expected more. "This brother-in-law, Bruno, the one you say is following you, he's been a lot harder to track down. Being an ex-cop, he knows how to stay under the radar. And you're right, he's using his old police connections to hunt you down. But not being able to use his police informants is hamstringing our detective. He's trying to track Bruno's car, but it's a hard thing to do without the proper software. He was in the town of Beaudesert a few weeks ago when you said you spotted him. And it seems he might have made it to Cairns. But that's not been confirmed."

Again, Kee's heart lurched in her chest. Cairns was way too close for comfort. She and Benni had spent one night in the city and that'd been over a week ago now. They'd stayed on the outskirts of town, in a run-down trailer park, where it seemed not even the tourists liked to go. She and Benni had both badly needed a shower, and Kee was desperate to wash some clothes. She'd made sure to pay with cash, and they'd left first thing in the morning, slinking out at first light.

"Okay. That helps, thank you." Kee's mind began to race. Daniella's detective hadn't provided much that she didn't already know. All it did was confirm her fears in her mind. Thankfully, her car would be ready tomorrow. She began to feel the weight of her responsibilities press down on her. She'd been suspended in a certain kind of limbo over the past few days, but that was now at an end. Her peaceful interval was over, it was time to get moving again. Time to take back control over her own life, if that was even possible, while running from a vicious family determined to take her precious daughter away from her.

Instead of immediately returning to the kitchen, as Kee expected, Daniella hesitated for a second. "I would invite you to join us and the guests for dinner, seeing as how it's your last night here. But I understand your reasons for not wanting to mingle. And I admit, it'd also be breaking the adults-only rule at the resort. We don't want to be upsetting the guests." Daniella gave a small, wry shrug, as if to say, if it were up to her, she'd break the rule in a heartbeat, because Benni was worth it. "But how about I get Wazza to bring a meal to your cabin, instead?"

"Oh, yes, thank you. Benni would love that. She's become quite attached to him." Kee didn't add how attached she also had become. It was lovely of Daniella to effectively give Wazza the night off. Most nights the staff were expected to dine with the guests, it was part of the happy country community feel Daniella liked to display. "Oh, and Daniella, I want to thank you again for all the help. For everything you've done for me. It's been amazing. You've been amazing." An unexpected lump formed in her throat. She was going to miss this place, and all the people who'd made their past few days seem so special.

Daniela waved a vague hand in the air. "It was nothing. I would've done the same for anyone."

Kee wasn't so sure about that.

"I just want to say that I hope...everything turns out right for you and Benni." Daniella suddenly gathered Kee into a quick, fierce hug. Releasing her just as rapidly, so Kee was left wondering if it'd actually happened. "I know you won't agree with me right now, but you can't keep running forever. You have a young daughter who needs stability and care." Daniela pierced her with her fierce, blue gaze. "There will come a time when you'll need professional help."

What was she saying? That the law would catch up with her, eventually. That Bruno would catch up with her, eventually. She wasn't going to let that happen. But a tiny voice inside her head agreed with Daniella. At the moment, she was only thinking day to day, hoping to stay one step ahead. Until she could find a place to hide and come up with something more permanent.

Daniela pushed on, ignoring Kee's shake of her head. "If... when you need help, all you need to do is ask. I have access to lawyers and other expert advisors. I'll be here when you call."

Kee knew Daniela meant well. She might not be the most subtle woman in the world, but her heart was in the right place. "Thank you," she said. The words didn't seem nearly enough. Perhaps somehow, sometime in the future, Kee would find a way to repay all this kindness. She trailed after Daniella back into the kitchen, where happy banter filled the room. Kee sidled over to where Dale was still sitting with Kee. Julie had joined them and was teaching Benni how to do a simple card trick, using Dale as the guinea pig. Benni was completely enthralled.

Wazza gestured to her, holding up a plate full of food. Her stomach rumbled as she remembered she hadn't had a chance to try Skylar's finger lime cake yet. She went over, accepting the plate, and leaned up against the countertop with him. She watched the interaction of the Stormcloud family—because that's what they were, even the staff were more like family—with growing contentment. She wondered if these people truly understood what they had. A strong connection, a commitment to each other and to the resort. And then she wondered what it would be like to be a part of this.

Later that evening, Kee sat back in her chair with a sigh. "This wine is amazing." She held up her glass and saluted Wazza, who was sitting across the table. He held up his glass in return.

"Can I go play with my toys?" Benni asked.

"Yes, my bunny." Kee watched her daughter hop down from her chair. She really should get her ready for bed. Benni was yawning already; it'd been a big day. "We'll get you in the shower soon, and then off to bed."

"Can Wazza read me a story tonight?" Kee was about to say no, that Wazza had more important things to do, but then she stopped. This was the last night her daughter would spend with him. She turned to Wazza, a question in her raised eyebrow.

"Sure. You go and choose a book."

"Yay." Benni bounded off to the bedroom to pull out all her books. It was something Benni took very seriously. Each book had to be considered first before it was discarded. Kee had only brought a few of Benni's books along with them, but Daniella had handed her over a bag full of kids' books this afternoon, along with an odd assortment of other toys, saying they'd belonged to Dale and Skylar, and she'd been meaning to pass them on to someone else who needed them for ages. Benni had been over the moon with all the new stories to choose from.

Wazza studied Kee over the rim of his glass, blue eyes heavy and earnest. She watched as his gaze traced over her bare shoulders and down the line of her dress. She was suddenly absurdly glad she'd decided to throw this summer dress into her bag at the last moment. And also, absurdly glad she'd decided to wear it tonight for their dinner together. The hungry look Wazza had thrown at her as he came through the door earlier tonight had made her skin tingle, and she'd plucked self-consciously at the flirty hem of her dress which only came half-way down her thighs. It might be the last time she got to wear a pretty dress for a handsome man, and she didn't regret her impulse in the slightest.

Dragging her gaze away from his, Kee heaved a huge sigh. "I don't know how I'm going to repay everyone for their kindness," she said. "I mean Daniella has given me so much, and you—"

"You need to get over this guilt trip thing you have going."

"What?" She'd been going to add that Wazza, too, had given her so much, but he'd interrupted her before she could elaborate.

He put his glass on the table. "You keep saying that you need to repay us, and maybe in the city that's how it works. But out here, country people look after each other. They all made a decision the moment they saw you. They knew you needed help and welcomed you in with open arms. They could see that you're one of us."

One of them? Kee wasn't sure what he meant by that. Because she was as unused to living in the outback as any other city girl. She latched on to the one thing she knew made sense. "But Daniella and Steve have given me this cabin to stay in, and they've fed us all this gorgeous food. I don't want to be a charity case."

"Why not? There's nothing wrong with needing help now and then," he replied lightly.

His question stumped her. But when she stopped to think about it, things became clearer. It was true, her parents had always hated taking charity. Perhaps it was something to do with being immigrants in a strange country. When they'd first moved to Australia, they'd wanted to prove they could stand on their own two feet. They were a proud family and didn't want people's pity. She pursed her lips at him as she contemplated her family's history.

"This is only my belief, and I might be completely wrong, but I think Daniella is doing this as much for Benni as she is for you. There are very rarely kids at the station. I think she might have a secret longing for grandchildren. I've never seen her quite so besotted over anyone before. There's a softer side to Daniella that not many people see, but she really is a generous person underneath all that brusque exterior. And the same goes for Steve."

Wazza reached across the table and lay his hand on top of hers. "You've brought everyone here a little bit of joy. Don't undervalue that."

She looked down at his large hand covering hers. Tanned, with long, strong fingers, a callus evident on his thumb. Her gaze lifted to find his locked onto her. A flood of emotion washed over her. She was going to miss him. Terribly. He looked like he was about to say something more.

Benni shattered their moment by running into the living area, a book held high above her head. "I found the one I want," she said, placing it on the table in front of Wazza. He slowly withdrew his hand.

"My favorite," he said with a wink and a smile. "*Blinky Bill the Koala.*"

"Right, let's get you showered, young lady," Kee said,

concealing a sigh. There was no point in telling Wazza how she felt, she'd never see him again after tomorrow, anyway.

CHAPTER THIRTEEN

Wazza leaned inside the rear door of Kee's four-wheel-drive. It looked like Lefty had stacked everything he'd requested inside. He could see the brand-new tent tucked in front of two thirty-litre water containers—full of water—which Lefty had slotted into one corner of the rear cargo area. Two small, lightweight sleeping bags and a couple of rolled-up mattresses completed the list of things he'd asked for. Kee's pair of old jerry cans were strapped in against one side of the compartment. Wazza tapped them to make sure they held fuel. Yep, full to the brim. Wazza noticed a few items that hadn't been on the list, like a small gas camping stove and some steel pots and pans.

"I threw in a couple of things as well," Lefty said. "They were just sitting around my workshop, gathering dust." Lefty tapped the side of the car with a grease encrusted finger thoughtfully. Wazza had no idea how old the mechanic was, he seemed ageless. He'd been working in Dimbulah for as long as anyone could remember. A bit of a hippie, his long, gray hair was pulled back into a ponytail, teeth stained yellow with nicotine. The townsfolk often talked in hushed whispers, wondering what they were ever going to do if he chose to retire; good mechanics were like hen's teeth, especially way out here.

"Thanks, mate. You've done a bonza job," Wazza confirmed, closing the door. "Add them to the list of things I owe you for."

"Nah, it's all good. I never use them; you're actually doing me a favor by helping me declutter. Next thing you know, I'll be like Marie Kondo." Lefty waggled a bushy eyebrow in Wazza's direction, and Wazza gave a snort.

"Not likely, mate," he said, his sweeping gaze taking in the chaos inside Lefty's mechanic shop. There were car parts cluttering up every available bit of bench space, rolls of wire and tubing, drums of oil, and cans of grease. But Lefty was the best mechanic for hundreds of miles, and he could fix just about anything. He'd kept many of the local cars on the road long after they should've been destined for the scrap heap. "Come and I'll settle the bill with you now," Wazza added.

He headed toward the back of the workshop, where Lefty had his desk set up, also cluttered with piles of paperwork. Kee wasn't happy about him paying for her car repair, and she'd be even less happy when she found all the extra stuff he'd ordered in the back. But after their conversation last night, hopefully she'd take his offer with good grace. She needed to learn to accept help when it was given. It was good that Kee was heading off today. Skylar said Nash was due back in town this evening. It'd be much better if she was gone before he arrived home. Then Skylar wouldn't have to lie to him, and hopefully he'd be none the wiser about Kee's existence.

Wazza glanced to the front of the workshop, out through the enormous roller door to where Kee was busy unloading the Stormcloud Land Cruiser and transferring her and Benni's belongings into her own car. It looked like she'd already installed Benni's child seat into the back and was now carrying over their bags. Benni was on her knees, looking at something intently in the gutter by side of the road. Kee said something to her daughter, but Wazza couldn't catch her words. Probably telling her to stay off the road. Lefty's shop was in a quiet, dead-end street, one row back from the main thoroughfare. Benni would be safe enough, the only cars were those of the people who owned the other shops.

Lefty sat at his desk and pulled out a dirty sheet of paper from beneath a pile, handing it to Wazza. How the man knew where anything was in this jumble, Wazza couldn't guess. But it seemed to work for the old man. Wazza studied the bill for a few seconds. He would've paid whatever Lefty asked, especially after he'd gone above and beyond to tow the vehicle back to the shop. But Lefty made sure everyone understood exactly what they were paying for. Wazza found it was a sign of respect, to make sure he looked at each itemized detail. Everything seemed to be in order, including the list of camping items he asked Lefty to include. He pulled out his credit card and handed it over.

Lefty pursed his lips as he punched in the numbers to the machine.

"Looks like she and her young'un are off on a trip outback. You going with her?" Lefty asked conversationally.

"No. Got too much work to do back at the station. The second round of mustering starts in a week or two," he replied. Wazza knew he needed to get his head back into his job; he'd let things slide while Kee and Benni had been there, but now she was leaving, he could catch up on prepping for the muster.

"Will that other guy be going with her, then?" Lefty asked, peering down at the credit card machine as it beeped at him, and then handed Wazza his card back.

Wazza's hand froze, half outstretched. "What other guy?"

"There was a man in earlier this morning, asking when the

car would be ready. He called the woman and the girl by name, as if he seemed to know them." Lefty gave him a puzzled look.

Wazza's heart did a double tap. Who was looking for Kee? Wazza didn't want to ask outright if it was a policeman, not wanting to give anything away. "What did he look like?"

"Seemed nice enough. Tall bloke, dressed a bit fancy, in long pants and a shirt. Definitely not a tourist, that's for sure. He had a way about him, a hardness, kind of military, if you know what I mean?"

"What did you tell him?" Wazza snapped. "I need to know exactly what you said." It sounded like it could be the ex-brother-in-law from Kee's description. Bruno was an ex-cop. *Oh, shit, he'd found her.* Wazza glanced up, but neither Kee nor Benni were in sight.

"I...um..." Lefty hesitated, unsettled by Wazza's intensity.

"Did you tell him the car would be ready today?"

"Well, yes. I didn't see no harm in it. What's going on?"

"Shit, shit, shit," Wazza swore. Kee needed to get out of here. Now.

Suddenly, there was a scream from the front of the shop.

Wazza bolted past the car and out into the street, to see Kee scrambling to her feet, holding her head, blood trickling from between her fingers.

"He's got her! Bruno's got my baby," Kee screeched. She pointed down the road to a man running toward a car parked on the corner, Benni in his arms.

"Mummy," Benni cried over the man's shoulder.

Wazza reacted without thinking, sprinting after the man. He couldn't let him have Benni.

Wazza reached the sedan just as the man opened the back door and threw Benni inside. He grabbed the man and spun him around, landing a punch square on his nose. Instinctively, Bruno raised his hands to protect his face and

Wazza took the advantage, getting low and striking him in the solar plexus. Bruno doubled over in pain, but Wazza was under no illusions that the only reason he'd got in two good blows was because he'd taken this man completely by surprise. Bruno was an ex-cop. Wazza had no doubt he could handle himself in any fair fight, but he wasn't about to give a single concession. This man needed to go down so he could rescue Benni.

Wazza was by no means a trained boxer, but his father had made sure he could defend himself; taking him and his brothers out to the packing shed, watching them punch an old boxing bag over and over, until they ran with sweat, showing them how to duck and weave, throw another quick jab or an uppercut. He was also the youngest of four brothers, which said it all. He had his own collection of dirty tricks that'd helped him through many a fight with one or more of his brothers.

He aimed a kick at Bruno's knee and the man let out a howl of pain as his leg buckled.

"You," Bruno said between gritted teeth, slowly straightening, taking on a boxer's stance. "You're going down."

Uh-oh. Wazza raised his fists, ready to do whatever it took. They circled each other warily, dancing on the pavement. Bruno lashed out suddenly, and Wazza ducked just in time, receiving a glancing blow to the side of his jaw. More blows rain down on him, and it was all he could do to protect himself from the large fists which felt like blocks of iron landing on his body. He got in a few more punches, giving almost as good as he got. But he needed to end this now. If Lefty called the police—the station was just down the road—they'd be here within two minutes.

Even while he fought, out of the corner of his eye, he saw Kee appear at the side of the car, lean in and grab Benni while

Bruno was distracted. Then she disappeared. God, please let her get in her car and drive away. But when he chanced a glance across the road, she stood out front of the mechanic shop, Benni on her hip, her face a rictus of fear. *Get in the car. Get in the car,* he chanted over and over in his head. But she kept standing there. What was she doing? If it was him she was worried about, she needed to forget him and just go.

Bruno seemed to hesitate as he, too, glanced in Kee's direction. Then he stepped back and reached into his jacket pocket, pulling out a knife. Wazza stilled, watching him intently. A knife changed things. He'd never been involved in a knife fight, and he didn't want to start now. Time to get inventive. Time for some more dirty tricks. Sweat ran freely down his back.

A street tree, planted by the town council to give shade to the pathway, stood directly behind Wazza, about ten feet away. Slowly, he backed toward it, and the other man followed. Bruno lunged, Wazza deflected the knife with a desperate swipe of his hand, barely escaping the slice of the blade. Two more steps, and he was beneath the tree. Watching for his chance, he evaded another of Bruno's attempts to stab him. He grabbed a low branch, bobbing down at the same time as he dragged it back and let it go. It hit Bruno full in the face, propelling him stumbling backward. Wazza took the opportunity, rushing at his opponent straight on, smashing him to the ground. The knife was sent flying into the gutter. Wazza drew back his fist, ready to pummel the man's face, but he lay completely still, unconscious.

He'd knocked the man out stone cold. Bruno must've hit his head on the concrete as he fell.

Wazza didn't wait to see how badly hurt he was, or if he regained consciousness. He was on his feet and sprinting back to the mechanic shop as fast as he could go.

"Get in the car," he yelled as he ran toward Kee. She

jumped, as if in a trance, and went to buckle Benni into her seat. Lefty was standing at the front of the shop, gawping.

There was no time. Bruno could wake up at any moment. Wazza made a snap decision. He opened the driver's door and jumped in. She needed his help. She couldn't do this alone. He couldn't let her do this alone. "I'm coming with you," he said, willing her to hurry.

Kee didn't argue, naked fear still smeared all over her lovely face. She seemed to be in shock, working on autopilot.

"Don't tell him which direction we've gone, if he wakes up. Don't tell him anything," Wazza commanded of Lefty, winding down his window to stare at the old man.

"Your secret's safe with me, son," Lefty promised. "These out-of-towners get so uppity sometimes, they need to be put in their place. I might say he just tripped and fell from his own stupidity."

If the situation had been different, Wazza might even have smiled. "Better to say you didn't see anything," he advised instead.

"Right." Lefty nodded sagely. "I never saw a thing."

"Thank you." Wazza put the car in gear and checked that Kee had her seat belt on, then began to drive out of the warehouse. Halfway onto the road, he stopped the car. "I'm just going to grab something from the other car," he said, feet already hitting the pavement. Running to the driver's side, he reached in and grabbed the satellite phone off the cradle on the dashboard. Then he sprinted around to the rear door and yanked it open, retrieving a hamper of food Skylar had prepared for Kee. It was a surprise; he was supposed to give it to her just before she left. The whole mission took him less than twenty seconds as he headed back to Kee's car, still idling in the driveway. He suddenly remembered the keys to the Stormcloud vehicle were still in his pocket, and he pulled them out and tossed them to Lefty. "Look after these until

Steve can come and collect the car," he said.

Then he was back in the driver's seat, shoving the hamper on the floor at Kee's feet. "Hang on," he warned. The vehicle roared out of the shop and onto the street. Wazza stared at the scene of carnage as they passed by. Bruno was still lying prostate on the path. No one else was around. At least this wasn't the main street, which would've been crowded with locals and tourists alike. He gunned the motor, and the car leapt down the street, screeching around the corner as he turned left, taking them into the back streets of Dimbulah.

Benni was sobbing in the back seat and perhaps it was this noise that finally drew Kee out of her shocked silence. "It's okay, my baby. It's gonna be okay." She reached between the seats to take hold of her daughter's hand, the only contact she could manage with her seatbelt on.

"Why was Uncle Bruno so mean?" Benni asked between sobs. "He hurt me when he picked me up. And he said the *S* word, too."

"It's okay," Kee repeated. "You're safe now. Bruno didn't get you. Wazza saved you." She looked across at Wazza, as if seeing him for the first time.

She didn't say anything for many long minutes, waiting for her daughter to calm down, while Wazza navigated through the back roads, the houses beginning to dwindle, until they were out on the open road. Kee dabbed at her forehead with the corner of her T-shirt. From what Wazza could see, it wasn't bad, a scrape from where Bruno had knocked her to the pavement. He'd make sure to check it the next time they stopped.

Benni's sobs became sniffs, and finally she stopped crying, and Kee turned back to the front of the car. Her gaze zeroed in on him, and as if she finally grasped the situation, she hissed at Wazza, "What are you doing? You can't come with us. That wasn't the plan."

"Well, I'm coming. At least as far as the border." He set his lips together, hoping she took that as a sign not to argue.

"No, you're not," she said, louder this time. "I'm not letting you do this. Pull over. Right now."

CHAPTER FOURTEEN

Kee decided that Wazza had a stare like a blue-eyed hawk when he got angry. And boy, was he angry now. She could tell he was reining in his emotions, probably for Benni's sake as much as her own, but his knuckles were white where he gripped the steering wheel, and his scowl was deep and dangerous.

"Look, Kee," he said, a muscle in his jaw twitching. "I know this wasn't part of the plan, but things have changed. You're in imminent danger now. I can't let you face that guy alone." He never took his eyes off the road—which was a good thing because he was driving like they had the devil on their tail, and perhaps they did.

Oh, God. What had they done? Was Bruno after them this very moment? Or was he still lying unconscious on the pavement?

"I know the back roads in this area. I can keep us off the main drag and out of sight. Take the dirt tracks and find the unused camping spots, so he'll never find us." *Without getting us lost.* He didn't need to say the words, the implication was there for her to hear. She glowered at him. How dare he suggest she wasn't up to the task? But then again, perhaps she wasn't, because she *had* got lost.

There was another reason she shouldn't let Wazza join her. That damn attraction sizzling just beneath the surface. She'd already kissed him twice now, the second time, she'd even instigated it. If she didn't want things to go further, then the absolute last thing she should be doing was sitting in a car with him for the next three or four days. She wasn't about to get involved with another man, not when she was running for her life. Not when all she cared about was keeping Benni safely by her side. There was zero room in her world for a romantic liaison right now. Even if the cowboy sitting beside her set the blood zinging through her veins and did something strange to her guts every time he gave her that crooked little smile.

Her thoughts skittered across her mind like a drop of water on a hot griddle pan. What to do? The image of Bruno carrying Benni away replayed over and over in her mind. She'd nearly lost her daughter. Bruno had nearly succeeded in taking her. What would she have done if Wazza hadn't been there?

"Is Mr. Cowboy coming with us?" Benni asked from the back seat, startling Kee out of her musings.

She stared at Wazza's profile, biting her lip. Jaw set, eyebrows lowered, he looked as serious as she'd ever seen him. And dammit, now wasn't the time to decide that he was perhaps even more sexy when he was serious than when he was smiling. *Concentrate on the problem at hand.* That Wazza was trying to railroad her into taking him with her. She didn't like to be backed into a corner. She didn't want him to think that he could just come in and take over. Because she'd had enough of men thinking they could order her around, telling her what to do. She also had to remind herself that he wasn't Jakov, however. Or Bruno. Needed to remind herself that Wazza was kind and generous, and only had her and Benni's safety as his utmost motivation. She knew that Wazza would stop the car and get out if that's what she demanded of him. Stand by the side of the road and watch her drive away, if that's what she really wanted.

He glanced in her direction, blue eyes finding hers, spearing her with his resolve. Trust. Trust and accept help. That's what their conversation had been about last night. And that's what she needed to do now.

"Yes, okay," Kee replied, closing her eyes for a second. God, was she doing the right thing? "As far as the border, then," she qualified.

"Thank you," Wazza said, with a grim smile that acknowledged how hard the decision had been for her.

"Yay. He'll keep the bad people away," Benni said, a little subdued, the commotion with Bruno clearly still top of her mind. Until that second, Kee hadn't really thought about how her daughter saw this whole crazy situation. She hadn't told her about her father being in jail. Hadn't mentioned anything at all about them being on the run from the police and Jakov's family. Benni hadn't asked too many questions, either, happy to go along with Kee's version of them being on an adventure, on the surface at least. Kee had tried to keep her stress and fear hidden from her daughter, but maybe enough had permeated through so that Benni knew something was inexplicably wrong. And there was no hiding what had just happened at the auto shop. Benni had been terrified. Perhaps that was why Benni had taken to Wazza so quickly and was clinging to him now. She saw him as a sort of knight in shining armor, someone who could help keep the *bad people away*, as she'd put it, even if she had no idea who they might be. Kee suddenly realized she could no longer hide their plight from Benni. Her poor little girl was making assumptions about what was going on around her, whether Kee wanted her to or not. It was beyond time Kee sat down and had a proper chat with her daughter, but now was not the place. Later tonight, once they'd found a safe spot to camp, Kee promised herself.

"Oh, no," Benni cried out.

"What?" Benni whipped around, worried that her daughter had been more badly hurt by Bruno than she first let on.

"My blue hat. We left my blue hat in Wazza's car. We need to go back and get it."

Kee let out her breath in a gust of relief. Was that all? "I'm sorry we left it behind, bunny. But we can't go back and get it. Not with…" Kee left the sentence unfinished. She'd also left her new hat behind, but that couldn't be helped.

"But I need my blue hat." Benni's eyes filled with tears, and Kee felt torn. She was sorry for her daughter, she really loved that hat. But her overwhelming emotion was irritation. The nightmare of Bruno and the past half hour crushing her beneath the weight of what-ifs, turning her fear into anger. She wanted to snap at her daughter that it was only a hat and they'd been lucky to get away with their lives.

Before Kee could say anything she might regret, Wazza interrupted, saying, "I promise to try and get you a new one at the next big town we stop in. Okay?"

Benni nodded, but wasn't completely mollified, continuing to pout for the next half an hour.

"I need to call Steve on the sat phone. Let him know what's happened," Wazza said, interrupting her thoughts.

Kee nodded and rummaged around on the floor at her feet to find the phone he'd dumped down there when he'd jumped back into the car.

"Can you dial Steve's number for me? It's button number one."

She did as he requested, then put the phone on speaker and lay it in his lap.

Her heart was still racing, and she pushed a hand on her

chest to try and calm it as she listened to Wazza relate the happenings of the past half an hour to his boss. Steve took the news with relative calm—but then Steve seemed to take everything in his stride. Wazza told him the complete truth, not leaving out any details. Said that he was committed to helping Kee, and he didn't know when he'd be back, and apologized for leaving them a man short, especially with another muster looming.

"A man has to do what a man has to do," Steve said. "You keep Kee and that gorgeous little girl safe and let me worry about running Stormcloud."

"Thanks, boss." Wazza's voice was gruff, and perhaps Kee was imagining the slight edge of emotion in his tone. "Before you go, can I pick your brain about road conditions up there near the border? What about Nine Mile Road? That should be open this time of year, shouldn't it?"

"Sure," Steve replied, and began to spout names of places, which roads were better to take, which turnoffs to look for, and likely spots they could use for a campsite. His information was probably priceless, but most of it went over the top of Kee's head. She pretended to listen anyway, not wanting to interrupt him. Finally, after ten long minutes, Wazza ended the call, promising to keep in touch.

"Good. That's good." He seemed to be talking to himself, so Kee didn't answer immediately. "Did you understand any of that?" he asked.

"Not really," she admitted.

"That's okay. I'll give you the abbreviated version. But at least we have the kernel of a plan." He pursed his lips thoughtfully, the serious frown with that cute little line marring his forehead lifting slightly. "So, the quickest way to get to the Northern Territory border is to take the main highway through Georgetown and on to Normanton. That's about a day's drive."

"Yes, I think I already Googled it, and I'd decided against going that way, it'd be too easy for anyone to find me, or a cop to pull me over," Kee replied, happy that she knew that much. At least it showed she wasn't a complete idiot.

"Good decision," he agreed. "Another, less-travelled way, is to go up to the Mitchell River and then back around, still arriving in Normanton in the end. It's longer and less likely we'd see a cop car, but it's a bitumen road, and there'll still be plenty of locals and lots of trucks and road trains."

"That was the way I was headed," Kee mused. She didn't add, before she'd tried to take the wrong turnoff and got lost.

"It's a better alternative, but still not great," he said.

"It didn't seem like there were many other options, at least not on the maps I was looking at." Kee glanced out the window at the dry scrubland racing by on either side of the car. They were still on the main highway out of Dimbulah, and she wondered where Wazza could possibly be taking them.

"Aha, that's where local knowledge comes in. Steve has given me a few ideas. We're going to head across to the Gilbert River on an overland track. There's a dry creek crossing that should be easy going now we're well out of the wet season, and we should be able to make a good camp for the night. The turnoff is coming up soon."

"Good." Kee would be relieved to get off the main highway. She had a terrible premonition of Bruno racing up behind them in his big, expensive, four-wheel-drive, trying to run them off the road, or calling the cops and telling them where she was.

"It's a long drive, we might not get there until it's nearly dark."

"That's fine." As long as they were going in the right direction and off the main road, it didn't really matter how long it took to get there.

"Then tomorrow we're going to take Nine Mile Road and hopefully camp next to the Norman River tomorrow night. That one is a mine-access road, and hopefully the gate has been left open. After that, we might have to head into Normanton to stock up on supplies, or we might be able to keep going on to Nicholson, which is right on the border, we'll just have to play that by ear."

"Why are you telling me all this?"

"Because you need to know." He looked her full in the face. "It's important. In case we get separated...or something happens."

Kee didn't like the sound of where this conversation was going. Now that she'd decided that having Wazza along was a good idea, she suddenly didn't want to lose him. And she didn't like the fact that Bruno had nearly abducted Benni right from under her nose. How had he found her, she wondered, for the hundredth time? Had he tracked her car registration somehow, while it was waiting to be fixed in the shop? She was pretty sure he hadn't known she was staying at Stormcloud, otherwise he would've appeared out there, probably with a whole squadron of police, to back him up.

Voicing her thoughts, she said, "I have no idea how Bruno found us. Was it just dumb luck? Or is he tracking me somehow?"

"I'd like to know that, too. Lefty mentioned someone had been looking for you this morning. I assumed it was Bruno, but I didn't get a chance to ask, because that's when he snatched Benni. Bruno could've been in town for days, for all we know. I asked Steve to gather what information he could. The town will be most likely be absolutely buzzing by now. These kinds of things don't happen often in Dimbulah. Steve needs to be careful who he talks to and what he says, because we don't want to implicate you. Or me, for that matter. It all depends on how Bruno fared after we left him unconscious. If he ended up in hospital, there will be a police investigation, and Nash will have to get involved."

"What if he just woke up and got back in his car and drove away?" Kee voiced the other viable option.

Wazza shrugged. "It's just a hunch, but Bruno seemed to be working on his own. Using any information he can get from the police, but not giving them what he knows in return. Otherwise, why didn't he have the local constable waiting there to arrest you when you arrived to pick up your car?"

The more Kee thought about it, the more she agreed with his theory. "But why is he working alone?"

"Don't know. I'm not up with the rules surrounding family law. Perhaps he thinks if he can snatch Benni from you and take her back to the parents, then they'll retain custody until the trial. But if the cops get to her first, then she may go into foster care, until custody can be decided." Wazza gave another shrug. "We could ask Daniella to check up on the facts for us, if you like?"

Kee hated to ask anymore of Daniella, but Wazza was right, if they could figure out Bruno's motivation, it might help. Give them an advantage, even.

"Mummy?" Benni spoke up from the back seat.

"Yes, bunny?" Kee turned to face her daughter.

"I wish we could have brought one of the puppies with us." Benni looked hopefully at Kee, and she had to quash an exasperated sigh.

"I told you, a puppy wouldn't like to be in the car with us for so long. Maybe when we get someplace where we can settle down, I'll get you a puppy." The words had just popped out, she hadn't really meant to say them. What had she let herself in for now? She made an effort not to make empty promises to her daughter. Was this one she'd be able to keep?

"Really, Mummy? Yay." Benni clapped her hands together

in delight.

Wazza glanced at her out of the side of his eye, but wisely said nothing.

A few minutes later, Wazza said, "Here comes the turnoff."

Kee searched the road for any sign, but there was nothing. Scrubby trees lined the road, casting shade in some spots, but outside the line of vegetation, the outback looked as dry and hungry as it always did to Kee. Wazza slowed the car and then turned onto something Kee might have called a goat track. She would never have found this on her own, not in a million years. Surprisingly, once they were past the turnoff, the track opened up to a wide gravel road.

"I'll find us a spot to stop in half an hour or so and we can dig out something to eat. And take a look at that scratch on your head. Are you hurt anywhere else?" Wazza asked.

"I scraped my knee and elbow when he pushed me to the ground. That's when I hit my head, as well. But nothing major. I did worse riding on the yellow devil the other day." Her attempt at humor didn't lift his mood, however. He nodded, keeping his eyes on the winding track ahead.

The plan had been for them to stop by the local grocery store, so Kee could stock up, and then Wazza was to buy Kee and Benni lunch and they were going to sit and eat it in the local picnic area next to the river, before they headed off. It was now well past lunchtime and Kee's stomach rumbled. Benni must be starving, as well, but for now she wasn't complaining.

Nearly an hour passed before Wazza finally decided it was time to pull over. By then, Benni had started to grumble that she was hungry. Wazza found a stand of tall, straggly acacia trees and pulled up in the shade. They both got out and stretched their legs. The heat hit her like a sledgehammer. The countryside hadn't changed at all since they'd left the main road, just more open woodlands, with patches of shrubby bushes Kee couldn't name, and the occasional sparse tree, branches reaching toward the blue sky, as if begging for clouds to cover the relentless sun and send down some much-needed rain. Kee didn't think she'd ever seen country as desperate as this before. Not a blade of green grass. Wazza had told her that in the wet season everything was lush and verdant, but Kee was having trouble imagining that. Funny, but when she'd been living—and working—at Stormcloud, she'd been aware of the dry country surrounding them, but it hadn't seemed to bear down on her like it did out here. Here it felt so desiccated and scorched, and slightly menacing. You really had to know what you were doing to survive out here. It suddenly hit her as to exactly how lucky she'd been that Wazza had come along when he did and found them at the bore. Perhaps if she'd left it until she was desperate for help, it might well have been too late. She shivered at the thought, in spite of the heat.

Kee opened the rear door and unclipped Benni from her child seat. The girl bounded out, glad to be released from her prison, just as Wazza deposited the wicker hamper he'd thrown in the car earlier and an old blanket in the shade of a tall bottle tree, its bark pockmarked with age.

Suddenly, Wazza was standing in front of her, touching her forehead with care. Her reaction to his presence was instant. She wanted to stretch her arms around his waist and pull him in closer, as her blood pounded through her veins.

"You're right," he murmured. "It's not too bad. It's stopped bleeding. I'll clean it and put a bandage on it after we finish lunch." His fingers lingered longer than they should on her face as he gazed down at her, an unreadable emotion flickering across his face.

"Come and get some lunch," he called loudly to Benni, who was hunkered down in the middle of the gravel road, watching a line of ants march across it. Then he backed away, and it was as if the moment had never happened, striding over to the little picnic spot he'd set up in the shade.

"Skylar packed a few things to see you through," Wazza said by way of explanation, as she wandered over to where he was setting out plates and boxes of food. "Some of this needs to be eaten today," he continued, pointing at a container of miniature quiches and another of roast beef sandwiches. Kee saw that there were ice packs at the bottom, to keep the food cool.

"That was so thoughtful of her." Kee went over and tapped Benni on the shoulder and shooed her into the shade, then sat down next to Wazza. Everyone had been more than generous during her stay at the station.

Wazza pointed out the foods that'd keep for a few days, half a dozen fresh eggs, tomatoes from Skylar's own garden, a couple of avocados, two loaves of her wonderful, seeded bread, a jar of homemade dill pickles, bags of nuts, small cans of tuna and some granola bars—made by Skylar, of course. Skylar had gone overboard, as usual, and Kee was flabbergasted by the abundance of delicious things, none of which she would have ever thought to pack. Which reminded her she hadn't had time to stock up on any foodstuffs before they left Dimbulah in such a hurry. Wazza might be right, they may have to risk a trip into Normanton to replenish. But this should see them through the next couple of days. Right at the bottom, there was even a bottle of white wine. Kee wondered when they'd ever find the time to drink that.

Kee handed Benni a plate with two bacon and chive quiches and a bottle of water that Wazza had produced from the rear of the car. Benni bit into the little pasty with gusto. Less than a week ago, Benni would've looked at the quiche with distrust and probably refused to eat it. Kee owed a lot to Skylar for broadening her daughter's palate.

She glanced over at Wazza, who hadn't touched his plate.

He was staring at the vehicle, as if it were guilty of some heinous crime, muttering something under his breath. She thought it might've been, *"We need to get rid of this car,"* but she couldn't be sure. She'd paid good money for this car. She knew it might make it easier to track them, but a lot of her equity was tied up in the vehicle. It might be a little old and have rust in some places, but it was doing a great job of handling these dirt roads. If they dumped her car, she'd have nothing to live off later on. There was no way she was letting him get rid of it.

CHAPTER FIFTEEN

After backing the four-wheel-drive as close as he could get without hitting the trunks of a large stand of trees, Wazza shut off the engine with a sigh. It'd been a long drive, over six hours on gravel roads all the way. After stopping three times to let Benni go pee, and twice more to have a drink and a snack—that child liked to eat, or maybe it was more likely boredom—they'd finally arrived at Gilbert River. He'd driven over the rocky ford and then chosen to go a few hundred meters farther downriver before he found a spot that looked suitable to set up their camp. The sun was getting low on the horizon, but they still had a good hour or more of daylight left.

"This looks good," he said, stretching his arms behind his head. There was an expanse of flat ground in a clearing above the riverbed, free of rocks and debris directly ahead—it looked like it'd been cleared for this exact purpose by previous campers. Overhanging branches of three large gum trees laced together to form an almost impenetrable canopy above, lending them shade, and even more importantly, seclusion.

"There's no water in the river," Kee replied, leaning forward to peer through the windshield, eyeing the river skeptically.

"A lot of rivers are dry at this time of the year. But there might be a couple of deeper pools that still hold water farther down. We can take a walk later, after dinner, if you like."

"Sounds great." Kee was making a good show of keeping her spirits up, probably for Benni's sake, but he could see the stress of the day etched into the lines around her eyes.

They both turned to look around at exactly the same moment, to see if Benni had woken up and their heads banged lightly together. Benni had fallen asleep about an hour ago, and she looked so cute and innocent, with her head propped on the backrest, her mouth slightly open, and Dolly still firmly clasped in the crook of her elbow. Kee had mentioned that after she'd told Benni they were leaving Stormcloud this morning, Benni had spent a long time picking out her clothes, changing her T-shirt four times before she'd finally decided the one with the unicorn on the front was the best one to wear on this new instalment of their journey. From Kee's facial expression, Wazza had known that she'd been driven to distraction by her child's indecision. But Wazza guessed that perhaps it was Benni's way of waging some sort of control over her life. The apple-green unicorn T-shirt only made Benni look even younger and more innocent than ever. As their heads clashed, Kee stared at him for a second and gave an embarrassed giggle, before turning back to face the front, rubbing the spot on her temple where they'd come together. He caught a glimpse of the bandage on the other side of her head and was grateful she hadn't been hurt worse when Bruno had shoved her to the ground. She'd been an appreciative patient as he'd cleaned the wound and applied the bandage after lunch, giving him a brave smile, even as he dabbed the dried blood away. Which was a good thing, because it'd stopped his mind from wandering onto images of him beating the snot out of Bruno for hurting her.

"I guess we should start setting up camp while we still have some light?" It came out as a question, but he could hear the edge of accusation in her tone. She was still a little piqued at Wazza's presumption, filling her car with the things he thought she needed. Kee had been speechless after she discovered all the new camping gear in the back of her vehicle. It was at their first stop, right after they'd eaten a late lunch, devouring Skylar's delicious quiches and sandwiches. Kee had opened the rear door and stared, dumbfounded for many long seconds, documenting all the equipment that'd somehow miraculously appeared in her vehicle. Then she'd narrowed her eyes, raven brows winging down in a frown, and shot him a look.

"Wazza, can I talk to you for a second?" Her dark eyes had gone a dangerous shade of inky black. "Over here." She beckoned him with a crook of her little finger, then watched intently as he got up, dusted the non-existent dirt off his jeans and sauntered over with what he hoped was a good dose of cowboy nonchalance.

"Yes?" He said, going for casual indifference. He didn't care if she was mad at him, which she probably was if the clench of her jaw was anything to go by. And such a gorgeous jaw it was, giving her face an almost heart-shaped appearance. His gaze traced the soft lines of her face and he almost forgot she was mad at him.

"What's all this?" She waved a hand dramatically over everything stowed in the back.

"Things you needed to make your life on the run a lot easier."

"We did fine sleeping in the back of the car," she snapped.

"I know you did," he shot back evenly.

She made a huffing noise and rolled her eyes. "Men. You always think you know best."

He merely shrugged. He didn't want an argument. All he

wanted was for her to accept his gift with good grace. He knew she would've bought all this if she could afford it. But she was such a novice at surviving in the outback, she didn't even realize how much these things, like a tent, extra water, extra fuel, could make living on the run easier, or could even save your life.

"I'm going to pay you back for this," she said, studying the pile of supplies.

"You don't need to do that, I—"

"I *am* going to pay you back for all of this," she'd said in such a low voice that it made him think it might be perilous for his health if he continued to argue.

"Fine." He'd held his hands up in surrender.

Kee hadn't said much for the next hour in the car, just glared out the window, until Benni had to stop for a pee. After she'd taken Benni behind a tree to do her business and then left her drinking from a bottle of water in the shade, she'd pulled Wazza aside.

"I know you're only trying to help," she said, holding up a hand to ward off any comments until she'd finished. "And I know you said I need to accept help because I'm bad at it. Maybe that's true. But I also don't like being told what to do by a man. I've had enough of that to last a lifetime. So, can you please back off?" Her dark-brown eyes had flashed with determination, rosebud mouth pursed into a thin line.

"Yes, I can do that," he'd replied, and they'd got back into the car and kept driving. She was clearly upset, and he didn't like to see her that way. But she had a point. He'd imposed his judgement on her; decided what she did and didn't need and then acted without asking, thinking he was doing her a favor. If it'd been the other way around and someone had interfered in his life in an unwarranted way, he was sure he'd probably have acted similarly. Possibly with a lot less restraint and dignity than Kee had. He spent a long time pondering exactly what Kee had had to put up with from her ex-husband. She was clearly struggling to regain some self-respect and independence. Perhaps it was time to find out more of what'd gone on in her marriage, so he could understand where she was coming from. He decided to ask her next time they had a few moments to themselves.

Wazza opened his door and stepped out at the same time Kee did on the other side of the vehicle. The heat hit him hard after the cool of the air-conditioning in the cabin. Drawing in a deep breath of desert air, he slapped his hat on his head and went around to pull open the rear door.

Kee appeared with Benni on her hip a few moments later, still rubbing sleepy eyes. The pair watched as he pulled equipment out and dumped it in a pile next to a large tree trunk.

"That tent says it's for two people," Kee said, leaning over and poking the bag.

"I'll sleep outside. It'll be fine, I'm used to it. There's a spare tarpaulin in the back I can use to keep me off the ground." Wazza had never intended to sleep inside a tent with Kee, even if it'd been big enough for all three of them. That was a sure road to long nights of no sleep as he lay there thinking about her, mere inches away. Stopping himself from reaching out to touch her. Ever since he'd kissed Kee, he could think of nothing else when she came close. He wasn't sure even having Benni sleeping next to them would be enough deterrent to rid him of his lustful thoughts.

"If you're sure." She was frowning at him, but there might've been a hint of relief in her voice.

"I'm sure," he replied.

They got to work. He showed her how to erect the tent, which was very simple, a few poles and a flick of the wrist, and it was up. Kee would've been happy to leave it like that, but he insisted she peg it down, as well. You never knew when the wind might pick up in the middle of the night. Benni wanted to help, so he got the hammer and wrapped his hand around hers—engulfing her tiny hand in his enormous one—and they hammered in a few pegs together. Then he talked Kee through setting up the small gas stove and they pulled out Skylar's hamper of food.

"How do fried eggs and tomatoes on toast sound?" Kee asked, after rummaging around in the basket for a while.

"Yay," Wazza and Benni chorused together, and then both had a fit of giggles.

"You two are a pair of silly gooses," Kee said, not unkindly.

Wazza found an old dead log, and after checking underneath for snakes or any other creepy crawlies, he pulled it over to their makeshift campsite, so they had something to sit on. He unpacked the tin cups and plates that Lefty had given them, lining them up along the log for Kee. The food smelled delicious, and his stomach rumbled. Kee seemed to have got the hang of the gas stove quickly enough, she had a frying pan full of eggs and tomatoes on one burner, and bread toasting over the open flame of the other. Benni sat close by, watching every move her mother made. He had to smile. A mini version of Kee in the making. He wondered if Kee even realized how much her daughter followed in her footsteps, wanted to please her. Watching them made him understand exactly how much a child depended on their parents, needed their parents' love and support. Then it struck him how little he knew about being a father. Had he been kidding himself that if Karri had survived, they could've pulled off being parents together? Would little Ava have looked at him with such concentration and wonder? And uncomplicated love?

He shook his head and walked away from the domestic scene of mother and daughter. After a few seconds of deliberation, he went over to the hamper and pulled out the bottle of wine. It was still cool from the ice blocks on the bottom. It might not be the most appropriate time, but boy, he could do with a drink right now. Better to drink it while it was still cold. He found the corkscrew at the bottom of the hamper—because of course Skylar had included one—and drew out the cork.

"Dinner's ready," Kee called, ladling eggs on top of the toast on the three plates. She helped Benni clamber up onto the log, and handed her the plate, food already cut into bite-size pieces.

Wazza nudged her shoulder and handed her a tin mug full of wine. She raised a quizzical eyebrow, then took a small sip. Her face lit up in delight. "Courtesy of Skylar, I assume?"

He tipped his hat by way of acknowledgement. They both settled on the log, plates resting on their knees, staring at the dry riverbed. The cicadas were singing full throttle tonight—they always got louder toward the end of the evening—and a flock of white cockatoos wheeled overhead. A slight breeze tickled the leaves above as the heat of the day finally abated. The isolation suddenly struck him. They were alone out here, possibly the only people for a hundred kilometers, or more. But this thought didn't bother him. Instead, it filled him with peace. It was one of the reasons he loved living in north Queensland, you could get away from the madding crowd, and enjoy nature at its rawest.

"It's kind of beautiful," Kee said, through a mouthful of food. "In a deadly kind of way," she added. "Sort of like how a leopard leaping for its prey is beautiful, yet deadly."

He'd never heard it described like that before. But then the famous poem by Dorothea Mackellar suddenly came to mind.

"Her beauty and her terror-
The wide brown land for me!"

He spouted the words vaguely remembered from his time at school.

"Yes, exactly," Kee said, a large smile engulfed her face. Christ, she was so pretty when she smiled.

He took a sip of wine, letting his gaze drift over the vista in front of them.

"I guess I never really stopped to look at it before," Kee said, thoughtfully. "It's always just been a whole lot of dry country to me, made me thirsty just looking at it." She chuckled softly.

An hour later, Wazza listened to the sounds of Kee putting Benni to bed inside the tent as he set up his improvised swag. He angled it just right so he could see through a gap in the branches up to the night sky. The two glasses of wine—he hadn't indulged in any more, he needed to be sharp for tomorrow's drive—had mellowed his mood nicely. He watched the silhouettes play across the tent wall, backlit from the LED lantern inside, and a part of him wanted to be in there with them, partaking in the nighttime ritual. Kee's voice was a low rumble, the words indecipherable as she read a book to Benni. Then things went quiet, the light was turned off, and Wazza assumed they'd both fallen asleep. He lay back, hands behind his head, and stared up at the night sky. The quiet sound of a zipper being drawn down alerted him to Kee emerging from the tent, flashlight in hand.

"Oh, I didn't realize you'd gone to bed." The beam of light flicked over him quickly and then dropped away.

"I haven't. Not really. I was just watching the stars."

"Do you mind if I join you? Benni's asleep, but I'm still wide awake."

"Not at all." He shuffled sideways a little, making room for her on the tarp.

She lay down next to him, head on his pillow made from a folded coat, not quite touching. She'd loosed her hair from her customary braid, and it fell long and satiny across the coat. "It's gorgeous," she sighed as she stared up into the heavens. "I only really noticed how clear the stars are out here on the night when we were stuck at the bore. You don't get this view in the city."

"No, you don't," he agreed.

They lay in silence for many moments, appreciating the view above. The Milky Way was sprayed across the sky as though an abstract artist had painted the nighttime with their brush. Individual stars were so clearly defined against the velvet backdrop, Wazza felt as if he could reach up and touch one.

"One of the many things about this land that keeps me here," he said.

"So, you like living on Stormcloud? You like your job?" Kee asked conversationally.

"I love my job." As he said it, Wazza realized just how true it was. He thought about the email still waiting for an answer, dangling the offer of a new job. He finally knew what his answer should be. Thank you, but no thank you. He'd stay on at Stormcloud for a while longer, because there was no reason to leave.

"Working there isn't merely a job," he said, rolling his head slightly so he could look at her. "It's a way of life. The boss and the rest of the staff aren't just workmates, they're good friends, lifelong friends."

"I'm beginning to see that." She shifted on the pillow so they were eye to eye. "There's not many jobs in the world you could say that about."

"No," he agreed.

"So, you're truly happy here? Want to spend the rest of your life out here?" He couldn't see her face well in the dark of the night, making it hard to decipher the intent behind her question.

He decided to go with the truth. "Yes. And no. Not sure I'd go so far as spending the rest of my life here. But who knows what the future holds? I guess at the moment, I have nothing to tie me down, no responsibilities, no mortgage, nowhere to be." They'd touched on the subject of him being single already, that he hadn't had a girlfriend in over two years, but she'd never really delved too deep into his past. He didn't want her to think he was going to stay at Stormcloud as the leading hand for the rest of his life, grow old and gray and never achieve anything beyond that. That wasn't what he meant.

"That's not to say that I wouldn't move on if there was the right inducement. But then again, I might also stay, if the… situation were right." *If the right woman came along*. He couldn't say that, because Kee definitely wasn't the right woman. His tongue was getting tangled up with his thoughts. Perhaps the two glasses of wine had gone to his head more than he'd been aware.

Karri and Ava sprang to mind and before he knew it, he blurted out, "I want a family one day. Kids and a wife. I would've married Karri if she wanted me to."

"What?" Kee turned completely onto her side to stare at him. "You were nearly married?"

"No. Not really." Now look what had he gone and said. But she was looking at him so expectantly. He couldn't remember the last time he'd spoken about Karri to anyone. He'd just let her death fester inside of him, like an open sore. What would she say if he told her? "Did anyone tell you about the girl who was murdered on the station?"

Kee hesitated fractionally. Then she said, "Oh," as if the last piece of a puzzle were falling into place. "Yes, Julie mentioned it."

Trust Julie to be the one to say something, she was an open book, bright and breezy, not letting anything get her down. She wouldn't see the murder and the trouble Dale and Daisy had endured when they discovered who the murderer was as something that needed to be kept quiet—unlike Daniella, who liked to sweep everything under the carpet. Julie had always thought it was better to talk about things than to let them smolder under the surface.

Kee went on. "Julie didn't say a lot. It was more about Daisy and Dale's relationship than spilling sordid details of the murder," Kee hurried to clarify. "She claimed she was so grateful for Daisy, so glad that she'd been there for Dale at one of the hardest times of his life, when one of your staff, a local indigenous girl, was murdered by another one of your staff. She went on to say it was a hard time for all of you. That sounds awful. It must've been a terrible time for you all."

"Yes. It was a huge blow, everyone took it hard, me especially." He took a deep breath and plunged on. "Not least of all, because Karri and I had been dating for a little while before she was…well, you know."

"Oh, God, that's terrible." Kee reached out and took his hand, her touch soft and soothing. "I'm so sorry." He clasped her fingers tightly in his, the physical connection helping him sort through his feelings.

"Yeah, so was I. Not least of all, because for a time, I was suspect number one." He remembered that time as a swirl of mixed emotions, each one strong enough to carry him away on the torrent. Grief at the loss of Karri. Fear that there was a murderer hiding in their midst. Anger when he was wrongly accused and then arrested. Sheer relief when they let him go. More anger that anyone could possibly have believed he'd kill anyone, let alone Karri.

Kee gasped and covered her mouth with her other hand. "Oh, my, I didn't know that. How horrible for you! How could they even think you'd do something like that?" she said, disbelief coloring her tone. "Anyone who's known you for even a day would realize you aren't capable of murder."

"Thank you," he said, touched that she'd jumped so

eagerly to his defense. "I got over it, I guess. And no one at Stormcloud really believed I was guilty, anyway. Steve was the first to make sure I had proper legal representation."

"I can see now why you haven't had a girlfriend since then," Kee continued quietly. "That must've been so hard to cope with." Her hand tightened its hold on his and he became aware of just how soft her skin was against his work-roughened palm.

Wazza nodded thoughtfully. It was so nice to have someone who'd just listen to him, not pass judgment and not try and tell him he needed to harden up and move on. Funny, he'd meant to ask her more about her life married to Jakov, but instead he was spilling his guts to her about his own problems.

Could he tell her the last bit? So, she really had all the pieces to fit to the puzzle. Did he want her to know this much about him? Why not, asked a small voice?

"That wasn't the worst part. It wasn't until later that we discovered Karri had been pregnant. With my child." It was this loss that'd stayed with him the longest, the one that still ate at him, even now.

"Oh." Kee's other hand came up to stroke his face. "You lost a child, as well? That's unthinkable to me. I could never...I wouldn't know how to cope..." Then she moved closer and enfolded him in her embrace.

His traitorous body immediately went into overdrive the moment she lay her chest against his side. Maybe it was this surge of feeling that prompted him to say, "I gave her a name. The baby. In my head. I called her Ava. I think I would've made a good dad." He'd never told anyone else, these were his innermost thoughts, so why was he spouting them at Kee as if he'd known her all his life?

"Yes, you would have made a great father. Just look at how good you are with Benni, she loves you."

"Mmhmm." He was only half-listening to her now. Of its own accord, his hand slid up and underneath the nape of her neck, her long hair wonderfully soft against his palm. She looked up at him then, starlight reflected in the dark pools of her eyes. Gazing at him, he could just make out her lips curling into a small, knowing smile, something erotic replacing the compassion showing in her eye's mere seconds ago, and his cock went hard in an instant. His other hand slid down to cup her ass, pull her into his body, so there was no space between them. He wanted to kiss her. Wanted to glide his hands all over her naked body. She was only in shorts and a T, but he still had on his jeans and shirt. Way too many clothes stood between them.

It was too much. His lips found hers and he kissed her. Hard. Claiming her mouth as his own. She was so sweet. Hot and sweet, like a drug that he couldn't rid from his system. Her hands became busy with his buttons and suddenly his shirt was hanging open, her palms buzzing over his chest.

The tempo of her breathing became ragged. As ragged as his.

A sound pierced through the fog blanketing his brain. It took him a moment to realize it was only the bark of a night owl, but it was enough to bring him back to his senses. Brought him back to where they were and what they were doing. Reminded him that Kee's daughter was sleeping not too far away. Slowly, he ended the kiss.

Kee gasped and withdrew. "What's wrong?" she whispered.

Their chemistry was off the Richter scale, but he didn't want to complicate her life. Shit, it was already way too complicated already.

"Nothing," he replied. "And everything."

CHAPTER SIXTEEN

"What's that noise?" Kee lifted her head to study the sky from her spot perched on the edge of a large river rock, curious. The cool of the early morning was already giving way to the coming heat, and she'd bowed to Benni's wish to take her down to the river for a quick visit to find a *pretty green leaf*, before they got in the car to continue their journey. Wazza had been crouched down next to Benni, helpfully holding all the green leaves she gave him. He stood and followed her gaze.

"Oh, shit," Wazza swore and ran toward the car. "Get under cover. Now," he commanded over his shoulder. Kee startled for a second, before picking Benni up under one arm and heading for the safety of the trees in the same instant a helicopter buzzed over the horizon. It was a mere bright speck in the sky, flying high and fast. Was it looking for them? Kee thanked their lucky stars that Wazza had already dismantled the tent and packed most of their camping gear away. He'd also backed her car in beneath a tight clump of trees last night. At the time, she'd wondered if it was worth going to such lengths to hide themselves; they were so far from anywhere, it was ridiculous. Now she praised his efforts. Wazza was throwing the green tarpaulin he'd been using as a makeshift swag over the roof of her car, probably to hide any telltale glint off the metal.

She reached the relative safety of the tree canopy and ran to where Wazza was already crouched by the rear of the car.

"What's wrong, Mummy?" Benni asked, a mixture of fear and curiosity in her wide eyes. Then a flash of understanding crossed her face. "Are we hiding from Uncle Bruno?"

Kee grimaced. Why did Benni have to be such a perceptive child? She'd had a quick talk with her last night in the tent before they settled in to read a book before bedtime. Told her she should no longer trust Uncle Bruno. That if Benni ever saw him again, she should run away. She tried to downplay it, not wanting to scare her daughter, but needing her to understand that Bruno could no longer be believed. Thankfully, Benni hadn't questioned why, and hadn't asked about her father, either, which surprised her.

Instead, she'd said something equally surprising. "What about baba and dida?" Benni asked. "Do we still trust them? Are we ever going to see them again?" She hadn't been upset, merely curious, her little face screwed up in a solemn frown, trying to understand the intricacies of the grown-up world.

"I'm not sure, my bunny."

"I miss them," Benni had said. "Baba makes good *krofne* doughnuts, and she gives me good hugs."

"I know," Kee had said, smoothing Benni's hair away from her forehead. Life weaved such a tangled web sometimes. Benni only knew the soft side of her paternal grandparents, the side that loved her with all their heart, and she loved them back unconditionally. She was too young and innocent to understand the twisted motives behind their love, and how they were prepared to use their grandchild as a pawn in their son's sick games of power and control. Kee wasn't willing to destroy her daughter's innate trust in them; not yet, at least, so she said no more.

After Benni had fallen asleep, exhausted by the day's endeavors, her question had repeated around and around in Kee's head, making her wonder. Making her think about her own parents and her sister. Her family. Family was important. They were family that Benni hadn't even met; didn't even know existed. Perhaps it might be time to try and reconnect with her family. They were all she had left. Her circumstances had changed dramatically from six years ago when she incurred her father's wrath by marrying Jakov. Would he be prepared to forgive her now? If she extended a plea for help, would he want to get to know his only grandchild, or push her away again?

"I'll make sure our campsite is better hidden tonight," Wazza murmured in her ear, drawing her back to their predicament. The buzz of the helicopter was getting louder, and she held her breath as they listened to it pass by. Not directly overhead, but to the north of them.

"Maybe it was lucky we weren't on the road already," he said finally, standing up and straining to peer through the canopy above.

"Do you really think they were looking for us?" Kee asked.

Wazza shrugged and said, "Hard to tell. It could've been a mustering contractor on his way to a job, or a landowner heading to town for supplies." He lifted those broad shoulders in another imitation of a dismissal. "Better to be safe than sorry," he added, face lighting up with a smile. "But maybe we should thank Benni and her leaf collection, after all." Wazza raised a finger and pointed it at Benni, and she squealed with delight, as he waved his finger in ever decreasing circles until it collided with the exact place on Benni's side that he'd discovered was her ticklish spot. Benni squirmed so hard in her arms that she had to put her down and she ran behind the car, still giggling. Kee smiled up at Wazza, thanking him with her eyes for keeping their situation light, knowing he didn't want to scare Benni unnecessarily. She'd meant it last night when she'd told him how good he was with children.

"Let's get going," he said, humor leaching from his face as he leaned down to grab the last remaining items still waiting to be packed, as well as the tarp covering the car, shoving them in the back and slamming the door.

Soon they were back on the road, a dust trail rising for miles behind them. The track was the same as yesterday, red gravel with wide edges, stretching straight and true on toward the horizon. The surrounding country was also much the same, short, brown grass, bleached almost red by the dust and heat, spread across flat plains dotted with patches of scrubby eucalyptus trees and acacia shrubs. The occasional conical-shaped large ant hill, often as tall as she was, breaking up the monotony.

Kee set up the Wiggles on the kiddie music player she'd found amongst the bag of toys Daniella had given her. It came with a stack of tiny square tapes that slotted into the machine, filled with different children's music from the nineties. It was old and clunky, but it did the job, and Kee helped her put her earphones on. Benni's face took on a faraway look and her head bobbed from side to side as the music filled her ears. Without Benni's constant chatter, it was quiet in the car.

Now was as good a time as any. Kee cleared her throat. Why was this so hard? Wazza had bared his soul to her last night, surely she could do the same in return. Their talk last night had disclosed things about Wazza that even she hadn't begun to guess. Such a big, strong, stoic man. No one would predict the depths to which his emotions ran. Losing his unborn baby had really affected him. Her heart felt it might break wide open when he'd spoken his dead daughter's name aloud. She couldn't help but offer him comfort, she was only human, after all. It had been the key that unlocked one more of the seals around her heart. She realized he was pulling down her wall of defenses, one brick at a time. She might be falling for this man. What a pickle she was in.

She cleared her throat a second time. "Wazza, I was wondering, can you call anywhere in Australia on that satellite phone?" Her eyes drifted to the phone in the console between them, avoiding his gaze.

"Sure you can. Who do you want to call?" he asked in a lazy drawl.

"My parents," she half-whispered. Wazza knew the bare bones of her estrangement with her parents. He didn't realize how deep the wounds ran, or how her father's pride had ruined everything. She was terrified he wouldn't even take her call. And what if he didn't? Would it even matter?

"Okay," he prompted, but when she didn't respond, he asked gently, "How long since you've talked to them?"

"Six years," she answered dully.

Wazza's mouth formed a straight line. "So, you haven't seen them since you got married? Did they even come to your wedding?"

"No. And they've never even met Benita." She stared out the window at the passing trees.

"Oh, wow." He made a small noise in the back of his throat that Kee couldn't interpret, but she didn't dare look at him. What must he think of her? "Well, at least now my family doesn't seem so screwed up anymore," he joked.

His attempt to lighten the mood eased her misery a little. "They don't know about any of what's going on with me and Benni," she confessed. "They know that Jakov is in jail. Pooja, my sister, called me after it was splashed all over the newspapers." Kee could just imagine her father, Vijay, sitting in his brown, corduroy armchair, feet up on the footrest, a knowing twist to his mouth, thinking *I told you so, daughter of mine*, over and over when he heard the news. "But even then, my parents refused to talk to me, running all their communication through Pooja." It rankled Kee that not even once had they reached out to offer her any kind of help, either financially or emotionally. Vijay would've seen it as a form of penance for Kee, letting her find out the hard way how her bad decisions affected her.

"So, why didn't you tell them about the grandparents trying to take Benni away?"

"I don't know." It was Kee's turn to shrug. "It all happened fairly quickly, and I guess I didn't want to hear any more of their negativity. I just wanted Benni back." They certainly wouldn't have condoned her methods of stealing her daughter right from under the grandparent's noses.

"And so why do you think they might help you now?"

"I'm pretty sure if I admit I was wrong and beg for forgiveness, my father will suddenly become all magnanimous and supportive. It's all about managing his pride, you see. His male ego." Kee knew it was more than that because it was also her pride that'd stopped her from calling him in the first place. Perhaps she was more like him than she thought. Which was a scary idea.

"Hmm," he growled. "I hope you don't think all men are like that?"

"Not at all," she hurried to assure him, placing a hand on his knee, then quickly removing it. She glanced surreptitiously into the back seat, but Benni was still listening to her music, making Dolly dance on her knee to the rhythm.

"That's just how my father works."

"Next time we stop you can give it a go, if you like," he said, not quite managing to hide the dubious quirk of his mouth.

The next stop was an hour and a half later. Wazza pulled over onto the verge beneath the shade of a stand of trees.

She'd offered to drive, but so far, he'd refused all offers. She was going to make more of a concerted effort, she couldn't let him drive all the way, not when she was quite capable.

He turned to face her across the cabin. "We have to cross the main highway up ahead. After it leaves Dimbulah, it curves south for a way and then swings around to head north again, while we've been cutting straight across country."

"Oh, right," she said, unclipping her seat belt. It'd be nice to get out and stretch her legs.

"I'm just going to walk the last little way and check that it's all clear."

She had no idea what he might be expecting to find, a police roadblock, Bruno waiting right there for them to enter the highway, as if he was some omniscient clairvoyant. Not likely. She raised her eyebrows in mock amusement.

"Shall I take Benni, so you have some peace and quiet to make your call?"

Oh, that's why he was taking a walk. It wasn't about him at all; it was about her. She was such an idiot sometimes. "Thank you, that'd be great." Her stomach fell at the idea of talking to her parents. She could do this. For Benni's sake, if not her own. Benni deserved to know she had a whole other set of grandparents who might love her even more unconditionally than Jakov's. And truth be told, she needed their help, if only Vijay could get past his pride and offer it.

Wazza showed her how to use the sat phone, then asked Benni if she wanted to go for a walk to find some interesting insects. She danced beside him as he strolled down the track, her little sneakered feet leaving puffs of dust in her wake.

Kee took a deep breath and stared at the phone in her hand. She could do this. Pressing each button precisely, she dialled her parents' number and waited.

"Hello?" The voice was that of her mother, but it was different somehow. Older, frailer.

"Mamma? It's me, Kee," she spoke haltingly into the phone.

There was a moment's hesitation. "Keiyona? Is that really you? Oh, my! Oh, my!" Her mother sounded like she might be about to weep, and she could imagine her hands fluttering around her face as she often did when she was upset. Her father's deep voice sounded in the background, and her mother shouted something unintelligible back at him in Hindi. "We've been so worried about you," her mother continued. "Tell us what is going on?"

Before Kee could open her mouth, her father's voice boomed through the phone. "Keiyona, is that you?"

"Yes, Pappa." She kept her voice strong and steady. She was no longer a meek little mouse who bowed to her father's every wish.

"I'm so glad you got in contact with us. Your mother has been worried sick. The police have been here, asking us all kinds of questions, but we have told them nothing."

The police? Kee frowned. If the police had spoken to her parents, then they must know what was going on with her and Benni. Now she thought about it, of course the police would follow up all avenues to recover a supposedly kidnapped child, even though her parents knew nothing. Perhaps it was a blessing in disguise that the cops had been in touch.

Her father's voice brought her back to the present. "We want to help. You and the little one. We hoped you'd contact us, and we have been thinking, coming up with plans to help you."

Wow. This was a complete turnaround. It seemed her parents had changed their minds. They wanted to be involved in her life. In Benni's life. A huge weight lifted from Kee's shoulders, and she felt sudden tears form. She blinked them away, but her chest remained tight. Six years she'd been frozen out of her family. Now, all of a sudden, they wanted to welcome her back into the fold. The feeling of comfort was unbelievable. Maybe, just maybe, things might work out all right. Kee wasn't stupid enough to think that there wouldn't be recriminations and hard conversations to come. But that didn't matter right now. Her family was on her side. She didn't have to do this all alone anymore.

Not that she had been doing it alone, a little voice reminded her. Warwick Nobles had been there for her when she needed him.

Kee was grinning from ear to ear when Benni and Wazza returned.

Wazza took one look at her face and said, "The phone call went well, then?"

"Yes." She couldn't help it, she rushed up and threw her arms around him. "They want to help," she said into his neck.

"Me too, me too," Benni demanded, raising her arms so Wazza could pick her up and include her in the group hug, a tangle of arms and legs.

Kee didn't mention the type of help her parents were suggesting. Because she still wasn't sure she'd got her head completely around it yet. And she wasn't sure how Wazza would take it. He was already breaking the rules helping her this far, he might balk at her father's extreme idea, and she wouldn't blame him.

Benni giggled in Wazza's arms, and he quirked an eyebrow at Kee as if to say, *your daughter is something else*. A surge of happiness lifted Kee's spirits. When Bruno had appeared in Dimbulah, she'd thought all the hard-won peace and contentment she'd found staying at Stormcloud had disappeared in those few seconds of violence. Now it came back to her, how much she enjoyed Wazza's company, how much he made her emotions come to the boil.

"You can tell me about it when we're back on the road,"

Wazza said, putting Benni down as he tipped his hat back to stare down the gravel track. It made her realize they still had a long way to go. The trip would've taken them a third of the time if they'd stuck to the main road. But taking the long way around was also helping to ease something wound up so tight inside Kee, she felt like she might snap in two. Apart from the chopper this morning, and a dusty truck wheezing its way along the road near the river crossing, they'd seen no other people. Kee wondered where Bruno had got to. They had no idea how badly Wazza had hurt him. He could be in a hospital in a coma, for all they knew. Although, Kee doubted that, Bruno was strong and stubborn, and like a junkyard dog with a bone when he wanted something. If he'd recovered and jumped straight back in his car to follow them, he could be on their tail right now. Or he could even be ahead of them. But how would he have guessed which direction she was taking? She could've gone north, south, east, or west, for all he knew. Would he guess she was heading for the border? She hoped not.

Shaking her head to rid it of unwanted thoughts of Bruno, she said, "I'm driving." She held out her hand for the keys. Lifting her chin, she looked him dead in the eye, daring him to say no. His blue eyes sparkled with mirth, and something else.

"Just don't get us lost." He threw her the keys and backed away before she could pummel him for his impudence.

CHAPTER SEVENTEEN

The Norman River still had a few large pools scattered along the mostly dry riverbed, even at this time of the year. Which didn't surprise Wazza; the Norman River flowed all the way to the Gulf of Carpentaria, where it became wide and fast, an estuary full of saline water. This far inland, the water was fresh, but Wazza still advised against swimming in it, which Benni had begged to do in the large pool they'd found a little way downstream. The water was deep and dark, but also stale, and had a slight odor. She might get sick if she swam in there. Even so, he also gazed at the water longingly; it'd be so nice to be able to cool off from this heat. But Benni had to be content with poking around the rocks at the edge, squealing in delight as a school of tiny fish darted away from her stick. Wazza had already warned her to be on the lookout for snakes, and he'd also checked the area twice. It was the sort of place where they liked to congregate at this time of year.

Kee had agreed wholeheartedly with Wazza's decision not to let Benni go in the water, reminding her daughter that she needed to stay close to Wazza by the edge because she hadn't learned to swim properly yet. Then, right before she'd turned around to leave them by the pool and start preparing dinner, she'd shuddered as she stared at the water, and murmured,

"And I don't know about Wazza, but I won't be able to jump in there and save you, because I can't swim, either." Her soft confession surprised him, but she'd already turned her back and walked away. No wonder she'd been eyeing the deep pool with distrust, and pulling Benni back if she got too close. It suddenly dawned on him that perhaps that was why she'd become so hysterical the day Benni had disappeared at Stormcloud, and she thought Benni might have gone into the billabong. Because she wouldn't have been able to rescue her.

Now, the sound of Kee preparing dinner drifted to him on the hot breeze. They were having tuna pasta, with the last of the tomatoes. Skylar's food reserves were running low. They'd eaten the avocado and the remains of her homemade sourdough for lunch, and Benni had munched through the whole jar of nuts during the day's drive. He'd discuss it with Kee after dinner, but they may have to call into Normanton to replenish supplies, especially if she hoped to make it all the way to Darwin. Not for the first time, he made a silent plea that Kee would let him accompany her all the way. If she chose to send him home once they crossed the border into NT, he'd abide by her wishes, but there was still a long way to go to get to Darwin, and Wazza would much rather be by her side. He could map out a route that'd keep her off the main highway, but not take her on such isolated back roads as they'd followed for the past few days. That would be suicide, if she got stuck, or lost again, she may never be found in the huge vastness of the top end of the Northern Territory.

She was actually not a bad driver, although Wazza had sometimes struggled to keep his comments to himself if she hit a pothole or took a corner a little too fast. He'd liked the way the tip of her tongue came out to the corner of her mouth if there was a particularly tricky section of the road. He'd found himself so distracted by the sight, he'd even forgotten to correct her when she took a steep hill at too high a gear, making the engine work harder than it should. An easy mistake to make if you weren't used to four-wheel-driving on a dirt road. Her small hands were dwarfed by the large steering wheel, and she had to sit up really tall to see over the dashboard—he must remember to find her a pillow or something to raise her up next time, he couldn't believe she'd driven this car so far while not being able to see properly. But instead of being annoying, Wazza had found himself enjoying the spectacle immensely.

He'd used the chance while Kee had been driving to make a few calls on the sat phone, the first one to Steve to find out what kind of stir their little scene had caused in Dimbulah. He was thankful to hear that Lefty had managed to keep the whole thing quiet, and the fight hadn't even been reported to the police. From Lefty's account, it seemed Bruno had revived soon after Wazza and Kee had turned the corner and while still groggy and holding his head, had got into his car, and driven away, even though Lefty tried to stop him. That was the last they'd heard of Bruno. Steve had tried to sound out Nash to see if they were looking for any persons of interest in the area. But he couldn't say too much without tipping Nash off that Wazza was somehow involved in his strange questions. Steve said that it didn't look as if the police were actively hunting for Kee and Benni, nothing had changed in the quiet town of Dimbulah as far as police action. But that didn't mean much. Nash was good at keeping things close to his chest.

Wazza wasn't sure how helpful Steve's intel was, all it really told him was that Bruno was definitely back on the hunt for them. Would he be able to guess what direction they'd gone in?

The second call was to his family farm in Goulburn. He spoke to his brother, Mark, who seemed slightly surprised to hear from him. Wazza kept his call short, asking how the orchard was going—it sounded like they were in for a good year, which made up for the past two bad ones—and telling Mark he was just checking in as he was taking a few days *holiday* to regions up north, and he didn't want his family to worry if they couldn't get hold of him. Mark and Todd, the two eldest sons, had taken over most of the running of the orchard, and his parents were now semi-retired. It was good to hear Mark's voice. It'd been too long since Wazza had visited home. Mark said Mum and Dad were doing fine, tough as old boots, the both of them, but Wazza decided he'd make a trip down south as soon as he got Kee sorted. One thing this situation had taught him was that family was important.

"Dinner's ready," Kee's voice drifted down the riverbed to him.

Benni's head popped up from behind a large rock. "Oh goodie, I'm hungry. Come on Wazza." She took his hand, a serious frown on her little face. "But watch out for those bloody snakes."

He winced and hoped her mother didn't hear her using that word. He'd slipped up when he'd told her to be careful, and now he was probably going to pay for it for the rest of his life.

Picking their way between the rocks, they made their way up the riverbed and onto the bank near the campsite. This one was even better than the one at Gilbert River. Four old river gums, bark pale as clotted cream, created a natural amphitheater on a crest of the riverbank. Clumps of tussock grass formed little hillocks on an otherwise flat area beneath the trees. A set of horizontal river rocks shaped into a natural staircase led down to the level of the river, where there was a small beach made of soft, white sand. He still didn't want to risk a fire, which would've been nice to sit around at night, but the temperatures were warm enough that they didn't need one. He'd found a spot between two tussock grasses to set up the tent, close to the largest tree trunk and hopefully out of sight of any aircraft. Although they hadn't seen any more choppers since this morning, Wazza remained vigilant. Not that he mentioned his fears to Kee.

Half an hour later, Wazza dropped his tin plate on the ground with a clatter. "That was bloody delicious." He smacked his lips together. "You could apply for a job as a camp cook with those skills," he added.

"A what?"

"Camp cook. During muster, when all the ringers are out at the stock camp, they usually have a designated camp cook. It's practically a full-time job."

"Oh. I didn't know that." Kee gave a pleased little smile. "But I'll keep that in mind. I'm going to need a job when I get to Darwin."

Wazza didn't have the heart to tell her that the life of a camp cook was spent trailing from one stock camp to the next for over half the year. A hard life, but some people loved it.

"Talking about cooking, we don't seem to have a lot of food left," she said, also laying her empty plate on the ground.

"Yes, I know. I'm thinking we might need to call into a town tomorrow. To stock up on supplies before the drive to Darwin." He carefully avoided the topic of exactly who would be going to Darwin.

"I think that's a good idea," Kee said after a few seconds. "Would we be able to find somewhere to wash up, as well? I'd really like a shower," she admitted. "This red dust gets into everything. And Benni is impossible to keep clean."

"I know," he admitted. They'd all had a bowl bath this morning, where he filled a metal bowl with enough hot water for them to wring out a washcloth and use it to clean their faces, under arms and other important bits, but it was fairly unsatisfactory. "There's a town called Karumba north of Normanton, and right on the coast. It's off the main highway and if we stay out of the Main Street, stick to the outskirts, we should be fine. There must be a mum-and-pop grocery store somewhere, rather than going to the central shopping district of Normanton. And I know of a tourist park where you can pay five dollars for a shower."

"Five dollars, that's outrageous."

"Water is a scarce commodity out here," he said, standing and offering her his hand so he could pull her up. She stood close, not releasing his hand straight away, staring up at him with hooded eyes. He was the first to break away, meandering over to fill the metal bowl they used to wash the dishes, while Kee went to pick up Benni's plate. "I'll clean up from dinner while you read to Benni, if you like?"

"That would be wonderful." She straightened from where she'd been bending over and knuckled the small of her back. Wazza caught her profile as she stared downriver toward the large pool of water, and he was struck by just how exquisite she was. Even covered in dust and rumpled by sitting in a car most of the day, her flawless brown skin glowed in the rays of the setting sun. High cheekbones and rosebud mouth, with a little snub nose, her beauty called to him. Watching her, he knew he didn't merely hope Kee would let him continue their journey together, he *needed* to stay with her. He suddenly couldn't imagine being without her. How would he cope if he had to go back to Stormcloud without her? Life would be bland and colorless without her—and Benni—in it.

What was happening to him?

He was becoming way too attached to Kee, that's what was happening. But it was happening against his will. As if she'd cast a secret spell over him. He knew if he had to wave goodbye to them at the border, his soul would never be free of her, even if he never saw her again his whole life.

Twenty minutes later, Wazza was laid out on his swag, staring up at the skies, much the same as last night. And just like he'd hoped, Kee emerged from the tent the same as she had last night and made her way over to where he lay.

"Can I join you?"

"Of course." He shuffled over to make room and extended his arm so she could snuggle into the crook of his shoulder.

"I've been looking forward to this all day," she sighed, laying back so she could look up to the heavens, as well.

"Me, too." It was the simple truth. Him and Kee alone, with only the stars to keep watch. A companionable silence descended over them, with only the music of the cicadas singing in the trees above to keep them company.

Suddenly, a dingo howled, low and mournful in the distance.

"What's that?" Kee shuffled closer, and he hid a smile.

"A dingo. He won't bother us, don't worry." He liked the way she nestled into him, her hand draped over his stomach, head resting in the hollow of his chest just beneath his collarbone. She'd let her hair free again, and he had a crazy urge to stroke his hand down the length, feel his fingers tangle in the locks.

"Really? I always thought they were a bit of a myth. I've never seen one, certainly not in the wild."

"Oh, no, they definitely exist." He gave into temptation and stroked his fingers lightly through the silken span spread out down her back. He wanted to kiss her again. Would she let him after he'd practically pushed her away last night? The same reasons he'd stopped last night still existed, but they were veiled by his overpowering yearning to taste her, touch her, consume her. It obliterated all logic and reasoning. Rolling up onto his elbow, he peered down into her face. Her thumb traced lazy circles on his stomach, through his shirt.

She was looking at him like she wanted him as much as he

wanted her. Then she smiled, slow and sexy and heat streaked down his spine, like a shaft of lightning, straight to his cock. His mouth was on hers and she moaned as his tongue delved deep, tangling in a deluge of lust. Her hand slid up the side of his ribs and he angled his head so he could kiss her deeper, harder.

At last, he had to come up for air before he consumed her whole. "God," he panted, leaning his forehead against hers. "That feels so good. You feel so good."

Her only answer was her hot breath on the side of his neck, as she ran her tongue along the soft spot behind his ear. This was so much more intense than anything between them before.

I'm falling in love with you. The words echoed around and around in his brain, and it was all he could do to keep them safe behind his tightly clamped lips.

Her hand darted between them and squeezed his erection through his jeans. Wazza moaned, getting lost in his carnal desire. Suddenly, she pulled away, and he wanted to cry out in despair. Then he realized what she was doing as she pushed on his chest, rolling him over. He hardly dared breathe as she settled on top of him. Taking control.

Hands as nimble and quick as a cat undid the button on his jeans and slid down the zipper. And then slipped inside to grasp his rock-hard cock. A surge of molten lava burned through his veins, and he let out a groan. This was a new side of Kee, the take-charge kind of woman, that he suddenly liked a hell of a lot.

Whoa. Hang on, he needed to apply the brakes here, before things went too far.

Lifting his head, he asked, "Should we do this? I mean, Benni…?"

"She sleeps like the dead," Kee panted. "She won't wake up."

All this time he'd been worried about Benni finding them. He wished he'd known this little gem of information earlier. But perhaps Kee had kept it from him for just this reason.

Her dexterous fingers were now undoing his shirt buttons, baring his naked chest. "I want this. I need this."

If she could abandon all propriety, then so could he.

He reached up and tugged at the hem of her T-shirt, and she lifted her arms obligingly so he could drag it over her head. Kee's plain, white bra glowed against her dark skin in the starlight. Impatiently, she reached around and unsnapped the back fastener, lowering the straps over each shoulder to reveal…everything. Her pert breasts bounced enticingly, and his mouth went dry. Not small exactly, just right, they suited her beautiful body perfectly.

He let his gaze wander over the gorgeous curves of her hips, where the waistband of her shorts rode low, across the flat planes of her stomach and then up again to stare at her breasts. His palm slid up to cup her cheek as the air around them buzzed with tension.

He needed to get her naked. If she wanted this, then so did he. More than she could know.

Tensing his stomach, he flipped her over with one, smooth move. She gasped, then grabbed a handful of his hair, dragging his mouth down to hers. His shirt flapped open, and he got to his knees, discarding it with a grunt. Boots, blue jeans and boxers followed in quick succession, but not before he retrieved his phone from the back pocket. At the time he'd slipped the condoms inside the cover, he hadn't held any hope that he might use them, and yet…a part of him must've hoped this night would come.

Still on his knees, ready to drop and cover her body, he saw her staring, gaze sliding appreciatively down the slabs of his stomach to rest on his erection. If the way she licked her lips was anything to go by, she liked what she saw. Before he knew it, Kee had wriggled out of her shorts and panties and was lying naked beneath the stars, allowing him to look his fill. She was a beautiful woman, and he was pleased to see that she owned that fact. Too many women were self-conscious of their bodies, but Kee seemed to have no qualms about him checking her out.

"Come to me, Cowboy," she cooed. Then giggled softly at her use of the nickname. Warm hands reached up to stroke his erection, sliding like silk over his skin. Drawing him down to her. Quickly, before he forgot completely where he was, he sheathed himself and then lowered down slowly, hovering above her, enjoying the exquisite feeling of his skin meeting hers, chest crushing her breasts, thighs coming together.

Heat surged to Wazza's groin as he slid between her legs until his cock nestled into the point right at her core. Sinking slowly inside her, he watched her face as she gasped and then surged to meet him, locking her ankles around his back with an urgent whimper. They moved together to a rhythm immemorial, her gasps of fervor rising with each thrust.

Tension built deep in his belly, sensations threatening to overwhelm him as he thrust faster and faster. His legs shook and he couldn't catch his breath as he came closer to climax. He didn't want to leave Kee behind, but he needn't have worried, her cries were building in the back of her throat as she arched her spine, thighs tensing around him.

Suddenly Kee became as still as a statue, back curved, hips risen to meet his, and then she issued a sound from somewhere deep in her chest, and Wazza let himself go, barely conscious of anything except the fierce sensations surging through him.

It took many seconds for him to come back to his body.

Kee was limp in his arms, her head lolling to one side, completely satiated, and he chuckled as he kissed the side of her neck. A feeling of complete and utter contentment filled him.

And that's when he knew. It was totally mad, but he couldn't shake the feeling that'd been building ever since he first saw her by that bore. He needed to get it out in the open.

"I think I'm falling in love with you," he murmured.

"That's just the sex talking," she sighed and turned her lips up to touch his. "And it was damn good sex, I have to say."

She was blowing him off, didn't think he was serious. And perhaps that's where he should leave it. But he couldn't help himself.

"It's not just the sex." He leaned in and kissed her forehead. He'd given her his all, worshipped her body with his, now it was time to bare his soul. "And I'm not asking for anything in return." He drew back and heard the catch in her breath as she finally focussed on what he was saying. "But I'm really glad I met you, Kee. And I meant what I said."

She sobered, her dark eyes fixed on his face. "I'm really glad I met you, too, Warwick." His gut squeezed at her admission. It was a start. "For Benni, as well as for me. We both care for you, a lot." Her eyes were dark pools in the starlight, but he could tell she was giving him the truth. Of course, she had to guard her heart. She had a daughter to consider.

It was enough for now. He didn't need any more from her.

Rolling off her, he relieved himself of the condom. He'd dispose of it properly in the morning.

"If you don't mind me asking, exactly how many of those do you have handy?" she asked, turning onto her side to watch him.

He waggled his eyebrows at her. "Wouldn't you like to know, my little vixen?"

She giggled and threw herself at him, arms around his neck, unabashedly wrapping her legs around his, leaving him wishing he had a whole box handy.

There were three condoms in total, and they used them all that night together under nature's canopy. Kee got up and checked on Benni twice, reporting back to Wazza that she was sleeping sideways across the mattresses with Dolly kicked to the side of the tent, forgotten. Afterwards, he wrapped them both in his tarp to keep the bugs away, and they slept in each other's arms until the first rays of light touched the world.

Wazza was the first to open his eyes. The morning air was cool, a whisper of a breeze flowing up the river and over their improvised love nest. The sky was indigo, but he knew the sun wasn't far below the horizon. Lying there, with Kee in his arms, he felt completely at peace. Propping his head on his hand, he stared at the skyline, watching the last star dissolve into the fledgling blue as dawn approached.

Kee stirred in his arms and opened her eyes to stare into his face. He liked that he was the first thing she saw that morning. With a light flutter of her lips over his in greeting, she turned onto her back, using his arm as a pillow so she could look up at the growing daybreak.

Pink clouds were arranged like a row of seashells against the rising blue. Wazza had seen many sunrises in his life, but this one was particularly breathtaking.

"Dawn skies have always been my favorite," Kee whispered.

Today, he couldn't agree with her more.

CHAPTER EIGHTEEN

I think I'm falling in love with you. The words still made Kee's heart beat faster every time she thought of them. And she thought of them a lot. Risking a quick glance, she took in Wazza's profile as he drove. Strong, square jaw with three days' worth of stubble, high forehead, straight nose, lips curled up in a slight smirk, with those blue eyes of a hawk. He was good-looking, there was no doubt about it. Her gaze lingered on his lips a second longer than it should've. Oh, what a revelation those lips had been last night. Scorching her skin with his kisses. Her whole body felt languorous and lethargic, as if she'd feasted on Wazza's body and was completely satiated now. She couldn't believe she'd actually gone through with it. It was true that Benni slept like the dead most nights, but they'd still taken a risk. What if Benni had woken? Had called out for her mother? But she hadn't. And Kee regretted not a minute of it. It'd been the best night of her life. But now, reality came crashing down over her little bubble of intimacy. That'd been the first and the last time she would make love with Wazza. It'd been a night of carnal sin, a night where she'd allowed herself the freedom to take what she wanted. But now duty rode her like a heavy cloud. Benni's safety was all that mattered, not her stupid heart.

Wazza had been careful not to mention her plans for after she crossed the border. She knew he was hoping she'd ask him to come with her. But she still hadn't decided. It was complicated. Her growing feelings for him made her want to be selfish. Want him by her side. Was it even fair of her to ask him to leave his whole life behind to help her and Benni? Then there was his declaration last night. Was she just leading him on if she let him come with her, perhaps going to break his heart? Maybe that was the best reason of all to leave him at the border. And she still hadn't told him what her father had proposed over the phone yesterday. She was sure he wouldn't like that, either.

Returning her inspection to the track unfolding ahead of them, she thought about what Wazza had said this morning. This track followed the Norman River north, most of the way to Normanton, where they would re-join the highway. They were taking a risk, returning to the main road, but Wazza assured her it was only for twenty kilometers or so, then they'd be through Normanton and onto the less travelled road toward the coast and the little town he'd mentioned. Kee was excited; Wazza said the town was on the Gulf of Carpentaria. This area was often called Gulf Country; even more Wild West than the outback, if he were to be believed. And while she'd heard of it, she'd never dreamed she'd actually come here one day. Wazza was regaling Benni with tales of the huge fish they caught at the mouth of the Norman River, called barramundi. Scaring her with stories of the greedy saltwater crocodiles that also lived there, and how sometimes a fisherman would have his catch stolen even as he reeled it into his boat by a marauding crocodile. Kee hoped they didn't meet one of those.

"Do you think we'll see a crocodile?" Benni asked, brown eyes wide with wonder. "Will they eat me, too?"

Wazza laughed. "I really hope they don't eat you.

Although you might make a tasty little morsel."

Kee smiled along with their happy banter. But she needed to talk to Wazza, preferably without her daughter overhearing. "Would you like to listen to some of your music?" she asked, fiddling around in the back pocket of the seat until she found Julie's old music player. This thing had been an absolute godsend, she needed to remember to ask Wazza to thank Daniella again profusely for her gift. Kee scrolled through the little tapes and found something called "The Kidboomers Playing Kindyrock". Whatever that meant, it sounded right up Benni's alley.

"Here you go." She handed Benni the earphones and then tucked the little player down the side of her child seat.

"I take it that means you want to talk," Wazza said as soon as she faced forward again, waggling one eyebrow at her.

"You're so perceptive." She caught herself reaching to put her hand on his knee. It wouldn't do for Benni to see any public displays of affection; it'd just confuse her. But it was hard not to touch him sometimes.

"I wanted to ask your opinion on something my father mentioned yesterday."

"Shoot," he replied.

"My dad made a suggestion." She bit her bottom lip, hesitating. "When I told him I was most likely going to end up in Darwin—"

"Was that wise?" He growled. "Telling them where you're going?"

"I trust them," she said honestly. "Even though my father disowned me, he'd never betray me." Kee wasn't sure she could explain it to Wazza, the way Vijay's twisted pride worked. Betrayal was worse than death in his eyes. He may never want to see her again, but he'd never give her up to the police. "Anyway," she continued, "He wanted to meet us in Darwin. Him and my mother. Said he'd buy us tickets to anywhere in the world I wanted to go."

It took Wazza a few seconds to grasp her meaning. "What, you mean leave the country? Wouldn't that be illegal?"

"I guess." She gave a small shrug. Vijay had even offered to go with her and Benni, or meet up with her later, in whatever country she ended up in. It'd touched a chord deep inside her, that her parents were prepared to put their lives on hold, defy the law to help her and their granddaughter.

"But everything I've been doing over the past month has been illegal, so that's no different. I could perhaps take Benni back to India. Re-connect with the rest of our relatives," she added hesitantly.

Wazza made a scornful sound. She'd been right in guessing he wouldn't like this idea. It was by no means the answer she was looking for, but she wasn't going to discount it completely.

Lifting her chin, she narrowed her eyes. This was her life and her decision, in the end. "Is it really that much more of a stretch from what I've already done? In the eyes of the law, I'm a kidnapper. I'll probably go to jail."

"Not once they see you're innocent, that you were framed by your jealous ex-husband," he replied quickly. His mouth was set in a firm line of unease, a slash of red against his tanned face. He slowed the car to steer around a large pothole before he continued. "And yes, I do think smuggling her out of the country is taking this thing to a whole other level. If you do that, it escalates everything, you may never be allowed back into Australia."

She almost said, *would that be such a bad thing?* Even as far back as a week ago, her answer would've been a resounding *no*. There was nothing in Australia to hold her here. But now she'd met Wazza…things were different.

"You do know that Australia has an extradition treaty with India?" he added with a grimace. "I don't think that idea would work."

"Oh, I hadn't thought about that. I guess it doesn't have to be India, though." She furrowed her brow in thought.

"Yeah, you could go to China or Russia," he said, a sarcastic note creeping in.

She glared at him. He was being no help. The cabin was quiet the rest of the way to Normanton, as Kee considered her options. Which all seemed to be bad ones, no matter which way she looked.

Had she seriously been considering her parent's offer? Possibly. It probably went deeper than a mere desire to get out of Australia, it was also tied to her need to please her parents. She'd just reconnected with them and didn't want to lose them again so quickly. If she agreed to this crazy plan— and if they joined her at some stage—at least she'd be doing it with her family, enfolded in their embrace once more. That wasn't to say they'd reject her if she refused their offer. Vijay had made it clear he'd do whatever she decided, and all they wanted was to help keep the granddaughter they'd never met safe.

A line of trees appeared in the distance and Wazza sat up straighter in his seat. The highway must be up ahead. She held her breath as they turned onto the bitumen road. Not a single vehicle in either direction. She let out the breath.

"Not too long now," Wazza said reassuringly.

Kee scanned the line of road stretching out before them intently. A truck appeared over a hill, coming toward them. It swooshed past with a buffeting of backdraft. Then an older model four-wheel drive flashed past a few minutes later. Not the type of car Bruno had been driving. None of them was a police car, either. Kee let out another relieved breath.

But the cars became more numerous the closer they got to town and Kee began to sweat every time a new one appeared.

"It'll be okay." Wazza touched her arm. She was being

stupid, she knew it. Rolling her shoulders, she tried to relax. Then she glanced at Wazza and saw his pinched mouth and tight eyes and knew he was just as worried as she was.

They came to the town limits, passing a sign proclaiming that the Normanton newsagent sold Gold Lottery tickets.

More cars now, one every twenty seconds or so, and then they were into the town proper. Wazza took a right-hand turn, away from the sign pointing to the Main Road.

He zigzagged his way through the streets, Kee craning her neck around to look at passing cars, trying to discern their make, or see into the driver's face. Was that Bruno? It looked like him. But they were past that car and turning into another side street before Kee could take another look. In the end, she glimpsed four vehicles exactly like his, and two more men she was sure were Bruno. Then she saw the distinctive red-and-blue lights atop a white cruiser farther ahead of them, and she nearly ducked down in fear, but the squad car turned a corner and was gone. Neither of them spoke for the whole ten minutes as they traversed the town. Her nerves were a wreck by the time they passed through Normanton and out the other side, on the road to the coast. God, was it going to be this bad every time they went through a town? What about when she reached Darwin? Was she going to jump at every shadow, check every car that passed her on the street? After only two days out of civilization, and she already preferred the isolation of the bush.

"I was sure I saw Bruno," she muttered out of the side of her mouth.

"Me, too," he replied. Then he let out a gust of air and banged his hand on the steering wheel. "I think we need to get rid of this car," he muttered, half under his breath.

This time, she didn't disagree with him. She felt like she had a beacon on her forehead, broadcasting her whereabouts to whoever was interested.

"Are we there yet?" Benni's voice came from behind Kee. She'd removed the earphones and was staring expectantly at the dwindling town flashing by on either side.

"Nearly, bunny." Kee reached around and patted Benni's knee.

"Can we buy a new blue hat soon?"

Kee sighed. That child was never going to let that hat go.

"I'll look for one for you," Wazza replied diplomatically.

While not a main highway, the road to Karumba was still bitumen, and more than a few cars passed them by, keeping Kee's anxiety levels high. She swiveled her head to see a couple of cars following along behind them. But they were too far back to see any details clearly, and Kee decided she was going to go crazy if she kept expecting every car to be Bruno.

Eventually, Wazza took a right-hand turn and then a left, and houses began to appear haphazardly along the edge of the road, most of them the older style, small, fibro cement places that looked more like fishing shacks than anything else. Some had a few scrubby trees in the front yard, but most had parched, brown lawn and not much else. A few kids hung out along the gravel edge of the road on their bicycles, watching the cars drive by with little interest. Now and then, Kee caught glimpses of a swathe of water off to their right through the trees. Wazza had said this was a coastal town, so that must be the Gulf. He'd also warned them the water was full of crocodiles and the locals didn't swim in the ocean. What a waste. Suddenly, Wazza slowed and turned off into a wide gravel driveway. A large sign with the word POOL was the only indication that this was the entrance to a tourist park.

He pulled up around the back of a wooden building bleached almost white by the sun, with OFFICE scrawled on the front door.

"You both wait in the car," he said, not taking his eyes off the small house. "I'll sort us out some showers." He didn't need to say that the less she was seen in public, the better.

"I want to get out," Benni whined.

"Soon. We're going to have a nice shower in a minute," Kee soothed.

Wazza was gone for an eternity, or so it seemed. Even though he'd parked the car in the shade, it was heating quickly without the air conditioning going. Kee opened her door to let in some air.

Then he was striding toward the car, long legs eating away the ground, face hidden beneath his hat as he came toward the car. Kee willed him to lift his head, she needed to see his face to make sure they were still okay. Still safe. Opening the door, Wazza held up two keys fixed to a large piece of wood each: one pink and one blue, and grinned.

"Your shower awaits, my ladies." He handed her the pink key and slid into the driver's seat. "We can use the laundry facilities as well, I paid extra."

Kee fleetingly thought it might be nice to spend the night here, tucked up in one of the air-conditioned cabins, able to eat off a table instead of an old log. Admittedly, they were very rustic, and probably basic inside, but she quickly banished the idea. It wasn't worth the risk.

Wazza drove down the maze of internal roads through the tourist park, eventually arriving at a squat, brick building somewhere in the middle. He backed the car in behind a row of shrubs that at one stage might've been an attempt at a hedge but had now grown wild. She applauded his attempt at hiding her car from view.

"Are you ready to take a shower?" he asked Benni.

"Ready as we'll ever be," they both chorused back, and then filled the car with their gleeful laughter.

Sobering, she unclipped Benni from her seat, and watched

her daughter wander around the car, staring at all the new sights and sounds. She wondered what Benni made of all this. The constant traveling, sleeping rough in a different place every night. She seemed to take most of it in her stride. She was a happy kid, resilient and outgoing. But she'd taken to carrying Dolly with her wherever she went, and right now she was clutched tightly in her arms as Benni explored around the car. Kee's heart shifted in her chest at what she was asking her poor daughter to do; what she was putting her through. She needed this to be over, so she could finally give Benni the stable environment she needed.

"Take your time," Wazza said. "I'll take a quick shower, then the manager said there was a convenience store just down the road where I can buy the essentials. And I might ask around to see if anyone is selling a car, as well."

"Really? What would we do with this one?" She was suddenly, stupidly, attached to her car. It'd got her this far, after all, even if it had let her down at the bore site. But then, if it hadn't broken down when it did, she wouldn't have met Wazza.

"We could possibly leave it somewhere. A storage shed or something. Come back for it later, once…things settle down. Or sell it, but that might not be a good idea."

"Oh, all right." Kee wasn't sure that would ever happen, but he was right, the car was like a neon sign for anyone looking for them. A different one might give them the breathing space they needed to make it to Darwin.

An idea began to form. Perhaps this was the chance she needed to let Wazza go. If he found her a new car, she could ask him to take her old car back to Stormcloud for her, where it'd be safe until she could come and claim it again.

"I think there's a kid's playground over there." Wazza pointed to a spot overhung with trees between them and the road, and Kee could just make out the shape of a set of swings and a slide. "You can wait for me there, if you like."

"Can we? Can we, Mummy?" Benni pleaded. Kee couldn't remember the last time Benni did something as normal as playing in a playground.

She pushed the hair falling loose from her braid, tucking it behind her daughter's ear, touching the tip of her nose affectionately. "Of course we can."

Kee rummaged through their bags to find some toiletries and clean clothes and took Benni by the hand and led her to the right of the building, where the sign said *ladies*.

The amenities were old and shabby; the floor covered in sand, but the shower cubicles were bigger than she expected and the feeling of finally being clean for the first time in days overcame any of her distaste at the austere facilities. Benni sang her favorite song, while Kee worked up a lather of shampoo in her hair and Dolly sat on a ledge watching them both. For a fraction of a second, Kee wished Wazza were in here with her. She daydreamed of running slippery hands over that gorgeous cowboy body, all muscle and hard planes. A shiver ran through her at the thought, then Benni dropped the soap and all nefarious thoughts fled. What was she thinking? She'd already decided that last night was never going to happen again. And if Wazza managed to find her a new car, that might be all in the past.

They took their time getting clean, brushing their teeth at the sink, and she applying moisturizer, a luxury she didn't often get time for. Then Kee stood Benni on a plastic stool in front of the vanity mirror and braided her hair while it was still wet. With no hairdryer handy, it was the best option. The heat of the day would soon dry it. Then she did the same for herself. Leaning into the mirror, she examined her face under the fluorescent lights. There were dark circles under her eyes, which were to be expected after last night's pursuit of pleasure. She'd got used to wearing no makeup. There was no point while she was on the road every day, and it now felt like a frivolous pastime. Her brown skin was smooth and clear. Her eyebrows could do with a little maintenance, but otherwise she decided she didn't look half bad, considering how she'd been living over the past month; the worry and doubt that'd been plaguing her. Looking closer, she decided there was also a glow about her that hadn't been there before, either. She touched her cheek with her fingertips, remembering the feel of Wazza's lips as they trailed down the side of her face, from her temple to her jaw and back again.

Kee stuffed their dirty clothes into her bag and thought about using the laundry. It was nice to be wearing clean clothes, and they'd run out soon.

But then Benni looked at her with big, brown eyes. "Can we go to the playground now?"

"Sure, bunny." She packed up all their belongings and took Benni by the hand. "Just let me check it's all okay first, all right?"

"To make sure Uncle Bruno isn't there?"

Kee grimaced, but decided it was time to stop sheltering her little girl so much. "Yes, that's right." They'd already had one conversation about Bruno. And soon she'd need to find the right time to tell her she had a whole other set of grandparents that she'd never even met.

Kee held tight to Benni's hand as they cautiously approached the playground. She could hear children's voices raised in merry laughter, and Benni tugged, impatient to race over to the slide. They emerged from behind the trunk of a eucalyptus tree, and Kee stopped to observe the area. The playground was a large sandy bowl, with a set of swings, a slide, and a set of metal monkey bars, surrounded by large tropical trees with leaves as big as dinner plates, providing much needed shade. Two children, a boy and a girl, siblings by the looks of them, played on a large rope construction, built to look like a spiderweb. They didn't stop their bickering, even as they noticed Benni and Kee approach. There were no adults in sight, which surprised Kee at first. Then she decided that this might be a good thing. If the parents were prepared to let their kids play unsupervised, this was probably a safe place to do so. Still, she observed the area warily, checking to make sure it really was safe.

Finally, she let go of Benni's hand, and like a puppy loosed from a leash, Benni zoomed toward the park, making straight for the ladder up to the slide; her favorite thing in the world was zipping down the polished-metal, landing on her feet with a whoop and running around and doing it all again, and again, and again. Kee was often in awe of her child's boundless energy.

Taking a seat in the shade on an old, wooden bench, she settled in to watch Benni. The day was already hot; the sun blazing overhead in a bright sky, the buzz of the cicadas almost deafening. Lethargy overtook her, and she had to resist the urge to close her eyes. This wouldn't do, she needed to stay alert, keep her eyes peeled for any sign of Bruno or the police.

"Hiya, gorgeous." A hand touched her shoulder, and she nearly leaped out of her skin, turning around with a squeak of fear. "It's just me, sorry to scare you," Wazza apologized, when he saw the fear on her face.

Kee took a deep breath, and then another. "No, I should've been paying more attention," she admonished herself, as Wazza took a seat next to her on the bench. Benni waved at him from the rope construction—it seemed she finally had her fill of sliding, and had decided to join the other kids testing out their climbing skills. Wazza waved back, smiling at Benni's antics. Then he lay a hand on her knee, in an unconscious move of comfort, and she stared at it for uncounted seconds. To the outside world, they might look like a happily married couple watching their child playing without a care in the world. If only that were the case. Kee suddenly desperately yearned for that fantasy to be true. She could see it, her and Wazza married, he'd take to Benni as if she were his own child, and they could live a simple life, together in Darwin.

"I think I might've found someone who'll sell us a car," Wazza said, bursting her fantasy bubble.

CHAPTER NINETEEN

Wazza drove slowly down the pothole-ridden track. Was this the right place? He'd followed the guy at the convenience store's directions on the hastily scrawled note. He had said this place was a tad difficult to find, but this was getting ridiculous, even by country-people's standards. The air conditioning in the car was pumping, but it was getting hotter in here, as the humidity pushed in on all sides.

"Are you sure this is where we're supposed to go?" Kee voiced his concerns. She looked down at the note in her lap, and then peered through the windshield again. Vegetation closed in around the vehicle, making it feel claustrophobic. They were deep into the floodplains of the estuary formed at the mouth of the Norman River; the track following the slowly winding river inland. Every now and then, they'd catch a glimpse of sparkling water through the trees clustering along the river's edge on the left. And to the right, the land opened up to smooth, grassy plains, full of tall sedges and the occasional salt flat. The theme from the movie *Deliverance* ran through his head and he wondered again what he'd got them into.

Wazza shrugged, trying to seem unconcerned. "The guy said this man lived off the grid. Seems like a lot of folks out here do." They'd passed a few other shacks—there was no other word for them—hunkered down on the edge of the river, but the road seemed to be taking them to the end of the world. "If we don't find this place in the next five minutes, I'll turn around," he said, and Kee gave him a sideways glance, as if to say, where in hell would they find a place to even turn the car? The scrub had become so thick on either side, they might only have one option, and that was to keep going forward.

When Wazza had strolled up to the counter at the convenience store, arms laden with food supplies such as bread and tins of baked beans, he'd casually mentioned to the man behind the cash register that he was looking to buy a car, and did he know anyone who might have one for sale? Wazza was used to the open friendliness displayed in most country towns. People helped each other out, mostly, especially if you looked like you belonged. But this coastal town seemed to have a different vibe. The man, dressed in dirty overalls, with a scruffy beard and sharp, blue eyes that seemed to miss nothing, had looked him up and down before answering.

"Yeah, I might know a bloke," he'd drawled. "Depends what you're looking for."

"Something old, but reliable. Preferably cheap." Wazza had said with a friendly grin. The man hadn't returned his smile.

"Bloke called Diesel could have an old Toyota, if you're interested. He used to be a mechanic; keeps a few vehicles he's rescued that he likes to tinker with."

"I might be interested," Wazza had shot back. "Where does Diesel live? Would he mind if we dropped by?"

"Diesel is usually at home, if he ain't out fishing." The guy behind the counter lifted his head and stared out at the puffy, white clouds on the horizon and then to the where the ocean was hidden by a row of trees. "Tide's running out right now, nearly dead low on the flats, so he won't be fishing at the moment."

"Right. Thanks," Wazza said, piling his purchases into a large paper bag. "If you could tell me how to get to his place, that'd be great."

"Tell him George sent you. I'll draw you a map," the man drawled. "So you don't get lost."

Wazza nearly laughed at the absurdity of that comment as he continued to stare through the front windshield.

"I don't think..." Kee trailed off as the trees suddenly opened in front and they emerged into a clearing. A tangle of buildings met their gaze, some leaning precariously at an angle, as if the next strong wind might blow them down. The driveway led to an old house perched on the edge of the river around hundred meters away. Lining the driveway on each side, there must've been at least fifty cars, all parked at right angles to the track and all in various states of disrepair.

One glance at Kee's face said it all. Dismay and uncertainty were evident in the twist of her mouth. And he didn't blame her. But they'd come this far, they may as well check this guy out. Perhaps in amongst all these wrecks, he had one or two working vehicles that might suit.

As he approached the house and pulled up in the only area not overgrown with weeds, or stacked with engine parts, he noticed a large jetty with a pontoon at the end and a boat tied to it, reaching out into the river.

"Maybe you should stay in the car," Wazza said slowly.

"I want to get out," Benni whined.

Kee took one look at Benni and said, "We're coming with you."

He waited outside the car while Kee unstrapped Benni and brought her around to the front and put her on her feet. Then they all stared at the car graveyard with fascination.

"Look at all the cars," Benni said in wonder.

"Yes, well, don't go near any of them," Wazza warned. "There might be snakes."

"Really?" Benni's eyes went wide, and she made a large detour around the nearest car.

"And don't go near the water, either, Benni," Kee said loudly, as Benni skipped ahead of them down the track toward the house. She was right to be worried; that water was moving fast. Really fast. What had the guy at the shop said? The tide was on the way out? Wazza had heard about tidal estuaries and how much water moved up and down them during a single tidal cycle. But this was like nothing else he'd ever seen.

They all trooped up the two steps and onto the dilapidated front veranda together, Kee glancing around nervously. But the house seemed to be deserted, and even though Wazza knocked three times, no one answered.

"It doesn't look like anyone's at home," Kee said, a relieved note in her voice.

"Hey, what do you want?" A man appeared around the side of the house. He was tall, really tall, with an old baseball cap pulled down over long, lank hair, and a set of overalls so covered in grease it was hard to see where the gray of the fabric began, and the grease ended. The man glared at them suspiciously, piggy eyes narrowed and long beard bristling.

Wazza placed Kee and Benni behind him, then took the steps down into the front yard, squaring his shoulders and putting on his best smile. The man might be taller than him, but he was thin and weedy. Wazza could take him if he had to. But he really hoped it didn't come to that.

"I'm Wazza," he said, stretching out his hand. "You must be Diesel. George at the convenience store said you might have a car you'd like to sell." The man didn't take his hand, and so Wazza dropped it. But his face lost some of his open distrust.

"George sent you, huh?" His stare landed on Kee and Benni, still up on the veranda. "And who might they be?"

Wazza hesitated. Perhaps they should just get out of here, forget all about another car, and keep moving. Then Kee stepped forward. "My name is Kee, and this is my daughter, Benni." Benni poked her head around from behind her mother's legs and Wazza was reminded of the first time he'd met the pair when Benni had done the same thing.

The man perked up at the sight of the little girl. "Well, hello there." He took out a filthy rag from somewhere deep in his pocket and wiped his hands. "I've got a granddaughter about your age," he said, with a smile that showed two missing front teeth. "Her name's Tabitha. She comes out to visit me on weekends with her mother, sometimes."

Really. Wazza very much doubted that. But the man's whole demeanor had changed since he'd spotted Benni, and Wazza would take that advantage.

"It's actually Benni and her mother who need the car," he said, subtly getting between Kee and the old man as she and Benni came down the steps.

"Is that so?" Diesel's face lit up. "Well, in that case, I might have something to suit you. Come this way." The old man shuffled away around the corner toward the rear of the house. Kee shot Wazza a look, but they followed him slowly, Benni holding onto Kee's hand.

The sight that greeted them around the back of the house made Wazza stop in his tracks. Four vehicles were lined up next to each other in a gravel clearing, all in immaculate condition, in complete contrast to the broken cars around the front.

"It's my hobby, you see. I like to do up cars, make them run again when no one else can. Then, if the right person comes along, I sell them. But it must be the right person, mind you."

This old bloke was half crazy, Wazza decided. But if he could help them out, Wazza was prepared to live with it.

"Which one is your favorite, little lady?" Diesel leaned down and looked at Benni.

After a moment's hesitation, she pointed to the one on the far end, nearest the river. "The red one," she said, then glanced up at her mother.

"Great choice," replied Diesel. "Red is my favorite color, too. Come and have a look at it." He beckoned them onward.

It was a Toyota Hilux ute, with a double cab, which meant there was room for Benni in the back. It looked to be in good condition; Wazza noted there was no rust evident in the body as they got closer, which was surprising for an older vehicle in a coastal environment. Maybe it'd been garaged for most of its life.

"I just finished this baby last week. I even polished her paintwork; she came up a treat."

"It's pretty," said Benni. "I like it."

Kee still hadn't said a word, but she raised her eyebrows as Benni pulled her toward the car. Wazza wasn't so sure it was the one they wanted. A red four-wheel-drive would stand out amongst all the other plain white ones on the road.

"Hop in the front seat, little lady," Diesel said, taking obvious delight in Benni's interest in the car, opening the driver's door for her.

Wazza lifted Benni into the seat and peered inside. The upholstery was in a great state, everything shiny and clean. This guy really took pride in his work. Benni sat Dolly carefully on the passenger seat beside her and began to play with the knobs, turning on the windscreen wipers and pretending she was driving the car, bouncing on the seat with merriment. Diesel smiled his gap-toothed smile and nodded his head, enjoying Benni's antics. Wazza felt a pang of sorrow for this sad old man. He obviously lived alone, his cars his only love. If Tabitha was really his granddaughter, then it was a shame he didn't get more time to spend with her.

Kee tugged on Wazza's arm, pulling him aside a little. "Can we afford this?" Kee asked in a whisper, dark eyes fixed on his.

But Diesel must have the sharpest hearing known to man because he replied, "Don't worry, love. As long as the car is right for the person, then I'll only ask what you can afford to pay."

The guy sounded crazier by the minute. But it was to their advantage. Wazza had more than enough in his savings account to cover the cost. Hell, he could probably buy Kee a brand-new car, if that was what she wanted. But he also knew she wanted to be able to pay him back at some stage. She'd already said she'd pay him for everything else as soon as she got settled. And the price tag of more than a couple of thousand dollars would send her into a panic attack.

"What about this other one? The white Land Cruiser." Wazza pointed to the vehicle on the other end of the line. It looked to be an older model, not nearly as flashy; or expensive. More like what they needed.

"That's a good car, too." Diesel stroked his beard thoughtfully. "Do you wanna take a look?"

"Yes please," both Wazza and Kee said in unison.

Diesel turned to lead them down the line of cars. "Come on, Benni." Kee held her arms out for her daughter.

"I want to stay in this one," Benni pouted. "I like driving this one." And she bobbed in the seat, pretending to drive the car.

"She's fine, she can stay there for a minute," the old man called over his shoulder.

Kee wavered, unsure.

"She'll be fine for a few moments." Wazza took Kee's hand. There was no harm in letting Benni have a little fun. She was going to be stuck in a car for the next few days, at least until they got to Darwin.

"Okay. Behave yourself." Kee threw a warning glance at her daughter. They followed Diesel's bow-legged shuffle past the other cars to the one on the end. Wazza could still hear Benni talking to Dolly as they made their way to the Land Cruiser. Diesel already had the door open and Wazza took a look inside, then ushered Kee into the driver's seat; it was going to be her vehicle, after all, and she needed to approve. It was much bigger than her four-wheel-drive, but he thought she'd get the hang of it pretty quickly. He leaned in as Diesel pointed out the new radio he'd installed.

They listened as Diesel droned on and on about the upgrades he had done, and how it was practically rust-free, except for a little spot in the side roof panel. As long as the price was right, Wazza thought, this was the one.

What was that noise? Wazza lifted his head, puzzled. Kee was still sitting in the cabin, but it didn't seem like she'd heard. He was just about to tune back into the droning old man's monologue when the noise came again.

A muffled scream.

Benni.

He took two strides to the front of the car and peered down the line. Benni was no longer in the front seat of the red truck. Dolly was just visible in the passenger seat. Where was she? And why had she left Dolly? She would never leave Dolly behind.

"Benni," he exclaimed.

Kee looked at him through the windshield, a question in her eyes.

"Benni," he called again, taking a step toward the other car. A sliver of movement caught his eye, down in the long grass between the house and the river.

The figure of a man holding a struggling child appeared

briefly from behind the trunk of an old peppermint tree. It was only a split second, but it was enough.

Oh. Fuck.

Bruno.

It had to be him. He recognized the hulking shape of his shoulders and that regimental short hair.

"Kee. Bruno's got Benni," he yelled, breaking into a run. "Put her down, you fucker. You leave her alone." The other man was a good hundred meters away, close to the edge of the river. "Benni, hang on, I'm coming." His breath pounded in his chest as his long legs ate up the distance between them. He heard Kee's cry of anguish behind him, but he had no time to turn and wait for her.

The man let out a sudden yell, and dropped Benni. She took off like a startled rabbit, running fast toward the river.

"This way," he shouted. "Come to me, Benni." She was going the wrong way. If she ran toward him, he could save her. But she either didn't hear him, or was too spooked to obey. He kept running, trying to close the distance, he was now at the edge of the gravel carpark and lunged into the long grass, heedless of snakes or the large spider webs he ran through.

Bruno had taken off after Benni, swearing at the top of his lungs, which was only scaring her more. She headed straight for the little jetty that protruded into the river, then her feet were pounding down the wooden planks toward the pontoon. Where was she going? Didn't she realize it was a dead end? He put on another spurt of speed, but there was no way he was going to catch Bruno; he had too much of a head start. Bruno's heavy boots thumped onto the end of the jetty. The big man slowed to a jog, as if he knew Benni had nowhere else to go.

Wazza decided that if Benni had nowhere to go, then neither did Bruno. Perhaps it was a good thing, after all.

Suddenly Kee latched onto his hand, dragging him back, stopping his forward movement.

"We have to get to her," she screeched. "We can't let him get away. I'll never see her again."

"I know. It'll be okay." He took her by the hand and together they jogged toward the jetty.

Bruno was crooning to Benni. "Come here, lovely. It's okay. You remember me, your Uncle Bruno?"

"Get away from me," Benni screamed. She'd reached the floating pontoon at the end and looked up and down the river, searching for an escape. Reluctantly, she grabbed the gunnel of the boat—a smallish metal runabout that Diesel clearly used to do his barramundi fishing—perhaps meaning to jump in. Benni had most likely never been on a boat before and she looked back, fear evident in her eyes. "Mummy, help me."

Kee started to run forward, Wazza right behind her. Then Bruno pulled out a knife and in two strides, he'd reached Benni and grabbed her by the arm, hauling her up so that her feet dangled off the ground.

"Let me go," she yelled. "I'll—" The rest of her words were cut off as Bruno shook her like a rag doll. Then he pulled her in front of his body and put the knife to her throat.

Kee stopped dead in her tracks, right at the end of the jetty, and Wazza nearly ran into the back of her.

This was one huge shitpile of a stinking mess. *Think, Wazza. Think.* How were they going to get Benni back?

"Don't come any closer, or I'll cut her," Bruno warned.

Would he do it? Harm his own niece? Kill her? Wazza didn't know the man well enough. But Kee's gasp, and her whispered, "*Jebi ga,*" told him that perhaps he might.

"Don't hurt her," Kee pleaded.

"I won't, as long as you stay back." Benni thrashed weakly against him, until he shook her again and she went limp, staring at them with imploring eyes. Jesus, how had he let this happen? He was supposed to be protecting them. "And that means you, too, old fucker." Bruno tilted his chin to someone behind them.

Wazza turned just enough to see Diesel standing on the riverbank, a shotgun raised and pointed directly at the man and child on the pontoon. He snarled at Bruno, but said nothing. Wazza willed him not to discharge his gun, it looked as ancient as the man himself, and Diesel could just as easily hit Benni as Bruno. The old man might think he was helping, but this situation was going from bad to worse.

"Bring me the key to your boat," Bruno demanded of Diesel. He was going to use the boat as his getaway vehicle? Wazza hadn't even considered that. Bruno was standing in the corner of the pontoon, the small craft floating to the left, straining against its ropes as the river current tried to carry it away.

"I ain't getting you no key. You just put the little girl down, nice and easy, and I might not kill you."

With one arm, Bruno lifted Benni as if she were light as a feather, took two steps past the little boat, and held her out over the water, and then brought the knife to her throat again. "Bring me the key," he ground out between clenched teeth. "Or I'll cut her, and then throw her in the water."

Out of the corner of his eye, Wazza saw Diesel lower his gun. "What do you want me to do, son?" The question was directed at Wazza.

"Get him the key," Wazza replied, not taking his eyes from the man and girl in front of him. That might give them a few moments to regroup, come up with a solution.

Diesel grumbled, but turned away. "It's back at the house. Don't you do anything while I'm gone."

Not likely, Wazza thought darkly. He tried to telepathically will the old man to call the cops while he was inside. Not that they'd come in time. This nightmare would be over by the time they arrived, one way or the other.

All three stood, frozen in this bizarre standoff, afraid to move. Wazza came up with plenty of ideas, but discarded them all just as quickly. Talk seemed to be his best weapon here. If he could convince Bruno to let Benni go, then perhaps…

"Look, mate…" Wazza took a step forward and Kee's hand landed on his arm, a warning not to go any farther. "No one wants Benni hurt. Why don't you put her down and we can talk this over? What if Kee agrees to bring Benni to the nearest police station? Hands herself in? Then we can let the courts settle this?" Wazza knew Kee might disagree with him, but they had little else to bargain with at the moment.

"Nah, I don't trust the bitch," Bruno sneered. "Look how she turned traitor on her own husband. She don't deserve this little girl."

Benni gave a small whimper of terror. Wazza's heart ached for Kee's daughter, who was a picture of fear and misery, hanging like a limp kitten in Bruno's large hand. At least he'd stopped dangling her over the water and brought her back toward the pontoon. Wazza knew he would do anything for her. It was as if a piece of his soul was torn away every time she cried out. He almost thought he understood how desperate Kee must be feeling. But then, she was her mother. And she'd been prepared to do just about anything to keep her daughter by her side. So, perhaps he'd never understand the depths of a mother's love.

Kee tugged on his arm until he finally tore his gaze away from Benni and dropped his head to look at her. She stared him dead in the eye. Something in her demeanor had changed. Her shoulders were back, and her chin had come up. Defiant. That's how he'd describe her. A warrior princess. Wazza was struck by how beautiful she was in that moment.

What was she up to? He was about to ask, when she narrowed her dark eyes at him.

"You save Benni," she said emphatically. "Whatever else happens, you have to save Benni. Do you promise me?"

"What?" He had no idea what was going on in her head.

"Promise me," she ground out between clenched teeth.

"Of course, I promise, but—"

He got no further, because Kee took off at a sprint, body tilted forward, eyes fixed on her target. Bruno.

"Kee, wait—" What was she doing? How was this going to save Benni?

Kee hit Bruno full in the chest and they both went over the edge and disappeared beneath the water together.

Benni gave a yell as Bruno dropped her on the edge of the pontoon. She scrabbled to stay on her feet and, for a wonderful second, Wazza thought she'd make it. He lunged forward to grab her hand, but with a cry, she toppled into the water with a splash.

Kee. Kee was in the water with Bruno. She couldn't swim.

Benni.

Benni couldn't swim, either.

Wazza took two strides to the edge of the jetty, staring into the water, hoping for a miracle. Nothing. Not even a ripple. Where had everyone gone?

The silence was broken as something thrashed in the water. It was hard to tell, but it looked like Kee, and she was on top of Bruno, pushing him under. Then they both disappeared.

Kee. He had to save Kee. Without her, his life would be nothing. He loved her. He couldn't lose her now.

But where was Benni? Kee had made him promise.

Then suddenly, a little head surfaced for a split second, before disappearing under the water again, the current already carrying her farther downstream from where Kee and Bruno struggled just beneath the surface. He gave an animal howl of frustration. The two people he loved most in this world were in trouble. And he could only save one of them. Wazza dove in without a second's hesitation. He had no choice.

CHAPTER TWENTY

She fought him like a tiger. With everything she had. Tooth and nail. Anything to keep her daughter safe. Was Benni safe? She hoped she was standing on the pontoon with Wazza, unharmed and protected by him. But she really had no idea. All she knew was she needed to fight this man, so Wazza could get Benni away. And if she died doing it, then that would be worth the sacrifice. She *wasn't* going to let Bruno have her daughter. And she trusted Wazza to save her little girl. No matter what it took.

She'd had the element of surprise. But Bruno was a big man, and she knew his physicality would soon overcome her. She waited for the slash of the knife to come, for him to punch her, kick her, drag her down to the depths and drown her. But he did none of those things. After those first few seconds of disbelief, he thrashed around in the water, trying to get away from her. Floundering. Attempting to make it back to the pontoon.

It came as a shock to realize that Bruno couldn't swim, either.

But she'd use it to her advantage. Because her need was greater. She'd stay out here and fight until the bitter end.

Hanging on to his jacket for dear life, she towed him

backward underwater, away from the direction of the jetty. They'd been submerged for a long time now, and the urge to breathe was getting too great to ignore. She used him as a stepladder, clawing her way to the surface and gasping one bright, life-giving lungful of air, before she pushed him down again, thwarting his attempt to reach for a breath.

In that brief interlude as she raised her head for a gulp of air, she heard a commotion on the pontoon, Wazza's voice, but she had no time to see what was going on or if Benni was with him before she went down. She had faith in Wazza that he would do what she couldn't; rescue her daughter.

Bruno's struggles became weaker. The water was murky and she could barely see two feet in front of her. All of a sudden, his face was right there in front of her. Eyes wide, mouth open, bubbles leaking from his nose. Gone was the arrogant, cocky asshole with a swagger in his walk and an aura of entitlement. He looked as terrified as poor Benni when he'd held a knife to her throat, but she had no sympathy for him. He grasped at her weakly, but she pushed him away with hardly any effort. Then she watched as he drifted away from her on the underwater current.

The stream was strong, towing them steadily out to sea. Kee hadn't counted on being pushed this far away from Diesel's jetty. But then she'd never really counted on making it out of this river, either. Had Wazza mentioned something about crocodiles living in this estuary? They were found all over the Gulf Country. Kee had heard that drowning was actually quite a peaceful way to die. But being eaten by a crocodile, well, that was another matter. The thought of large gaping jaws and rows of sharp teeth had her fighting her way to the surface.

Her limbs were heavy and lethargic, her lungs bursting for air. But the sun beckoned to her, sparkling brightly through the lens of small waves above. Two more strokes and her head broke the surface, her mouth gaping as it searched for oxygen.

But she sunk straight back down beneath the waves again, and she panicked, swallowing water as she went. She hadn't been lying when she told Wazza she couldn't swim. Her parents feared the water. It wasn't something they instilled in their kids, like Australian parents did; that love of water, the way Aussies flocked to the beach. Her parents hated the beach. So, she'd never had official swimming lessons. But Jakov had taken her to the local swimming pool with him on the odd occasion—he loved to swim laps to keep fit—and while she'd been there, she'd often listened in on the children's lessons as she sat in the shallow end of the pool, with her toes in the water. The instructors had been teaching water safety as well as how to swim. And she learned that the best way to save yourself was to stop fighting and surrender. To lie on your back and let the water support you. Kee had tried it a few times in the shallow end, and found to her delight that she could indeed float.

Could she replicate that feat now, though?

Kicking her feet, she tried to get herself horizontal. Instead of thrashing her arms, she made small, swirling motions, around and around. And wonder of wonders, she floated to the surface. The first time it happened, she was so surprised, she immediately floundered and sunk like a stone again. Closing her eyes, she tried the same maneuver again, and it worked. Pushing thoughts of hungry crocodiles from her mind, she focussed on staying afloat. Small waves broke over her face, making her cough and splutter and start to sink again. God, was this going to work?

A drift of trees caught her eye. The far side of the riverbank was now closer than the one Diesel's house was on. Should she try and make for it? But every time she did more than float on her back, she began to sink again, so in the end she stopped trying. Was she going to end up out at sea? She banished that thought, as it did her no good. Her only aim was to stay alive for as long as she could. Past that, she did not know if rescue was going to come. Stay calm and controlled and let fate do the rest.

Something brushed past her arm, breaking her composed bubble. What was that? A fish? A piece of driftwood? Seaweed? A crocodile? She began to sink again. God, it was impossible to stay afloat. She was going to drown.

Her last thought was of Benni, her beautiful daughter. Wazza would look after her. Because he loved Benni. Just like he loved her.

* * *

He couldn't see her in the murky water. Couldn't find her. He'd swum to the place he'd last seen Benni's head go under, and then a little farther, allowing for the current, but she was gone. Nowhere to be found.

"Benni," he shouted uselessly, swimming in circles. Then he dove again, peering through the turbid water, trying to see things that weren't there. He surfaced again when his lungs felt fit to burst.

"Benni," he called again.

Wait. What was that? Something. A flash of pink in the brown water.

He swam hard, stroking out with long arms, going with the current, keeping his eyes fixed on that point of color.

Just as he reached it, the shape disappeared under the water, but he wasn't giving up that easily. Two more strokes took him to the spot, and he dived, down, down. Then his fist closed around a wad of pink material, and he climbed for the surface again. He had her.

"Benni." He held the little girl to his chest.

She flopped lifelessly in his arms. She wasn't breathing.

Wazza let out a sob.

"Benni. No."

Spinning in the water, he scanned the riverbank. It was around a hundred meters away. He could make it with Benni, but how many precious seconds would be wasted? But he couldn't do CPR in the water. He had to get her to dry land.

Without much hope, he turned on his back, resting Benni on his chest, and kicked for the shore.

A strange buzzing noise filled his ears. Then a boat pulled up alongside.

"Give her to me. Quick." It was Diesel in his little tinny boat.

Wazza handed his precious cargo up to the old man, and then hauled himself out of the river, nearly tipping the boat in the process. Water streamed from his soaking clothes, but he gave it no heed.

Diesel had Benni lying flat on the bottom of the boat, looking like a bedraggled pile of rags he'd drawn up from the depths.

"Let me. I know CPR." Wazza swatted the old man out of his way.

"She's got a pulse," Diesel said, clearly and calmly. "But you need to get her breathing again."

Everything seemed to come into sharp focus, moving slowly, as if Wazza were in a slow-motion movie. He could see himself as if from above, kneeling in the bottom of the boat, smoothing the hair back from Benni's face, then tipping her on her side to check her airway was clear. As if he were a robot, working on autopilot, all emotion suddenly gone. He had a job to do, and he knew if he did it right, Benni would come back to him. He checked for a pulse. It took him a few seconds to locate the artery in her neck. It was there, just as Diesel said it was, faint and thready, but there.

Her airway was clear, so he lay her on her back, gently tilted her head back, pinched her nose and administered a rescue breath. Then he waited. Counted to five and administered another rescue breath. Again and again, he did this.

"Wait." Diesel put a hand on his shoulder and they both peered down at the little girl lying in the bottom of the boat. Was she breathing on her own? It was hard to tell. He leaned in closer, listening for the hiss of air to pass over her lips. She made a small sound, something between a wheeze and a cat-like mewl. Then she gave a cough.

Wazza's heart kicked in his chest so hard he thought he'd been struck by a train.

She was alive.

"Benni," he said softly, lifting her head into his lap. "Can you hear me?"

Her eyes fluttered open, and she stared at him for moments without end. Then she tried to sit up, her head nearly colliding with his, and began to cry. Heavy sobs wracked her body, and he pulled her into his chest.

All emotion returned to him in a flood of sensations, and he found himself weeping, as well, tears falling down his cheeks. They sat like that for many seconds, Wazza holding Benni, until his tears finally stopped.

"You did a great job, son." Diesel patted him on the back and then patted Benni on the head. "You'll be okay. Both of you will be okay."

But his job wasn't done yet.

Wazza lifted his head. "Kee. We need to find Kee."

Diesel looked at him, compassion in his red-rimmed eyes. "Is she a strong swimmer, son?" Diesel looked hopeful, until Wazza shook his head. "Then, I'm not sure—"

"We need to at least look for her." Wazza stood, Benni enfolded in his arms. He had one of his women back, now he needed the other one, or his life would never be complete. Benni needed to get to hospital, to get checked over by a doctor. He knew that, but he also couldn't leave the river without looking for Kee. The small boat rocked as he moved, and Diesel ushered him to a bench seat at the front.

"Sit down, before you tip us all back in," the old man commanded. Then he clambered backward and started up the engine. The tinny surged forward as Diesel turned it to face down river, following the current. "If she's alive, she'll most likely be headed out to sea. Keep your eyes peeled," the wiry man instructed. "You watch the left bank, and I'll watch the right one. There are logs and old roots and all sorts of things sticking out into the water. If she managed to snag one of those, she might've been able to pull herself up..." Diesel trailed off, mumbling something about crocodiles to himself. Wazza didn't even dare think about those prehistoric predators.

He shaded his eyes, trying to see through the glare of the sun off the water. He'd lost his hat when he dove in, fully clothed. Benni was still cradled in one arm, but he focused on the water in front and to the left, looking for a sign, anything. She had to be alive. She had to be.

Diesel slowed the boat, and they motored down the middle of the river, searching. Around one bend, and then another. Surely, she couldn't have drifted this far?

"Over there." Benni lifted her arm and pointed. "I see something." Disbelieving, he followed the line of Benni's finger. It was the first time she'd spoken since he'd pulled her out of the water.

Wazza stared at something dark drifting in the water. He stood and placed Benni carefully on the bench seat. "Can you stay here for a second, bunny?" he asked softly.

She nodded. "Is my mummy okay?"

Wazza couldn't answer. Diesel maneuvered the boat closer to the object. Kee had been wearing blue denim shorts and a dark green T-shirt after her shower this morning. It was hard to tell if the object was a mat of green weed floating on the tide, or…

"It's her." Wazza didn't wait for the boat to stop, he dived into the water. She was floating face down.

For a moment, panic clawed at his brain. Karri had been floating face down, too. But this was different. He was going to save Kee. He had a chance to undo that terrible wrong from his past, if only he could save her. He refused to let the dread overwhelm him. Wazza reached her in under ten strokes and was pulling her back to the boat while Diesel was still shutting down the engine.

It was a lot harder to drag Kee into the boat. Diesel grabbed under the armpits, but the old man didn't have the strength in his skinny arms to bring her in by himself, so Wazza sloshed over the side like a wet seal and between the two of them, they soon had her laid out on her back in the bottom of the boat.

"Is Mummy okay?" Benni hovered beside him.

"She's going to be fine, honey." Diesel enfolded her in his arms, comforting her and holding her away so Wazza could do what needed to be done. He owed this old man a hell of a lot. Without him…Wazza didn't dare to think how he would've saved Benni. Or Kee. Because he was going to save her.

Kee's skin was cool to the touch, gorgeous lips which were normally rosy, and plump were tinged with blue. His fingers fumbled at her neck. There was no pulse this time. He gave a muffled groan as he tipped her onto her side. Water dribbled out of her mouth, but her airway was clear when he checked it. How long had she been face down? It'd been at least ten minutes since she knocked Bruno into the water. If she'd been under that whole time… How long had Karri been underwater before he found her?

No, he wasn't going there. He had a job to do, and that was

to breathe for her until they could get professional help.

Tipping her head back and pinching her nose, he gave two quick breaths into her beautiful mouth. He couldn't think about her beautiful mouth, couldn't think about kissing that mouth, feeling her warm breath on his cheek. He needed to concentrate. She was just a body, just a stranger who needed his help. Not the love of his life. Because if he let that thought creep into his psyche, then he was fucked. They were both fucked. Because he'd freak out and not be able to do what needed to be done.

He moved his hand to the center of her chest and began compressions.

"She needs help. We need a defibrillator. We have to get her to a hospital." Wazza ground the words out between chest compressions.

"Leave it with me. You just keep her alive," Diesel replied. Keeping Benni by his side, one arm wrapped around her small shoulders, he started up the boat and sent it full throttle up the river.

CHAPTER TWENTY-ONE

Wazza opened his eyes. His neck was sore as hell, and he adjusted his position slightly to try and unkink it. That's what you got when you slept in a chair half the night. A warm weight shifted slightly on his chest, and he stopped moving, not wanting to wake Benni. They'd both fallen asleep around midnight, exhaustion finally overcoming them. Benni had refused to leave his side, clung to him like a limpet on a rock. And he didn't blame her. So, he'd got as comfortable as was possible in a hospital chair and let her snuggle into his chest. Someone had draped a blanket over them both; probably that nice nurse, Peggy. That was the last thing he remembered.

Wazza rolled his head to the side so he could see Kee. She was still lying in the hospital bed, the same as last night. She hadn't moved an inch. With a tube down her throat and an IV line into her arm, she looked small and alone lying there. She was alive, but unconscious, and the doctors couldn't tell him how long she'd stay that way, or if there was any brain damage from lack of oxygen. They'd moved her from ICU to a private room late last night, which was one small mercy, because it meant he and Benni could be by her side. A pediatric doctor had come in at some stage to check on Benni, and given her the all-clear, which had relieved a little of

Wazza's stress. Benni kept asking for Dolly, but her little doll must still be sitting in the red vehicle back at Diesel's house. He tried to tell Benni that he would get Dolly back as soon as possible, but in his heart, he thought the toy was lost.

Light was sneaking in under the blinds, so it must be morning, but he had no concept of the exact time.

Aaron and Dale were flying the chopper up to Cairns this morning to be with Wazza. Be there for him as friends, as well as offer their help in any way they could. Wazza had to talk Daniella and Steve out of coming, too. They were both determined to be there. But after Wazza had appealed to Dale, he'd helped him talk them into letting Dale go, instead. He didn't want Kee to be overwhelmed when she woke up and he'd feel guilty if they dropped everything at Stormcloud to come and sit by her bedside. Because she was going to wake up. She was.

Wazza had called Steve late last night to tell him what'd happened. After the initial shock, Steve had gathered Daniella, Dale, and Julie around and put him on speakerphone, so they could come up with a plan. It made him so grateful that he had a boss and a team of friends who he could count on, who had his back through thick and thin. He found it impossible to communicate his appreciation properly, but he hoped they all understood how much they meant to him.

Yesterday was a blur of mixed emotions and fragments of images. He could hardly remember Diesel driving into the main dock of Karumba, screaming that they needed a doctor. Or the locals staring at them, fishing poles forgotten, until they scrambled up and ran to find the local GP and grab the defibrillator from its spot on the wall near the amenities block. He was still performing CPR on Kee, even though his arms were like leaden weights, and his shoulders felt like they were about to dislocate from his body.

Wazza had never used a defib machine, but he'd kept his nerve and followed the instructions as the robotic voice intoned its commands.

He had to do it twice, but the defibrillator was what'd eventually brought Kee back to him. At first, he could hardly believe what the machine was telling him; a pulse had been detected. He'd hovered over her face, placing his cheek close to her mouth, and had heard her shallow intake of breath. And then her equally shallow exhale.

Then a man had jumped into the boat and pushed him out of the way. "I'm a doctor," he'd said and so Wazza let him take over, waiting until the doctor confirmed his own diagnosis, that she was breathing on her own.

Then he'd grabbed the gunnel and retched over the side of the boat.

Afterward, Diesel told him it'd only taken them around five minutes to get up the river to town, but Wazza was sure it'd taken them five hours.

Once Kee was stable, the GP had called for the flying doctor to airlift her to Cairns, the closest hospital with an ICU.

Wazza had been prepared for a fight with the pilot, because he wasn't letting them go without taking Benni; she needed to be checked by a doctor as well, and she needed to be by her mother's side. But they'd surprised him by offering both him and Benni a seat on the airplane. Benni had sat in his lap the for the entire flight, which was over two hours, refusing to take her own seat, no matter how gently the nurses tried to cajole her. Wazza wasn't surprised. After everything that little girl had been through, he was the only solid thing she had left to cling to. She also refused to look at Kee, lying on the stretcher, hooked up to all kinds of machines. Wazza didn't push her on that, either, after she muttered, "That's not my mummy," quietly into his ear. He could understand what

Benni was feeling, because even in his grown-up mind, he hardly accepted that the motionless, pale woman was Kee. That wasn't the vibrant, beautiful woman he knew.

He glanced over at her again with a frown. *Please wake up, Kee*, he implored.

The door opened, and a nurse bustled in. "Good morning," she said brightly.

Wazza didn't recognize this woman. Benni twitched on his chest and then sat up suddenly.

"Hello, gorgeous." The nurse came over and bent down so she was at Benni's level. "Did you have a good sleep? Your daddy's taking good care of you, isn't he?"

Wazza didn't correct her, he merely sat up straighter in the chair, stretching out his legs with a groan.

"Is Mummy awake yet?" Benni asked, clambering down over Wazza's long legs.

"Not yet, honey, but she will be soon, don't you worry. This one is a fighter, I can tell."

"Really?"

"Really."

Wazza wasn't sure if the nurse's optimism was a good thing, or not. Should they be giving Benni false hope?

"Why don't you take your daughter and grab some breakfast down in the cafeteria," the nurse said with a kindly lift of her eyebrow.

"Sure." It was probably a good idea, although he doubted he'd be able to eat anything, but he needed to take care of Benni.

He had lots of things to do this morning. Top on his list was contacting Kee's parents. They needed to know what'd happened, and perhaps they'd even want to come up and be by their daughter's bedside. He could make some phone calls while Benni ate breakfast.

There was also the dilemma of what to do with Benni.

Last night, he hadn't let himself think about the future, about what might happen if Kee didn't wake up. But in the cold morning light, he knew he needed to at least consider the option.

He loved Benni like she was his own daughter, and he'd keep her safe and by his side for as long as he could. Hell, he'd adopt her in a heartbeat, if it came to that. But he understood that's not how the world worked. There was a custody battle with Jakov's parents to be faced. For a fleeting second, he considered taking Benni and fleeing back into the bush, so Jakov and his family couldn't get hold of her. That'd cause more problems than it solved, however, and he discarded that idea fairly quickly.

And there were also Kee's parents, who sounded like they wanted to be involved with Benni's life now that they'd reconnected. Kee's parents were the obvious people to take custody of Benni if anything happened to Kee, they were her closest kin. But poor Benni had never met her maternal grandparents. Wazza didn't think she'd take kindly to being shipped off to live with people she barely knew.

His heart ached for the little girl, who was now standing on tiptoe to look out the window at the ocean, as the nurse pointed out the beach below. All he wanted was for her to be happy. All he wanted was for Kee to wake up.

Moving to the side of her bed, he hesitantly raised his arm and stroked the hair back from her forehead. Her face was devoid of any color; her warm, brown skin was now washed out, and almost translucent. He dropped his arm and let his hand come to rest over the top of hers, which lay motionless on the bedclothes beside her.

"Come back to me, Kee," he whispered. "Please."

She lay calm and peaceful, like an unruffled lake. Had she even heard him?

With a sigh, he turned to collect Benni, when a finger

twitched beneath his hand.

"Kee?" He leaned in close, watching her face for any sign. "Can you hear me?" Her whole hand shuddered. Was she finally waking up? One of the monitors started to beep, loud and insistent.

"What's going on?" The nurse was at his shoulder in an instant.

"I'm not sure, but…" he gasped as Kee's eyes fluttered open. "Kee?" he said again, this time with wonder. The nurse took one quick look at Kee and punched a red button beside the bed. Then she leaned in to check Kee's IV line, pushing Wazza out of the way. But he didn't want to leave. Could this be true?

Benni pulled on his trouser leg. "Mr. Cowboy, what's going on?" She turned her fearful gaze up to him, tears swimming at the corners of her eyes. All Wazza wanted to do was hold Kee's hand, look into her gorgeous, brown eyes, and welcome her back. But he couldn't ignore Benni.

Reaching down, he scooped her up into his arms, and took a step back, just as two more nurses rushed into the room, quickly followed by a young doctor.

"What are they doing to Mummy? They're hurting her," Benni wailed, and Wazza drew her in and comforted her.

"It's okay, bunny. They're helping her. It's going to be okay." Wazza soothed the little girl as she sobbed into his neck. But he was nearly as shocked at Benni, as he watched a nurse draw out the intubation tube from Kee's throat.

Wazza was just wondering whether he should take Benni out of the room, away from the action that was upsetting her, when he heard a voice, raspy and hesitant from the tube, but still familiar.

"Benni? Where are you? I need to see my little girl."

Wazza shoved a nurse aside in his hurry to get to Kee's bedside. "Here. She's here."

"You saved her." Tears were streaming down Kee's face. She held out her arms for her daughter and Wazza ignored the doctor's protests, and placed Benni gently on the bed next to Kee.

"Of course, I did," he replied. "Did you doubt me?" He tried to make a joke, but she'd have none of it.

"Not for a second," she replied, deadly serious, voice still hoarse and frail. Then her focus shifted, and Kee stared into Benni's face. "Hi, my love."

"Hi, Mummy," Benni gave a watery smile, then rested her head on her mother's shoulder. The nurses continued to fuss around Kee, but she ignored them, concentrating only on her daughter. Soaking her in. Smoothing her hair with a gentle hand.

Finally, Kee's gaze came up to meet his. "Thank you," she said.

But she had no need to thank him, because this was the outcome he'd been praying for. He'd only done what needed to be done because of her. And because of Benni. There had been no other option, he would rather have stopped breathing himself, than to see either of them die. It was simple, really. Love made things simple.

Two of the nurses hustled out of the room, leaving the doctor and the nurse who had first entered this morning.

"It's nice to see you awake, Ms. Singh." The doctor was using his officious tone as he pried one of Kee's arms away from Benni's shoulders so he could take her blood pressure. "I need to ask you some questions and make sure you're okay." In other words, to make sure there were no long-term effects of her near drowning. "Do you mind if we...?" he started to reach for Benni, clearly meaning to remove her from the bed, while he ran his tests. Kee's eyes turned glacial, her mouth firming into a thin line as she subtly shook her head. There was no way she was letting go of Benni any time soon. Even though she'd just awoken from a near-death experience, there was one thing that would never change about Kee. Her devotion to her daughter, the way she would protect her without thought for herself. She was a lioness. Bold, courageous, and beautiful.

"That's fine, Ms Singh. We can work around you both, if that's what you'd like."

"Good," was all Kee said.

The doctor took up Kee's file from the end of the bed and began listing the tests he wanted the nurse to carry out. A blood test for this, a lung function thingamabob, an MRI scan for that.

Wazza ignored the medical professionals, he had eyes only for Kee.

"I love you," she mouthed to him over the top of the doctor's head, and his heart felt like it might explode.

* * *

"You have three cracked ribs from the resuscitation, which might take weeks to heal. And we need to keep you in to monitor you for the next few days, because you had water in your lungs." The doctor looked at her through his glasses, which were half-way down his nose. The doctor was young and quite good-looking, in a nerdy kind of way. She didn't care what he said, what tests she had to endure, or even how long she had to spend in hospital. She was alive, and so was her daughter, and that was all that mattered.

Well, not quite all.

Wazza mattered. She couldn't bear to think of her life without him in it.

They hadn't had a moment to themselves all day. What, with the doctors poking at her, the nurses fussing over her, and the police conducting a bedside interview—that'd been a little scary, but she'd told them the truth, now it was up to them to unravel the tangled web of lies and deceit that Bruno and Jakov and the Babić family had woven around her—all she wanted was a few moments alone with Wazza.

He was grinning at her from his spot in the chair in the corner, long legs stretched out in front, looking all gorgeous and dreamy. She willed him to get up and come over to the bed so she could kiss him. It was now late afternoon, and apart from the time he'd taken Benni down to the cafeteria for lunch, he'd sat there with her all day, refusing to leave the room.

"What? Sorry, I wasn't really listening," she admitted to the young doctor. She knew she was probably grinning like an idiot, but she no longer cared.

He glared down his nose. "This is serious, Ms. Singh. You nearly died." Oh, she was well aware of that fact. Well aware that she could've drowned; a few more seconds, and she might've disappeared under the water, and Benni may never have spotted her. She'd been given another chance. And she intended to make the most of her second opportunity in life. Starting with that big hunk of a cowboy still grinning at her from the corner.

"Yes, I know." She added what she hoped was a slightly pathetic sigh. "But I'm feeling really tired. Would you mind terribly coming back later to do…" She did not know what sort of test he'd been droning on about, and so she ended with a slight shrug.

The doctor—his badge said Dr. Carmichael—lifted his eyebrows, then lowered them again and turned to face Wazza. "You really need to impress on your wife how important these tests are," he said, before turning on his heel and stalking out of the room. Kee squashed a giggle. All the doctors and nurses were under some kind of delusion that she and Wazza were married. But she wasn't about to set them right because she quite liked the idea.

They both watched the doctor's back as he closed the door

behind him. As soon as he was gone, she ripped the oxygen mask off her face. "I thought he'd never leave," she sighed, lying back on her pillows and beckoning to Wazza. It was the first time they'd been alone all day. She needed to feel his arms around her. Needed to lay her head on his chest so she could hear his strong heartbeat beneath her ear.

She shuffled over, making room for Wazza to get on the bed, wincing slightly as her broken ribs twinged with the movement. His brow furrowed, and she could see he was about to refuse, worried because she'd removed her mask and afraid that he'd hurt her in some way. The only way he'd hurt her was by *not* getting on the bed. She wanted to yell at him to stop treating her like she was made of spun glass. She was as strong as an ox; she'd survived a fight to the death with Bruno, and then she'd survived the raging currents of the Norman River. She could survive anything.

Carefully, he lay on the bed beside her, tucking his arm under her shoulders, so she could use his bicep to rest her head and stretching his long legs out beside hers. The heat of his big body seeped into her, and her pulse jumped as his thigh spooned hers. He was still wearing the clothes he'd had on yesterday—all their stuff was still out at Diesel's place—and he was looking slightly rumpled and disheveled. But she didn't care. He smelled remarkable, like the ocean, slightly musky, just like Wazza. Snuggling into his embrace, she nuzzled his neck.

She let out a long sigh of contentment. *This* was what she'd been dreaming of. *This*, she could do all day. And all night.

"How long do you reckon we have?" she asked quietly.

Wazza knew exactly what she meant, because he gave a light shrug, and said, "Maybe half an hour." Dale and Aaron had taken Benni out for a gelato cone around an hour ago. Kee had watched them go, the two men towering over her little girl, each holding her hand as she chatted happily to them. Her heart had nearly exploded at the sight. The two men had arrived early this morning, just after Kee had woken up. But the nurse at reception wouldn't let them into her room at first, so they'd sat out in the waiting room for over an hour, until the nice nurse, Penny, had mentioned she had visitors, and she'd demanded they let them in.

They'd crept warily into the room, unsure what they'd find. But Benni had leapt on them with delight, so happy to see familiar faces. Aaron had flown them up in the station chopper and they'd been prepared for the worst, as last they'd heard, Kee had still been unconscious. Dale had surged forward, eager to hug Kee and tell her how happy he was to see her awake, while the more serious Aaron had hung back and chatted with Wazza, tilting his chin and giving her a thumbs-up.

"But I'd be more worried about that doctor coming back. Or one of the nurses. They don't seem to believe you when you say you're feeling great," Wazza continued.

"But I am feeling great," she implored. "I've never felt more alive. These broken ribs will heal, all these scratches and bruises will heal, and my lungs are going to be fine. I have the rest of my life left to look forward to. And I have you and Benni. Everything is perfect."

Wazza's brow furrowed again. "But we still have to get through the custody thing, and what if they—?"

"They won't," she said, with finality. "Everything will work out. I just know it." And she did know, she had a feeling in her bones that it would all end well. What she wasn't telling Wazza was that she'd had a sort of epiphany while she'd been floating on her back down the river. If she ever made it out alive, she vowed she'd never take life for granted again. She'd vowed to stop running and meet life head-on. She didn't believe in God, but something had infused her with whole-hearted gratitude, as well as a clear certainty that she would be fine, as would Benni.

"Kiss me," she demanded, tipping her head up so she could look into his face. The muscle of his bicep pillowing her cheek was solid and, oh, so warm. Lifting a hand, she traced the line of his jaw, delighting in the rough scrape of his stubble against her fingertips. Then she let it drift down to rest on his ribs, reveling in the feel of his expansive chest.

Blue eyes sparked to indigo, and her breath caught in her throat. "Well, if you insist," he finally drawled. At first his lips were hesitant, but her tongue darted out to meet his and she drew him in, wanting to inhale him, inhale everything about him. His mouth was warm and enticing, and heat flared in her veins. He angled his head so his lips could latch tighter onto hers, suddenly greedy and demanding.

"I've been dreaming of doing this all day," she sighed into his mouth. Her fingers tunneled through his hair and down his muscular neck to his broad shoulders.

"Me too," he admitted, drawing her in tighter. So tight her ribs complained, but she ignored them. She understood everything he was afraid to say out loud in that embrace. Every heightened emotion, every second of fear as he pulled her into the boat and then breathed life back into her. She understood he'd been terrified he might lose her. And that he was so glad to have her back. He didn't need to speak the words, because she felt exactly the same. He put his lips back on hers and she got lost for seconds without end in the carnal pull of him.

There was one thing that did need to be conveyed by more than mere physical embrace, however. Something he needed to hear.

She tilted her head back slightly, releasing his mouth, waiting until he opened his eyes and took her in. "In case it wasn't clear this morning, I'm in love with you."

His clear, blue eyes studied her. Wazza had already told

her he was falling in love with her. But she was suddenly hoping he'd say it again, just to be sure. Had she jumped the gun? Had his feelings changed? Wazza was a complicated man, with complicated emotions. She hoped his sleep-deprived brain hadn't suddenly come up with some reason he couldn't be with her.

"I love you, too," he said simply. "You are my lioness. Brave and beautiful."

Her eyes filled with sudden tears. He thought she was a lioness? Her heart swelled with emotions until it was enormous, felt like it was too big to fit into her chest. The past few weeks had been hell on earth, but with one bright, shining light showing her the way; Wazza. She loved him so much, it hurt.

He cradled her face in his big hands and kissed her. Gently, tenderly, and her heart ached with the exquisiteness of it.

CHATPER TWENTY-TWO

Kee shifted her weight from one foot to the other. She might've turned away and run back up to the lodge if Wazza didn't have his strong arm around her shoulders, steadying her. She'd thought she was ready for this, but all of a sudden, she was having doubts. What was she going to say to them? Would they even recognize her after all this time? Perhaps she should've chosen a dress for today, instead of her usual casual denim shorts and tank top.

The downdraft of the helicopter coming in to land shook the branches in the trees surrounding the helipad, so that leaves rained down on them like confetti. Kee held Benni's hand tighter and pulled her face into her thighs to protect her from the dust and other flying debris, remembering to grab Benni's blue hat before it was swept off her head. She shielded her own face in Wazza's shoulder, her loose hair whipping around both of them like flailing tentacles. He grabbed his hat with his other hand to stop it from flying off.

Daniella and Steve stood behind them, but the rest of the Stormcloud crew had diplomatically decided to wait up at the lodge; give Kee a chance to reunite with her parents in relative peace.

Then the helicopter was on the ground, the blades already

slowing as Aaron opened his door and hopped out, going around to the rear door to help the passengers disembark. Kee straightened her back and plastered on a smile. Two weeks staying at Stormcloud had worked wonders for her cracked ribs and compromised lungs. She was almost back to normal now, thanks to Daniella and Steve's kindness, insisting that she come to the station to recuperate.

"They're here, they're here," Benni squeaked excitedly, putting her hat back on her head. She'd practically lived in that hat since they'd returned to Stormcloud. Steve had rescued it from the vehicle after Wazza had abandoned it at Lefty's and kept it safe for her.

God, Kee hoped her parents didn't disappoint her daughter, she was so looking forward to meeting them. Kee had explained to Benni that she had more grandparents that she'd never met before. Kee had meant to tell her earlier, she really had. She'd made the decision while they'd been in Karumba, but things had gone so terribly wrong, so quickly, she'd never had the chance. But in the past two weeks, as Kee recovered, she'd told Benni about her Indian heritage and how nani and dadi and Aunty Pooja couldn't wait to meet her.

Then her mother was ducking beneath the blades, shuffling to meet the small group arranged around the helipad. She was dressed in a bright-orange sari that sparkled in the sunlight, long hair pulled back into a braid that ran down her back. There were gray hairs that hadn't been there before and her face was softer, slumped somehow. Her mother was old. The idea hit Kee like a sledgehammer. She could see her father exiting behind her mother, his cream linen robes flapping in the wind, and Pooja waving to her even while she was still in the helicopter. Her family was here.

Kee ran to her mother, arms outstretched. The look of

confusion cleared from her mother's face. "Keiyona, my beautiful one," she said, welcoming her embrace, and it was as if the last six years had never existed. She was back in her mother's arms. The familiar smell of cloves and spice and the faintest whiff of mothballs encased Kee, taking her back to her childhood. Kee suddenly, stupidly, felt like crying.

Pooja cannonballed into them, embracing Kee from the other side, so she was cocooned by her sister and mother, and Kee didn't even mind that they were crushing her sore ribs. Unexpectedly, they were all crying, sobbing on each other's shoulders. Kee was the first one to pull herself together.

Her father stood awkwardly a few feet away. "Keiyona." He nodded formally, his long mustache swaying. "Nice to see you again." That stubborn pride was still his greatest flaw. Still holding him apart from them all.

"Come here, you silly old man," her mother said through her tears. After a moment's hesitation, when Kee thought he might refuse, his face seemed to collapse in on itself and he moved toward them, taking Kee's hand in his and stroking the back of it gently. No words were needed as he stared into her eyes. Just like that, they were all forgiven.

Kee lifted her head and saw Wazza staring at them uncomfortably, Benni holding his hand. She beckoned them over.

Wazza removed his hat, wonder of all wonders, but hung back and let her introduce Benni to her new family first. Benni was suddenly shy and needed to be coaxed out from behind Kee's legs.

But her mother got down on her knees, disregarding the fact that the dust and prickles might ruin her beautiful sari, and held out her hand. "I dreamed about you, my little granddaughter," she whispered softly. "I dreamed about meeting you. You are so much taller than I thought." Her mother gave a joyful smile that lit up her face. "You're going to be much taller than your mother, yes? And I dreamed about how much fun we would have together."

Benni left the safety of Kee's legs and drifted toward her nani, as if mesmerized by her words. "I'm going to be taller than mummy?" she asked, glancing up at Kee.

"Of course, you are." Nani opened her arms and Benni slipped into them as if it were the most natural thing in the world to do.

Kee's tears started anew as she listened to her mother crooning all her soft endearments to Benni. All this time she'd thought they'd forgotten about her, shut her out of their lives. But all it took was one phone call.

Pooja also got down onto her knees—thankfully, she was dressed in more modern, appropriate clothes of jeans and a dark tank top—and added, "And I'm your auntie, and I've been waiting such a long time to meet you."

"You're Aunty Pooja," Benni said delightedly. "Mummy told me about you."

"Yes, I am." Pooja clapped her hands with pleasure. "And I hope she said nice things about me."

"Oh, yes, she did," Benni replied, serious now. Then she glanced up and saw her grandfather looking down at the little group clustered on the ground. "And you must be my dadi," she said with a little frown. Kee held her breath, wondering how her father would respond.

For the second time that day, her father did something shocking. He got down on one knee in the red dirt and looked at Benni earnestly. "I *am* your dadi," he replied. "And I am very, very happy to meet you."

"That's good," Benni said simply. Then she took a step toward her grandfather and tugged on his mustache. "You must've been growing this for a very long time," she said, awestruck. They all erupted into gales of laughter.

Kee wanted to introduce them to Wazza, but they were so

enraptured by Benni that she didn't have the heart to break into their little cluster of family bliss. She glanced bemusedly between him and her family. He shook his head and indicated it was okay, mouthing at her to leave them be. But she wanted them to meet the man who'd saved her and Benni. The man she was in love with. The man she wanted to spend the rest of her life with. Without him, there would be no family reunion. Hat still in one hand, he moved up and draped an arm around Kee's shoulders. She snuggled into his solid warmth, soaking in his dependable presence, and watching her small family reunion with a feeling of great contentment.

It was Benni who finally broke the bubble, by glancing up and spotting Wazza and Kee together. "Oh, you have to meet Wazza, too. He's a real live cowboy." She said the last part with such pride, Kee felt like her heart would burst.

Kee's dad was the first to get to his feet. Holding out his hand, he asked, "You're the young man who helped Kee and Benni? Who rescued them out of that river?"

"Yes, sir." Wazza returned her father's handshake, meeting his gaze with his own steady, blue one.

"Well, you deserve my absolute debt of gratitude. Thank you." Vijay squared his shoulders, but he was still no match for Wazza's height. "I wish..." Her father stopped and cleared his throat. Today was just full of surprises. "But no, that is in the past now. All we can do is move on. And I'm very glad you helped make this happen." Vijay waved his arm at Benni, still snugged up to her grandmother's knee, giggling at something she'd said. "This is the worst and the best thing that has happened to this family."

Wazza seemed stumped for how to reply, but Kee's sister stood and moved closer to Wazza.

"I can see why he stole your heart," Pooja said, an appreciative grin lighting up her face. "A mighty fine specimen of a cowboy you have here." She nudged Kee on the shoulder.

"Pooja," Kee exclaimed, surprised.

"Just stating the truth," her sister fired back, lifting a suggestive eyebrow in Wazza's direction. "Got any more good-looking cowboys hidden away up here?"

Kee goggled at Pooja. She could hardly believe her sister's brazenness; something had changed in her over the past few years. She needed to get all the minute details of her sister's life over the past six years, but after a quick glance at Pooja's hand, she could see no wedding band. Which meant what? Perhaps Pooja hadn't taken up the arranged marriage her parents had organized, after all. Maybe that was why her sister was now glancing appreciatively at both Aaron and Wazza. She was looking for a man of her own to fall in love with.

"Why don't we all take this up to the lodge?" Daniella spoke for the first time, breaking the awkward tension with her easy manner. "It's much cooler up there, and we have drinks and food, and a place where you can all sit down and get reacquainted."

"Great idea," Wazza agreed, reaching for Kee's hand. He was obviously still a little out of his depth with her family.

After Kee hurriedly introduced Steve and Daniella, they all nodded in agreement and followed Wazza and Kee as they lead the group up the hill.

"I'll help Aaron with the bags," Steve called out, as he jogged over to the chopper, where Aaron still waited and watched.

The next few hours were full of blissful, happy talk, as they all caught up on so many years lost. Everyone was there, filling the tables in the great hall with their talk. It was just after lunchtime at the lodge, but Daniella had suspended all activities for the afternoon, telling the guests they had some *free time*, so all the crew could be there to support Kee and Benni. Dale and Daisy sat with their heads together, chatting to Skylar and Nash, who sat opposite them at the table. Kee could hardly believe that Skylar had taken an hour off working in the kitchen to gather with the crew. Julie told her it was almost unheard of. But then she mentioned it was probably Nash's doing, he was always subtly pushing her to take more time to just enjoy life.

Daisy's brother, River, was also there. If Kee wasn't mistaken, he looked less withdrawn than the last time she'd seen him, his face lit up in an animated smile at something Daisy said to him. Dale had mentioned that River might take up a job offer from Daisy's mining company, and he was moving up to the Koongarra Station to live amongst the indigenous community in a few weeks' time, when a house became available. This place seemed to work wonders on everyone it touched, her included.

Pooja was sitting at the end of the table talking to Alek and Bindi. She kept leaning over and touching Alek's arm, which made Kee narrow her eyes. She needed to warn Pooja away from Alek. She could see why Pooja was keen on him, with his high Slavic cheekbones and stylish man-bun. But he had eyes only for Sasha, and Pooja wouldn't know that Alek was only being polite by not pulling away from her advances.

Julie and Aaron were talking to her parents over in a corner, seated on two comfy couches, Julie waving her arms around in great circles that made Kee think she was telling one of her larger-than-life tales again. By the look on her mother's face, eyes getting wider, her hand coming up to cover her mouth, she was probably right. Benni sat on Dadi's knee, laughing at Julie's story, blue hat pulled down, in an imitation of the way Wazza wore his. She hoped Julie wasn't scaring her parents off from station life too much.

Kee had convinced Benni to leave Winnie, their new

puppy, up in the shed with Kali and the other puppies. She thought a puppy might be too much for her parents to handle right at the moment. And Daniella didn't like animals in the lodge, either. Although she made an exception for Benni's new dog. Benni said the fat, roly-poly puppy looked like Winnie the Pooh and the name had stuck.

When Steve had presented the idea of giving one of Kali's puppies to Kee, her automatic reaction had been to refuse, at first. Kee still had no idea where she was going to live, or where they were going to end up. But her epiphany in the river made her take a deep breath and squash her initial response. She'd promised Benni a puppy, and here was Steve handing her one with an open heart. So, she'd agreed. And they'd all gone up to the shed and watched while Benni was told the good news. She knew exactly which one she wanted. A little girl, the fattest one of the bunch, with soft, brown eyes and a dark-brown coat. The puppy was still too young to be properly weaned, and Kee was secretly glad she didn't have to put up with puppy piddle all over her floor, and hours of midnight whining just yet, although that was all to come.

Daniella wandered over to where Kee was standing next to the bar, refilling glasses of water for her parents.

"You look happy," she said, smoothing back a non-existent loose hair in her immaculate bob. "Things seem to be going well with your family."

Her mother had already whispered into Kee's ear how much she loved Daniella's outfit. *"So classy and chic,"* Ritika had muttered, which meant she liked Daniella, but was somewhat intimidated by her, and Kee didn't blame her.

"Yes," Kee replied with a sigh of gratitude. But then that buzz of guilt tickled her stomach. Once again, Daniella and Steve were going above and beyond anything Kee had ever expected. Not only had they let Kee stay in the same cabin as before, so she had somewhere to recuperate from her injuries, but it'd been Daniella's idea to invite her family up, and she insisted they stay free of charge.

"I don't know how we can ever repay you," she began.

Daniella held up her hand. "You don't need to repay us, Kee." Her serious, gray gaze zeroed in on her. "You make Wazza happy. That's more than enough, in my books. For the past two years, after Karri died, he's been stumbling around in a sort of half-lived daze, keeping all those emotions bottled up, thinking none of us realized what was really going on with him. We've all been terribly worried about him. But then you came along, and it's as if you woke him up. You deserve our gratitude, not the other way around."

"Oh...uh..." Kee didn't know what to say. She'd never thought about it quite like that.

"Stop worrying," Daniella instructed her, softening her demand with a swift hug. Daniella's show of warmth made Kee's chest expand. "You're part of the family now, whether you like it or not." Then Daniella was off into the crowd, telling Alek at the top of her voice that she hoped he had a good movie lined up to show at the outdoor theater tonight.

Oh, wow. Kee had to hold back tears. Again. What was happening to her today? This was the third time she'd felt teary in the space of only a few hours.

Wazza wandered up, just as Kee wiped away a stray tear. "You okay?" he asked, wrapping his arms around her waist.

"Fine," she said, smiling up at him. "It's been a bit of an emotional day for me, that's all."

"I bet," he drawled, in that slow molasses voice that made her insides flip over. It dragged her back to memories of last night. Her and Wazza together. Dale and Daisy had offered to babysit Benni; Daisy had laughingly said it'd be good practice for Dale for when they had children of their own, much to his pretend horror. They'd had the whole night to themselves. Wazza had brought a picnic dinner to her cabin, but in the end, they'd hardly touched the food. She'd been too hungry for something else. For him. Her ribs had finally healed enough, so that she enjoyed every second of the attention he paid to her body. And her skin still buzzed at the thought of his muscular arms and gentle fingers stroking, turning her insides to molten lava.

"It's okay to be emotional," Wazza said, dragging her mind away from their erotic night. "I learned that the hard way. Bottling things up doesn't help, not in the long run. You went through a horrible time, Kee. And you made it through because you were smart, and strong and determined. But it's okay to lean on other people sometimes, as well."

"I know." She nuzzled his neck.

"I'm looking forward to our new adventure together. Just the three of us," he whispered into her hair.

And this was part of the reason she loved Warwick Nobles so deeply, because he loved her with all his heart, but he also loved Benni, without reservation, and without prejudice. He was a special man; one in a million, and she could hardly believe she'd been lucky enough to find him. Her life looked pretty much perfect now.

CHAPTER TWENTY-THREE

Wazza let his lips brush Kee's. A chaste kiss because her parents were watching, and not at all how he was feeling inside. He wanted to grab her around the waist and haul her up his chest, press their bodies together and drag her mouth up to his so he could taste her. Like they'd done last night. Last night would live in his memory as one of the best nights of his life; along with the night spent under the stars. Her stripped naked, watching him from the bed with dark, dark eyes as he slowly removed his jeans was an image that would stay with him for a long time. The way she'd pulled him to her, wrapped her legs around him and whispered his name into his ear as he'd plunged into her. She was the most beautiful woman he'd ever met. She was his true north. She and Benni were his reason to look forward to a bright future.

Kee regretfully disentangled his arms from around her waist. "I'd better take my parents their drinks."

"Yes," he agreed, watching her hips sway as she walked away. She glanced back once over her shoulder, eyes burning with a promise of what was to come tonight. He was grateful to Dale and Daisy for giving them the night to themselves, but from now on, they were going to have to find a way to make love with Benni in the house. He was going to have to get over his discomfort at knowing that Benni was asleep in the next room. She already seemed to have accepted him wholeheartedly, that he was there to stay. So, he needed to do the same.

Kee had finally told Benni that her father, Jakov, was in jail because he'd done bad things. Benni being Benni, she'd wanted to know all the details, how long was he in jail for, would they go and visit him and what bad things had he done? Kee answered as truthfully as she dared, telling her as much as a four-year-old could handle, because in the end Jakov was still her father. Benni had considered it all with a thoughtful frown, then she'd changed the topic and asked Kee if she still loved Daddy. Kee had told her the truth about that one, too. That while she and Jakov would always love Benni, they no longer loved each other. Then Benni had surprised Kee—that little girl was full of wisdom beyond her age—by saying that was okay, because now Kee could love Wazza instead. And Kee had agreed.

Wazza looked over to where Benni sat on her grandfather's knee as he leaned in and whispered something into her ear. Benni had taken to her new grandparents straight away. But that was Benni, so trusting, so unreserved, which made people open up to her joyfulness in return. His eye was caught by the bright-orange of Ritika's sari. It was beautiful, and Wazza could imagine Kee wearing something similar. It was a stark reminder of Kee and Benni's heritage, which Wazza had almost forgotten now that he'd become so familiar with Kee and her daughter. He never saw the color of her skin, never thought of her as any different. He made up his mind to discover more of the Hindu culture, learn about their festivals and their foods, their beliefs and way of life. It was a matter of respect for her heritage.

Which reminded him, he needed to call his mother. Arrange a visit for him and Kee and Benni down to the family orchard. His parents would approve of Kee. How could they not like a woman who was strong and wilful and whom he loved with all of his heart?

As he watched the interplay between grandfather and granddaughter, a sudden image popped into his head and he almost gasped. It was Ava. She was waving at him from across the room, smiling and holding up a pink everlasting daisy in her pudgy little hand. He hadn't thought of Ava or Karri in a while. He remembered back to the day, right before he'd found Kee and Benni at the bore, when he'd been talking to Ava as he drove. He now realized he'd only been half-alive back then. Half a man, the other half stuck grieving for a wife and child that would never be. Now he was complete. Ava smiled at him again and toddled off behind the leather lounge. Wazza wondered if he'd ever see her again. He'd never forget his little girl. But now with Kee… They hadn't discussed more children yet, of course, that was something to think about in the future. But Kee had looked at him yesterday, a cryptic twinkle in her eye, and said that Benni had told her she'd like a sister to play with. "Soon, please, Mummy. Because Wazza will make a good daddy, and I want to share him with my sister." And she'd told Benni that she was right, Wazza would make a good daddy, and that maybe they would think about it. But Benni was more than enough for him right now.

There was a commotion over at the table where most of the Stormcloud staff were sitting. Nash stood up and clinked his glass to get everyone's attention. He was wearing his police uniform, as he was still technically on duty and had taken an hour to come and be with his family before he went back to the office in town. A hush settled over the room.

"I have some good news, I think you'll want to hear," Nash announced. A tingle ran through Wazza. He hoped this was the news they'd all be waiting to hear.

"The custody case has formally been dropped." Nash raised his glass, and everyone clapped. Then Nash turned to face Kee. "You were right, Kee. Those claims your husband's family made about you have been proven to be false. Asking the court to analyze your hair to prove there were never any drugs in your system was a smart move. That's when their case really fell apart. They had no right to file that custody suit, and all parental rights have been returned to you."

Kee rushed to sweep Benni off her father's knee, twirling her around and around. Benni squealed with delight, even though she had no real understanding of what Nash had just said. Kee had kept from her the fact that her paternal grandparents were trying to take her away. They were pretty sure this would be the outcome, but it was great to have it confirmed. The courts hadn't looked kindly on the method Kee had chosen—kidnapping her own daughter—but they also understood she was doing it to protect her daughter and so they'd applied leniency to her kidnapping charge. She'd been given a suspended sentence and would need to carry out two hundred hours of community service work in lieu of incarceration. Kee was ecstatic with the sentence, as she'd half been expecting to go to jail. But the judge decided it was more important that she be at home to bring up her daughter. The judge had decreed the community service be carried out at a halfway house for single mothers who had nowhere left to go. It was a sobering thought, and Wazza knew Kee would find it hard to cope with the other women's despair and heartbreak, but the judge was trying to teach her a lesson in humility, he guessed.

Kee had spent many long hours at the police station in Cairns, giving evidence. Wazza had also been grilled, as had Steve and Daniella. They'd even flown Diesel down to interview him. Nash had described him as a very helpful witness. The old man was still dressed in his greasy overalls and baseball cap when Wazza had run into him in the hallway of the police station.

"I hope that little girl of yours is okay," Diesel had said.

"She's doing great, thanks to you." Wazza had slapped him on the back. He owed this man a debt of gratitude, if it hadn't been for him and his boat... The kindness of strangers, sometimes that idea still overwhelmed him. Then, from some deep pocket within his overalls, Diesel had produced Dolly, wrapped in a clean piece of tissue paper.

"I found this after you got on the airplane to go to the hospital. Give her back, will you?" Diesel looked at him, blue eyes expectant, and Wazza felt suddenly sorry for the old man, living all alone up there in the middle of the estuary, missing his granddaughter, and for a second, he wondered at the circumstances that'd occurred for Diesel to end up that way.

Nodding his head, Wazza said, "I sure will. She'll love to have Dolly back."

"You and your lady and Benni are all more than welcome to come and visit whenever you want," Diesel had added, before ambling off down the hallway.

"We might just do that," Wazza called after him. In fact, he'd need to do that soon, to retrieve Kee's car. But there was no hurry.

They'd found Bruno's body washed up on the beach at the mouth of the estuary two days after he'd tried to steal Benni. Or at least, what was left of his body, after the crocodiles and fish had had a go at him. Kee had been asked to identify the body, but she'd refused. She still had deep episodes of guilt and grief over the fact that Bruno had died. It was hard for her to come to terms with the fact she'd killed someone, even though she said she would've done it again to protect Benni.

Wazza had asked Nash if he knew how Bruno had found them, but Nash couldn't give him a genuine answer. Perhaps it'd been pure luck that Bruno had chosen to go north, toward the border. Maybe he'd deduced that was exactly where Kee would run. CCTV footage from Normanton showed Bruno's car arriving in the town the day before Wazza and Kee drove through. Perhaps he'd been aimlessly driving around himself, and recognized Kee's car and followed them. Perhaps he had contacts watching out for them in all the towns along the road to the border. But in the end, they'd never know, because dead men couldn't tell their tales.

Everyone was on their feet, congratulating Kee and Benni. Wazza left his spot by the bar and strolled over to where Kee and Benni were the center of attention. Pooja had Benni by the hands and was dancing in circles with her, while her parents and Daniella and Steve looked on.

He caught Kee by the waist and pulled her in for a kiss while no one was looking. "Shall we tell them?" he whispered in her ear.

She withdrew with a start, as if afraid of what he'd asked. But then a smile crept over her rosebud lips. "I guess now is as good a time as any. Are you sure you want to tell everyone at once?"

He nodded. He had to tell Steve and Daniella soon, so it may as well be now.

Tucking her beneath his shoulder, he raised his voice, and said, "We also have some news." A rush of nerves hit his gut, and he reached up to pull his hat down over his eyes, forgetting that he wasn't wearing it. Everyone turned to stare at him and Kee. Too late to back out now.

"Kee, Benni and I are moving to Cairns in a few weeks. I've been offered a job there." There was a moment's silence, and then the room erupted again. Questions and exclamations filled the room. It seemed like everyone wanted to congratulate them at the same time.

Wazza and Kee had talked about their future long into the

night over the past week. He knew with great certainty that wherever he went and whatever he did; it needed to include Kee and her daughter. He'd even been prepared to give up country life for good and move to the city, if that's what it took. At first Kee hadn't been sure what she wanted to do. Her job at the animal shelter had been fulfilling, but it wasn't really a career. A new city and a new start were fine in her books.

Tentatively, he'd told her about the job he'd been offered at the Gondwana Pastoral Company, acting as an agent to help hire and coordinate contract mustering crews for top end stations. With his experience as leading hand at Stormcloud, as well as his skill at using cutting-edge, low-stress mustering techniques and understanding the way mustering crews had to be matched to the ethos of a particular station, the company believed he'd make a great liaison between the contractors and the station owners. The job entailed a bit of travel, especially during mustering season, but he'd be stationed in Cairns most of the time. Allowing him to have a foot in both worlds. It'd been the job he'd been toying with on the day he'd found Kee stranded at the bore. And he was grateful he hadn't turned them down in those few days afterwards.

Kee was delighted with the idea. He assured her there were good schools in Cairns for when Benni was ready to start kindergarten next year. He also had enough money saved up for a good deposit on a house. Kee hadn't quite come around to this idea yet, she was still stuck on the fact she wanted to go into this as equal partners, and he could understand her point of view. He hoped for a cottage on the outskirts of town with a little bit of land. Living cheek to jowl with other families in suburbia wasn't his version of perfection. Luckily, Kee agreed with him.

"So, I guess this is you officially handing in your notice?"

Steve said with a laugh. "Good on you, Wazza. You know I'll give you a glowing reference if you need one."

"Thank you, boss." Wazza grinned at Steve over the top of everyone else's heads. He'd do everything in his power to help Steve find a good replacement for his position. He knew he was leaving Steve in a bit of a pickle, but Steve and Daniella would understand. Perhaps it was time for Dale to move up to the position of leading hand, he was going to take over Stormcloud at some stage, after all.

"I promise to come and visit you lots," he heard Kee say quietly to her mother, whose face couldn't hide her disappointment. They must've been hoping that Kee and Benni might move back to Sydney, but Kee had discarded that idea. She wanted a life where she was in control, not them. She was certainly going to include them as much as possible in Benni's life, but she would do it on her own terms. "And you're welcome to come and stay whenever you want," Kee added, as her father leaned in to hear what they were saying.

"We're sad you're leaving. But at least you're not moving too far away." Daisy raised her voice from the back of the crowd, where she and Dale stood hand in hand, watching the proceedings. "So you can come back for our wedding in December."

"Wouldn't miss it for the world," Wazza replied.

He *would* miss working with this wonderful crew. But he was also looking forward to building a new life with Kee and Benni. He knew Stormcloud would always welcome him back with open arms if he wanted to return, but he needed to start a new chapter right now.

Benni came up and grabbed his legs, hugging him tight. He lifted her up onto his shoulders, and she giggled with glee. Kee glanced up at them both, eyes full of love, and he pulled her into his arms. This was what life was all about.

Want to know more about Stormcloud Station?
Get your FREE and EXCLUSIVE Prequel Novella
MISTY SKIES
Read Steve and Daniella's story.

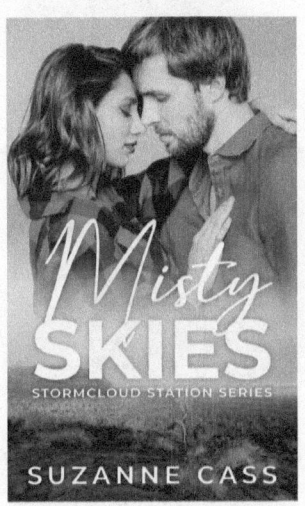

GO TO THIS LINK FOR YOUR FREE BOOK
https://dl.bookfunnel.com/xyuua14lyp

Stay in touch via my website
www.suzannecass.com

Facebook: www.facebook.com/suzannecassauthor/
Instagram: www.instagram.com/suzanne.cass/
Pintrest: www.pinterest.com.au/suzanne_cass/

If you liked Dawn Skies, you'll love;

Clear Skies

Fate and flooding rains brought them together. Secrets may tear them apart. Book 1.

Starlit Skies

They're polar opposites, with only one thing in common…
Book 2.

Crystal Skies

Her heart was shattered the night he disappeared…now he's back. Book 3.

Tangled Skies

Mistake number one was to risk her heart. Book 5
Coming soon.

Also by Suzanne Cass
NEW
Stormcloud Station Series
(A Stargazer Spinoff Series)
Small Town Romantic Suspense

Clear Skies
Starlit Skies
Crystal Skies
Dawn Skies
Tangled Skies

Stargazer Ranch Romance Series
Small Town Romantic Suspense
Combustion: Prequel Novella
Wildfire
Firelight
Snowbound: A Christmas Novella
Snowfall
Cloudburst

Island Bound Series
Mystery Romance (on an Island)
Books can be read as stand-alone
Bound by Truth
Bound by Silence
Bound by the Stars

Colors of the Earth Series
Small Town Romantic Suspense
Books can be read as stand-alone
Shadows in the Dust
Shadows in Deep Blue
Shadows of Red Earth
***

Romantic Suspense
Single Title
Island Redemption
Glass Clouds
Chasing Bullets

Love in the Mountains Novella Series
Small Town Short Romance
Novellas can be read as stand-alone
Rain on a Tin Roof
Lost and Found
Rescue his Heart

Please Leave a Review

The greatest gift you could ever give an author is to leave a review. You will be helping other people to discover this book and making a difference to me as an Independently Published Author. If you liked this book and want other people to read it to, please leave a review.

About the Author

Suzanne Cass is an Australian author who writes rural romance and romantic suspense abounding with passion and danger.

Her debut novel, Island Redemption, won the Romance Writers of Australia Emerald Award in 2016. Suzanne was also a finalist in the 2019 Romance Writers of Australia RUBY award.

She had always had a fascination with the tough resilience of people who live in our amazing red-dirt outback country. When not writing about the characters that inhabit her head, Suzanne can be found roaming the Perth beaches with her border collie, or encouraging from the sidelines as her two sons play sport.

Stay in touch via my website

www.suzannecass.com

Acknowledgements

Dawn Skies is the fourth book in the Stormcloud Station Series. The luxury eco-resort and cattle station is starting to feel like my second home and I find myself wishing it were real some days. Dawn Skies was a bit of a deviation from my normal romances, as Kee is a single mother with a gorgeous daughter, which adds another layer of conflict between her and Wazza finding true love. But it was an interesting dynamic that I really enjoyed exploring. All Kee wants is to protect her daughter. That is the heart of this story; a mother's unconditional love for her child. Love is complicated and it has many facets, that aren't always explored by a simple romance between two individuals. I enjoyed breaking the mould with this book, and all the single mothers out there bringing up their children the best way they know how have my upmost respect and admiration. You ladies rock.

To my beta readers (special nod to Rebecca who is my secret weapon when it comes to typo hunting) thank you for all your words of support and keeping me on the straight and narrow when it comes to my often creative spelling techniques.

To my wonderful ARC team, who are essential to an Indie Author like me. It's your heartwarming reviews that help keep me sane and keep me writing when imposter syndrome looms large.

Big thanks to my editor, Tanya Saari for putting up with my total inability to understand the comma.

Thanks also to the romance author community (my tribe) who are the best and most supportive people you could ever want to know. Romance authors believe that a rising tide lifts all boats, and the writers at the top of their careers love to help pull others higher. Together we are stronger.

My husband needs a special mention, as do my two beautiful sons, who are now gorgeous young men. Thank you for your unconditional love.

And last but definitely not least, I'm so very grateful to all the readers who have bought and enjoyed my books and who send me emails to let me know how much you love them. Thank you from the bottom of my heart.

www.ingramcontent.com/pod-product-compliance
Lightning Source LLC
Chambersburg PA
CBHW031949130726
47904CB00012B/597